A GANGSTA'S KARMA

Lock Down Publications and Ca$h
Presents

A GANGSTA'S KARMA

A Novel by *Flame*

Lock Down Publications
P.O. Box 944
Stockbridge, Ga 30281

Visit our website @
www.lockdownpublications.com

First Edition August 2021
Printed in the United States of America

Lock Down Publications
Like our page on Facebook: Lock Down Publications @
www.facebook.com/lockdownpublications.ldp

Book interior design by: **Shawn Walker**
Edited by: **Kiera Northington**

Stay Connected with Us!

Text **LOCKDOWN** to 22828 to stay up-to-date with new releases, sneak peaks, contests and more…
Thank you.

Submission Guideline

Submit the first three chapters of your completed manuscript to ldpsubmissions@gmail.com, subject line: Your book's title. The manuscript must be in a .doc file and sent as an attachment. Document should be in Times New Roman, double spaced and in size 12 font. Also, provide your synopsis and full contact information. If sending multiple submissions, they must each be in a separate email.

Have a story but no way to send it electronically? You can still submit to LDP/Ca$h Presents. Send in thc first three chapters, written or typed, of your completed manuscript to:

LDP: Submissions Dept
Po Box 944
Stockbridge, Ga 30281

DO NOT send original manuscript. Must be a duplicate.

Provide your synopsis and a cover letter containing your full contact information.

Thanks for considering LDP and Ca$h Presents.

About the Author

Matthew "Flame" Perry was born in Macon, Georgia but raised in a suburban subdivision named Homes of Lawrence (H.O.L. aka Da HOL) outside the western city limit of Boynton Beach, Florida. "Li'l Matt" was a modest youth that had his first run-in with the law at the age of eleven for retail theft. He gradually transitioned from a meek boy into a rapping, hustling THUGG OUT BOY (T.O.B.) called BlackFlame. Although his hard-working, upstanding parents made sure that he graduated high school in 2002, the street's grip on him tightened as he matured. His life took a dramatic turn after he witnessed the murder of his homie, Obel, on April 20, 2003. He soon developed an IDGAF attitude, which ultimately landed him in the Federal Bureau of Prisons, charged with six bank robberies and given a thirty-two-year sentence at the age of twenty-one. At the age of twenty-six, he started writing a book to escape his harsh reality. Upon completion of his first book (autobiography), he immediately started writing A Gangsta's Karma. Now thirty-seven, he is at peace, while perfecting his writing skills and continuing his fight for freedom.

Acknowledgements

First and foremost, it's a must that I thank GOD, THE BENEFICIENT AND MOST MERCIFUL MASTER OF THE UNIVERSE, for all that HE has done for me and my family. I thank HIM for HIS grace and protection, especially throughout the difficult and trying times in my life. I must now thank my mother, Hattie Mae aka HattieCake, and my father, Al aka Pops, for supporting and loving me without end. I'm forever grateful for you both and I can't thank GOD enough for giving me the strongest, most loving, caring and forgiving parents. Please forgive me for my actions that caused us to be separated. Always know that my actions aren't a reflection of how y'all raised me. Y'all gave me everything that I needed and more. And I thank you. I love you two to death. To my sister, Cherae aka RaeRae, thank you for being a great big sister and friend. Although there's nearly a nine-year age difference between us, our bond is one of a kind. You're like my second mother. I love and miss you. And thank you so much for taking care of our folks in my absence. I'm proud of the woman you've become and can't wait for the day to be able to officially call you Doctor RaeRae. Now this tribute goes to a very special woman that has been riding with me since the first day we laid eyes on each other: Amiyah Bertrand, aka Mama Mia bka my Haitian Sensation. No matter what we've been through, you never left or stopped loving me. To this day, I still wonder why you're dead set on sticking by my side. Some things I'll never understand, but I need you to understand that I'll truly always love you babygirl. Phoenix and Flame, together forever. I want to thank my phenomenal best friend Christana, aka Chrissy, and her wonderful family for their generosity, as the money and emails you sent and accepting my phone calls, has really helped me get through some of the darkest times of my life. Your friendship is deeply appreciated, warms my heart, and puts a smile on my face daily. I want to thank my Neekie Pooh, Tenisha Davis (R.I.P.). We met under unique circumstances, but I'm extremely happy to have had such an inspiring, brave, and strong woman like you in my life. The way you fought for your life, your never-give-up mentality, and your faith in GOD has motivated me to keep my head up and stand firm. I feel your presence daily. To everyone I mentioned above, you're all my guardian angels. And your prayers and love have kept me going strong. I'm forever indebted to y'all. To my co-defendants: James "JT' Winn, Charles "Pookey" Saulsby and Jimmie "Jimboe" Williams. I love y'all boyz. We stood tall in the paint. We didn't fold under pressure. And we took the 384 months they gave us without flipping. Y'all the realest niggaz in my Book of Thugz. Continue to be the stand-up men that y'all are until we hit the turf again, which will be soon. I want to shout-out my brothers from another mother and homegirlz from Homes of Lawrence (H.O.L. aka Da HOL): June Bug, Naldo, Boatwright, Brad, Sport, Drew, Darius, Mike Anderson aka Zo, JC, Herman, Da Polk Boyz, Hot Rod, Ree, Corey Bell, Amp, Nana, Woody, Buddy, Jesse Black, Nate, Truck, Li'l Junior, Kimboe, Greg, Kenny, Foy, Donnie and Derrick Dennis, Skylar, Flo, Meka Polk, Sabrina, LaShawn, Lydia, Tilly, Vanessa, Nicole and Brittney Guess. And all the others that I failed to mention because its too many to name. Thanks for the love and support and infusing the G-code into me during our upbringing in the hood. I'll see y'all soon. To my bros I met in the system that gave me advice and info for this book: Saeed from Washington Heights, Marquise Rogers from Greenville, Bill Weaver-Bey from DC, Chico Blick from Baltimore, Daryl Tanks from Miami, Eric "Blue" Gabe from Orlando, Cash and Chauncey James from Riviera Beach, Speed and the OG Kimmeye Parson from West Palm Beach, James "P" Perry from Boynton Beach. Thank y'all for the input which helped make this book credible. And Rest in Paradise to my bros Obel, Li'l Bruce and Courtney "Bump" Jones (Pleasant City). Miss y'all niggaz dearly. I want to thank CA$H for putting his faith in me and my artistic skills. And lastly, I want to dedicate this book to Ethel Mae Thomas, my G-ma and affectionately known as MaDear. Rest in Peace, MaDear. You left this earth to sit by GOD's side fifteen days after I got locked up. Losing you hurts me so much and I think about you every day. I love and miss you tremendously. I know you're watching over me and protecting me. GOD BLESS everybody above and I appreciate you all from the bottom of my heart.

CHAPTER ONE

August 17, 1988 4:42 am

West Palm Beach, FL

"Noooo!" cried the distraught, terrified little girl as she banged on the bedroom door. "I want out!"

"Please, Kilo! Don't do this in front of our baby!" Melina reasoned, attempting to maneuver by her assailant to get to her child.

"I told ya, bitch! That lil hoe ain't mines," Kilo declared, before backhanding the snot out of Melina, literally. Kilo's sheer power forced Melina over the bed and onto the floor. "That lil hoe ain't come from these." He grabbed his nuts. "She looks just like her dick-eatin', foot-draggin', crackhead mama!"

Oblivious to the pandemonium around her, the shaken little girl resumed trying her damnedest to get out. Her tiny hands were able to twist the lock on the doorknob. But she was unsuccessful at reaching the deadbolt lock that was just out of her grasp, so she continued to beat on the door. Unbeknownst to her, her efforts were of no avail, there was nobody around to hear the turmoil.

"Melina, shut her lil ass up befo' I do," Kilo demanded, snatching the frail, badly beaten Melina up by the neck.

"Pl-pl-please, Kilo," she muttered with a mouthful of blood, "Don't hurt her. Oh God, I'm beggin' you."

Kilo quickly glanced at the little girl as her pounding and cries for help became lighter and lighter. He turned back towards Melina, then tightened his fingers around her puny throat. He stared into her gloomy, bulging eyes and said, "You crossed me too, too many times, hoe. You lied ta me. You stole from me. So I can't ... I just ... I can't imagine lettin' ya get away wit tryna set me up. Now, cuz of yo' junkie ass, I got unnecessary blood on my hands."

"But, Kilo ... " was all Melina could say before Kilo's powerful hands cut off her air supply.

Totally out of it for God knows how long, Melina groggily lifted her throbbing head. The only reason she woke up, though, was because of the horrifying screams she repeatedly heard. Looking in the direction where the yelling was coming from instantly caused tears to pour from her swollen black eyes. *No, I must be having a nightmare,* she thought while praying to God that it was only a nightmare.

Suddenly, with newfound energy, Melina was on her feet so fast, the wave of lightheadedness that overcame her didn't faze her. Before she knew it, she was pummeling Kilo's back with all the strength she could muster in her five foot six, hundred and ten-pound frame. She landed a few solid blows, which interrupted Kilo from sodomizing the four-year-old little girl anymore.

Kilo rose from the bleeding, listless small body and uppercut Melina, shattering her jaw and a few teeth in the process. "Bitch, don't cha ever put ya hands on me!" he yelled as he stood over and spat on a dazed Melina. "Well, ya' know what? I ain't gon' have ta worry 'bout that problem, or any otha problems, from you. Know why?" He paused as if expecting an answer. "This time, da blood on my hands'll be well worth it. You an' that lil hoe of yours won't see a beautiful, sunny tomorrow."

Kilo's words were fading in and out. However, Melina clearly heard the last sentence. Kilo meant every word, and she knew it. So she began to pray. *I'm ready to die, Lord, especially after the rough, short life I lived,* she said unto herself, *but please spare my baby.*

Melina would never find out if her prayer to save her baby was answered, because her thoughts were cut short by a .45 caliber bullet.

Kilo was extremely tempted to let off another round from his Ruger into Melina's skull. Although he could have, being that gunshots in Pleasant City were just as common as gunshots at a shooting range, he chose not to waste ammo. *Mission complete,* he concluded, *so there's no need to hang around this bitch.*

"Good riddance, hoe," he cold-heartedly asserted. He made his way for the bedroom door before suddenly stopping in his tracks. He apathetically looked down at the once innocent, full-of-life but now deflowered, lifeless body of the little girl as blood streamed from her battered womb and rectum. "Sorry, baby girl, but charge it ta da game."

He unlocked the deadbolt and cleared the scene, leaving them both for dead.

Nevertheless, little did he know the little girl had the will to live, she was far from being out of the fight. She was so weak, though, after battling with Kilo while he sexually assaulted her, all she could do was lie there in a crumpled heap in silence.

As she lie there helpless in the morning's sun that flooded the room for what seemed like an eternity, she perpetually tried to block out the excruciating pain, along with the deafening sound of her mother's fatal gunshot. That tormenting gunshot brought with it immediate thoughts of the mother she hardly knew, and thoughts of how much she hated the man named Kilo.

Little did he know.

CHAPTER TWO

June 14, 2007 8:35 pm

Savannah, GA

"Damn, dawg! I thought you'd be back a week ago," JJ said. "You ain't answerin' ya phone. I swore sumthin' done happened ta ya, dawg."

"That's my fault, lil bruh," Bizzy replied, emerging from the 2008 Ford Mustang he'd rented. *The strip looks different*, he thought. "Some shit happened down in Tally wit my Pops, an' man, it's fucked up. Hopefully, er'thang be back on beat soon."

"I undastand, dawg. Say no mo'," JJ said with his countrified swag. He gave his main man dap. An awkward silence ensued as they posted on Rivers Avenue, letting JJ know that whatever happened to Bizzy in F-L-A wasn't good, not good at all.

Bizzy and JJ were two-of-a-kind, but paradoxically, they were also total opposites. First, there was the age difference. Twenty-four-year-old Bizzy was six years older than JJ. Then, there was the semblance, JJ was a gangbanging Blood, and Bizzy looked like an entrepreneur. JJ was thugged out to the max, with shoulder-length dreads and platinum on his teeth, ears, neck, wrist and fingers. He was five-foot-seven with a solid build and burnt rubber black. Bizzy, on the other hand, was Fortune 500 fresh, thanks to his pops' tutelage. He sported a low haircut with waves, dressed casual, and rocked just enough jewelry to not draw too much attention. He was six-foot-five, two-hundred-and-thirty pounds of lean muscle and brown-skinned.

The two met three years ago when Bizzy was in town visiting a cousin he had just found out existed. He made it his personal business to visit his cousin, Ant, that lived in the Fitch Village Projects on the eastside of Savannah, aka Seaport, with one thing in mind: expanding his network.

While researching the quality of drugs in the area, he ran into a fifteen-year-old hustler hustling outside a mom and pop store on Rivers Avenue. Seeing how bad most of the dope was in Seaport, compared to the work in Florida, he realized he could possibly take over the town, or at least get a large slice of the pie. He eventually began supplying Ant with a little of Florida's finest weed, coke and pills, after overcoming the trust issues he had dealing with "strangers." Subsequently, he also took the young hustler, JJ, under his wings.

Months passed, and each package he gave Ant was larger in quantity. He was fine with the fact that Ant and he were nothing more than just business partners. But Ant was envious of the bond he and JJ had. Bizzy liked JJ because of how street smart and ambitious the young'n was. He felt like Ant was a L-7, though.

Then, like he knew it would ultimately happen, the shit hit the fan. Word on the streets of Seaport at the time was that a jealous Ant was plotting to run him back to FLA and to permanently take over what the three of them had built. He eventually caught wind of the scheme Ant had in mind. Furious at his estranged cousin, he had JJ "take care of" Ant, which was also to test JJ's loyalty to him. The outcome was that Ant was never seen again, and JJ and he had damn near all of Seaport under their control since then.

JJ finally broke the silence by saying, "Dawg, I hope ya got some wood, white gurl or sumthin', cuz da streets need us. Look around an' see how shit done changed in a week witout us in da street, dawg. One week!"

Before answering, Bizzy examined his surroundings. Rivers Avenue was usually teeming with rambunctious people throughout the day. Gangbangers staking their territory and junkies hustling for their next fix should have been everywhere. But that wasn't the case. It was odd seeing the Ave like this on a blazing evening. *That just goes to show who runs this town*, Bizzy thought with a pompous smirk.

"I noticed when I turned on da Ave an' rode a few blocks, how dead shit looked," Bizzy said in his deep baritone voice.

"Yeah, dawg. Y' know why it's dead? Cuz er'body takin' they bread ta them crabs on da Westside in search of our shit. I been dry fo' almost two weeks now. I ain't tryna cop no backyard, so I'm 'bout ready ta make niggaz get down. I'm losin' my patience, I'm ... "

"Lil bruh, calm down. I got us. Just not rite now," he said, placing a firm, assuring hand around JJ's shoulders. "Hop in an' let's take a ride ta Pitbull's crib. I'll tell ya what da lick read in Tally on our way. It's some real bullshit goin' down."

JJ shook his head. "Dawg, y'know I don't fuck wit Westside like that."

"Lil bruh, just get in an' let's peel. I gotta proposition fo' Pit, if he's down. An' knowin' him, he'll be down."

During the fifteen-minute drive through the dense traffic to the westside, Bizzy explained briefly the ordeal taking place in Tallahassee.

Since Bizzy split his time between Tally and Seaport equally, his main reason to go to Tally was to re-up, and he'd drop by to see his oldest son if he chose. But, on his last trip back to Tally, he learned from a source that his father was under heavy surveillance by the FBI. His father left word for him to lay low in Savannah until things cooled down, while his father hauled ass to Miami. However, on the drive down from Tally to Miami, his father was pulled over by a Florida State Trooper near Fort Pierce, FL. His father had a federal arrest warrant for conspiracy to possess and distribute cocaine, and was currently being held in the St. Lucie County Jail with no bond.

He then goes on, telling how he spent his time discreetly selling work for the low to have money for his father's lawyer. His father had "jam-up" money, but Bizzy was unable to get to the safe in his father's closely watched home on Nicasagee Road in Tally, which was where the politicians and the rich lived. It took two long, stressful weeks to meet the lawyer's price. Once the lawyer was paid, he spent his last on a rental car, which was under a smoker's name, and drove his broke ass back to Seaport.

They finally pulled up to Pitbull's crib in Fairwood Projects. Bizzy could immediately sense JJ's uneasiness.

As if on cue with Bizzy's thoughts, JJ spoke. "Dawg, what we doin' out this way?" he asked impatiently while scanning his surroundings.

"Listen, lil bruh," Bizzy said, "I got three grand ta my name. I got no work, no money, an' I got no time ta get money from hustlin' rite now. We basically in da same boat, lil bruh, so I'ma stop us from sinkin'. We need help, an' Pit is da one that's gonna help us."

Still looking around cautiously, with a hand on the iron on his waist, JJ replied, "Dawg, you an' I both know we can't trust Pitbull. Da nigga name Pitbull fo' a reason, he vicious! He da type of nigga that'll kill his whole family if one of 'em cross him. Plus, he snort mo' coke than Rick James in his prime. We can't ..."

"An' that's how I'm gonna control him," Bizzy added. "We need him mo' than ever rite now. He a jack-of-all-trades type of nigga. Trust me on this one. I neva letcha down befo', rite?"

JJ didn't respond. He just continued to watch his surroundings.

"C'mon, lil bruh, let's go in, holla at this nigga an' get this money. Fast money!"

Boy, I sure hope you know what you're about to get us into, JJ thought as they exited the car and knocked on Pit's door.

CHAPTER THREE

June 19, 2007 11:45 pm

West Palm Beach, FL

"Devon, wake up. Baby, wake up," Miracle protested as she shook the body lying next to her. "Devon! Please, wake up."

Abruptly, Devon awoke, delirious. "Huh? Wha ... What happened?"

"You were havin' another bad dream."

Devon sat up in bed, soaking wet from sweating and trembling. *Fuck, after all these years, I still can't forget that day*, Devon thought.

"Was it that dream you never tell me about?" Miracle asked. She then began to wipe the sweat off Devon's face and neck with the T-shirt she wore. "Baby, you've had this same bad dream since I've known you, and you still won't tell me what the dream is about. Don't you trust me after almost three years of bein' together? I'm your ride-or-die bitch, baby."

Devon kicked the covers off and climbed out of bed, flat-out ignoring Miracle. "What time is it?"

"Damnit, Dee! I hate it when you do that shit! I know you heard me," she snapped.

"Bitch, miss me wit that bullshit! Tell me da fuckin' time an' shut da fuck up!"

Not trying to go through it tonight, Miracle sucked her teeth, grabbed her phone off the nightstand and sarcastically replied, "It's 11:47."

"Cut da attitude, Miracle."

Devon went into the bathroom to freshen up. After ten minutes or so, Devon was ready to bounce.

"Dee, I thought you said you wasn't goin' nowhere tonight. You promised we were goin' to spend some quality time. Just you and me," Miracle whined.

"I changed my mind," Devon said coldly. "I'm goin' ta da club ta check up on these hoes. They prolly in that bitch takin' it easy cuz they think I'm stayin' in. I'ma surprise those trick bitches."

"Well," she said as she climbed out of bed, "I'm goin' with you."

"Naw, just chill here. I'll be back." Devon grabbed the car keys, phone, .380, and wad of bills off the dresser and headed for the door. "Keep da door locked an' that pussy wet till I get back. Okay, baby girl?" Devon said, before walking outside into the darkness.

Living in an apartment in Pleasant City, aka Da City, on the corner of 20th Street and Beautiful Avenue, would certainly steer most to believe the area was a great place to reside. Oh, how deceitful that assumption was! Merely seeing a little of the nonstop drama and criminal activity, which took place in the area at any given moment, would cause most to think twice about riding through Da City just to sightsee. Simply not knowing someone personally, or not buying something illegal, in Da City made a person target practice.

"What they do, Dee?" somebody from a crowd of people gathered on the corner shouted, as Devon approached a candy apple green 2008 Dodge Charger on twenty-six-inch chrome floaters. "You gonna brang some of ya hoes back ta da crib tonite? I got plenty money like Plies!"

"What type ah bitch ya want?" Devon responded, playing along.

"It don't even matter. As long as da eater gobble this dick, fuck me an' a few of da homies, da bitch can be Somalian." The crowd on the corner erupted in laughter. "Make that a thick Somalian, cuz we break skinny hoes down 'round here like Dutches."

All Devon could do was smile.

***

It only took a few minutes for Devon to reach the destination. Once inside of Illusions, Devon immediately ducked off out of view at the bar and ordered the usual, a cup of straight Patrón. Tonight was normally a slow one, but the club was booming. *There better not be a single hoe back in the dressing room now with all this money around,* Devon thought.

"Oh shit," the DJ announced over the music. "If y'all niggaz brung ya old lady in da club tonite, ya betta handcuff her rite now, cuz my dawg Devon in da buildin' !"

The mentioning of Devon's name caused two reactions, a couple strippers tensed up, and a few niggas mean-mugged. Yet, Devon remained nonchalant as niggas and hoes approached to show love.

"Hey, Daddy," a stripper by the name of Rhapsody cooed as she stepped between Devon's legs. She was five-foot-five in three-inch heels and one-hundred-and-thirty-five pounds of pure thickness. She had on next to nothing, which was a bare-it-all pink lacy outfit. She sported pink highlights in her short black hair that complemented her Hershey-chocolate complexion. "What'chu doin' up in here? You 'posed to be at home. Well, anywayz, I missed you sooooo much, Dee. You miss me?"

"Y'all blow da bomb yet?" Devon bluntly asked, pulling the stripper close to caress her entire 36DD-25-44-inch frame.

"Tonite is good. I sold 'bout ten beans an' five bags of paint. I dunno if Peachez an' Jazzy sold ... "

"How 'bout you go holla at them hoes an' see if they need mo', cuz I'ma clear it soon. Hurry up, too." Devon slapped Rhapsody on the ass before she obediently went about what she was instructed to do.

While she was gone, Devon calculated that Rhapsody, Jazzy, and Peachez should have had about thirteen hundred dollars between all of them since the beans, aka X-pills, and bags of paint, aka powder cocaine, were twenty bucks a pill or bag. *I wonder if Star and Mystic got some bread for me at The Palace*, Devon thought.

"Here's fourteen hundred," Rhapsody whispered as she put the money in Devon's pocket. "It's still early, so we're definitely gonna need more."

"Go in my otha pocket an' y'all sell that." Rhapsody did as she was told and stuffed the small sandwich bag in her pussy. "At da end of da nite, collect my cut from Jazzy an' Peachez, an' I'll pick it up tomorrow at'cha crib."

"What about our tips?"

"Y'all can keep that since it's jumpin' on a usually slow nite." Devon pulled out a twenty-dollar-bill and placed it in Rhapsody's T-back. "Now, give Daddy a preview of what'cha gonna do ta me tomorrow befo' I go holla at Star 'nem at Da Palace."

Rhapsody smiled, then she seductively pirouetted and began to slowly grind into Devon's lap. *Damn, I may not be able to wait until tomorrow to tear this pussy up*, Devon thought as Rhapsody did what she did best.

June 19, 2007 11:57 pm
Savannah, GA

Throwing the car in park, Bizzy wearily said, "Lil bruh, I thought we'd neva make it home."

"That was a helluva road trip," JJ proclaimed, opening the passenger door immediately in desperate need to stretch his limbs.

"I told y'all it was gonna be worth it," Pitbull said from the back seat.

"I neva doubted ya, Pit," Bizzy said as he looked at JJ with an expression that said, *I told you so.* "Now let's go in da house an' see what we got."

Bizzy had a luxurious home in Port Wentworth on the southside of Seaport. With the best decor money could buy, he was very skeptical of exposing where he laid his head at, especially to someone of Pitbull's caliber. *It doesn't matter, because JJ and I are taking our operation to my other baby's mama spot in Orlando real soon*, Bizzy thought.

Once inside the mini mansion, Bizzy led the way into his game room. He immediately went to the bar to fix himself a drink.

JJ, meanwhile, literally collapsed onto one of Bizzy's La-Z-Boy chairs, and began snoring in a matter of seconds. Pitbull, with his six-foot-tall body that was made by a prison weight pile, toted two fifteen-gallon duffle bags and set them on the pool table.

"What da fuck! Get that shit off my Brunswick pool table," Bizzy yelled at Pitbull. "Set that shit on da floor, crazy-ass nigga!"

"Nigga, you can't even spell that. You fake scholar-lookin' ass nigga," Pitbull scoffed as he placed the heavy bags side by side on the floor.

"It's spelled f-i-v-e thou-sand dollars! Can yo' broke ass spell that?" he shot back. "Just dump that shit on da floor an' let's see what we came up wit."

Two days of planning was all it took. Now it was finally time to see the outcome. Pitbull put them up on a nigga he said he had been plotting to rob for the longest. He was really happy to learn that JJ and Bizzy would fund the money for whatever was needed to take to Greenville, SC, which was where the lick took place.

What made them choose the lick was Pitbull's guarantee that the nigga was caked-up in the woods. Plus, he said he owed the nigga a favor for fucking him over on a deal a while back. The lick went extremely smooth, a little too smooth for Bizzy's liking. But the only thing that mattered was they made it home safely, thanks to Pitbull's inside knowledge.

Pitbull phoned the nigga and asked for some work, after telling him to let bygones be bygones. Arriving at their destination three and a half hours later, the nigga, who sort of resembled an older Pitbull, answered the door with no hesitation. The nigga began to say something, and it seemed like he was going to hug Pitbull. But Pitbull upped his ratchet and shot him between the eyes, killing him before he hit the ground. Unaware and awestruck at what happened, Bizzy and JJ reluctantly walked behind Pitbull as he dragged the corpse into the house. Pitbull must've known exactly where to look, because they were back on the road within five minutes of pulling up to the house that was ducked way off in the woods.

"So, what we get?" Bizzy anxiously questioned. He walked from behind the bar to where Pitbull was kneeling by the bags. "What's in da bags? I been anxious ta find out da whole ride back."

Pitbull glanced at JJ as he slept, then he unzipped a bag. The contents in the bag were bricks of coke. He began unloading them, and the total came to be thirty keys.

"Damn, ya pot'nah was pushin' weight like a bodybuilder, huh?" Bizzy said as he picked up a block to examine it. "This look like some of that Florida gator."

"Maybe."

"You say you an' ya boy fell out a while back, rite? Well, if he gettin' paper like this, an' you broke as fuck, what y'all fall out 'bout?"

Pitbull glanced at JJ again to find that he was still asleep. He then unzipped the second bag and replied, "First off, we were gettin' money togetha fo' a long time, till my coke habit got outta pocket. He decided ta cut me off. But he said he would give me half of er'thang ta go 'bout my own bizness."

"So how da fuck ya broke? You snorted all ya dope an' blowed all ya money trickin' wit some ugly-ass bitches, huh?"

"Not really," Pitbull casually said as he pulled a chrome Desert Eagle out of the second bag and aimed it at Bizzy. "That nigga only game me a quarter of er'thang, which wasn't shit! That nigga thought he could fuck me since he was my uncle. An' I ain't 'bout ta get fucked over again by two soft-ass niggas when this shit is mine."

Without losing his composure, an unarmed Bizzy coolly responded, "What'chu 'bout ta do now? Merk us an' take er'thang?"

"That's exactly what I'm gonna do," he said, cocking the shiny Desert Eagle back.

Boc Boc Boc Boc Boc

When the smoke finally cleared, blood was already trickling from several decent-size holes in the body sprawled on the floor.

"It's a dawg eat dawg world," Bizzy said, standing over Pitbull's body.

"I told ya that nigga'll kill his family if they cross him," JJ said while getting up from the La-Z-Boy with a Glock 40 in his hand. "Dawg, I'm fuckin' glad ya planned this shit ahead of time, cuz we'd be stankin' like this bitch-ass nigga." He stood next to Bizzy. "How'd ya know he was gonna flip da script?"

"Truthfully, lil bruh, I didn't know fa'sho. It's just always good ta have a back-up plan fo' er'thang. 'Specially when ya dealin' wit a nigga that' s already throwed and snortin' heavy powda."

Bizzy then proceeded to look inside the second blood-covered bag. Inside, he found a shitload of money. He rifled through the bag quickly, estimating there was approximately a million dollars. So, in all, they acquired almost two million dollars! *Orlando, here I come*, he thought.

"What we gonna do wit this dead-ass nigga?" JJ asked. I neva did like his ass anyway." He kicked the dead body. "Pussy!"

"Wrap his ass up wit da plastic tarp in da garage by da washer, then put him in da Tahoe that's parked in there," Bizzy instructed. He then pulled out his Blackberry. "I'ma call my peeps ta clean this bitch up befo' I put it on da market. After that, we gonna take da Tahoe ta dump Pitbull sumwhere on da westside, clean da Tahoe up, an' come back here. Then we outta here. Tonite!"

"Where we goin' again?"

Smiling from ear to ear, Bizzy said, "Disney World."

CHAPTER FOUR

June 20, 2007 8:20 am

Fort Pierce, FL St. Lucie County Jail

"Demetrius Woodson," the female C.O. said, standing in the doorway of cell number three, "You have an attorney visit. Be ready in five minutes."

It's about fucking time, Demetrius thought as he promptly arose from the bottom bunk. Slowly, he made his bed before brushing his teeth and washing his face.

When he finished tending to himself, he shook his head at the man staring back at him in the mirror. *Boy, you picked a bad time to get jammed up.* He had too much on his plate right now to be locked up. He had major business to handle. He wasn't worried about the hundred bills he had to pay, because his accountant of many years was his power of attorney. Neither was he worried about the several personal businesses he owned, because they were established enough to run themselves. Nor was he stressing over Byron, the one child he knew was his, because he didn't allow Byron to be in the family business.

The family business was the only thing Demetrius was salty about. One thing for sure though, he knew things would continue to run smoothly. But the family was in the process of renegotiating prices with the connect in Peru. This important meeting that guaranteed the family would make billions a year was to take place in two days, and he wasn't going to be there.

"Demetrius Woodson, are you ready?" the C.O. said, breaking his train of thought.

"Yes." Demetrius proceeded to put on his blue uniform, then the C.O. escorted him to see his attorney. "Is my son still out there?" he asked his lawyer as soon as the C.O. left.

Demetrius' attorney for the last fifteen years was seated at the table. Matthew O'Hare was forty-six years old, Irish and well known throughout the state. His wisdom of the law, his gift of gab, and his "no bullshit" attitude, got Demetrius out of trouble many times over the years. Because of him, Demetrius either always received probation or time served, meaning that Demetrius never did hard time. However, since Demetrius was only getting in trouble with the state, Mr.

O'Hare sort of had his work cut out for him, dealing with Demetrius' first run-in with the feds.

"Well, Mr. Woodson," Mr. O'Hare said with a sigh, "let me start off by apologizing for taking so long to come consult with you. I had a very meaningful civil case in Jacksonville that I had to conclude first. Secondly, your son has paid me in full, and as of right now, he's not incarcerated. But he will be soon."

Demetrius just shook his head in disbelief.

"There is a federal arrest warrant," Mr. O'Hare continued, "for a Byron Woodson, your son, which he knows about, for illegal use of a cell phone. I know you're probably thinking, 'What the hell kind of charge is that?' Well, three cell phones used in the indictment were in Byron's name, linking him to the same conspiracy as you and nine others. Nevertheless, the good news is that's all they have on Byron, placing him at the bottom of the list. With that said, he's looking at a maximum of two years, since his record is flawless. So, I can get him six months to a year with a plea agreement."

"How much will that cost? To help him, that is," Demetrius finally spoke.

"Oh, forgive me, once again. Your son was included when he paid me, so I'll be representing both of you."

Way to think ahead, son, Demetrius thought.

Feeling more at ease now, knowing his son was okay, Demetrius finally took a seat across from Mr. O'Hare. "So, tell me, what's going on with me?"

"First things first, they denied your bond. Besides that, I really haven't gotten the chance to sit down and go over the specifics of the case," Mr. O'Hare said with a slight Irish accent. He opened his briefcase and pulled out a legal binder. He produced a packet of papers from the binder, skimmed through a few pages, then continued, "The government has indicted you for the conspiracy to possess and to distribute fifty kilograms of powder cocaine. Including you, there are eleven conspirators in the indictment.

"And, it says here … that they have you labeled as the leader and organizer of … the RockBottom Family, aka RBF. The good news is they did not indict you under the RICO Act. The better news though, is the government only possesses a single phone conversation for evidence. This conversation is between you and one of your co-conspirators, and I have yet to hear that evidence."

"Then they have no case," Demetrius excitedly said. "We can beat that with ... "

"Hold on, just one minute, Mr. Woodson. This is not the incompetent state DA office we are dealing with. Furthermore, the government claims to have two of your co-conspirators that are willing to cooperate with them in order to receive a lighter sentence."

The day Demetrius was apprehended, the feds knew exactly where to locate each person in the indictment, except for Byron. The feds simultaneously raided each conspirator's home, or followed them while they were on the road, and seized them all.

The next day, Demetrius learned by phone that he knew four of the nine co-conspirators personally. There was his younger brother, his two cousins and his confidant. These four guys were genuine players, and they lived by the code of the family. *It can't be one of them,* he reasoned with himself, *so it has to be two of the other five unknowns.*

Tyrell Woodson, Demetrius' younger brother, was a split image of Demetrius, except his skin was lighter and he was seven years younger. He'd been a member of RBF since age twenty-two, which was when RBF was starting to see money in the mid-nineties. He lived in Miami at the time, making his duty to retrieve the dope from the Port of Miami and transporting the dope to the family throughout Florida.

Demetrius' cousins, William "Bubba" and Robert "Obie" Jennings, helped found RBF with Demetrius. They were forty-five-year-old identical twins. However, they were easy to tell apart, because they made sure they didn't dress, talk or walk alike. Bubba, the oldest twin by two minutes, resided in Orlando, while Obie stayed in Fort Myers, FL. They were rarely seen in each other's company, let alone seen together with Demetrius. Everything was strictly business with them, making them trustworthy and reliable colleagues.

Thirty-eight-year-old Blaze and Demetrius had been conducting business together for almost two decades. He was the only person in the family Demetrius directly dealt with that wasn't blood. Bubba never did like the fact that Blaze was personally involved when it came to important decisions. Demetrius swore he was a good judge of character, deeming Blaze a member of the family. He had a home in Tally, but he handled his business in Gainesville, FL. Other than that, he was the only person Demetrius would talk to when it involved personal matters in RBF.

Giving up on thinking of who would snitch on him, Demetrius furiously asked, "Who are the two people?"

"I haven't the slightest idea, as of right now. I will have the names in a day or two," Mr. O'Hare said before packing up and rising from the table. "I will have my secretary send you some legal mail with all the information I have. This will be somewhat time consuming, so bear with me. If you have any questions afterward, do not hesitate to call me."

"I understand."

"Oh, by thc way, when you contact Byron, tell him to contact me ASAP. The sooner he turns himself in, the better my chances are of getting him as little time as possible." Mr. O'Hare handed him a business card, then informed the C.O. that he was finished with his client.

Once back in the pod, Demetrius immediately got on the phone, trying to reach his son. *Phew, I'm glad I kept Byron out of the family business,* he thought, *but I fucked up by putting those damn phones I used in his name without his consent.*

CHAPTER FIVE

July 6, 2007 1:55 am

West Palm Beach, FL

"Ummm," Miracle moaned, pushing Devon's face deeper into her juice box. "Yes, Daddy ... Yes, Dee … suck this pussy ... ooohhhh!"

Devon licked and sucked Miracle's pussy with such finesse that her pupils vanished into her head, her body convulsed, and her breathing became erratic, as usual. Devon's magical tongue should have been classified as one of the Seven Wonders of the World, according to every female that was blessed by that tongue.

"Say my name, bitch," Devon mumbled after slurping and swallowing the juice from Miracle's fifth nut in twelve minutes.

"Dee-Dee-Dee-Devon! I can't take ... no more. I want that ... dick now! Gimme that dick!"

Devon nibbled on her pink pearl before surfacing. "What'cha want? You want Mandingo tonite?"

"Yes, Daddy. I want all twelve inches tonight," she seductively said. She then flipped over and got on all fours, pussy dripping wet. "I want Daddy to bust this good pussy open."

In the dimly lit room, Devon still couldn't stop admiring Miracle's unblemished body. With measurements of 38F-27-48, she was a real Amazon. She earned the moniker Miracle her first day of stripping three years ago when the DJ said, "It's a Miracle how she makes a section of the pole vanish between her ass cheeks." Standing five-foot-eight and weighing one-hundred-and-seventy-five pounds, she had a flat stomach, toned, thick thighs and a firm, round ass from working out three days a week and stripping five days a week. She was twenty-two, and was of Jamaican, Haitian and Cuban descent. She had rich dark-chocolate skin that made her chestnut-colored eyes more vibrant.

Nevertheless, out of all those attributes, what Devon admired the most besides her beauty was how dependable Miracle was, and how they both shared the by-any-means-necessary mentality, which was why she was Devon's main bitch.

Devon strapped-up and commenced to slowly dive into Miracle's pink abyss. *She wanted all twelve inches, so I'm going to give her all twelve,* Devon thought with an egotistic smile. Miracle cringed after taking nine inches. “Aahhh ... that’s the spot,” she whimpered. “Fill me up, Daddy.”

Devon began to draw back inch by inch. “Say you want Daddy ta beat it up now.”

“Yes. I want Daddy to ... “

Devon didn’t give her a chance to finish before rapidly thrusting in and out of her heavenliness. Miracle’s upper body gave out, causing her to collapse face first onto the bed as the mixture of pain and pleasure consumed her body. After a while, with her pussy wetter than a pool, she spread her cheeks and started throwing her ass back, taking the whole foot of dick.

“I-I-I … I love you, Devon,” Miracle declared, as blissful tears streamed down her beautiful face.

Bitch, I know you do, Devon thought while continuing to butcher her insides.

***

Later that morning, Devon awoke to the aroma of cooked bacon. Noticing Miracle was not in bed, Devon peered through crusty eyes at the time on the wall. The clock read 10:37 am. Not much of a morning person, Devon crawled out of bed and proceeded to the bathroom to get right.

“I know you up, Dee,” Miracle called from the small kitchen, “C’mon before your food gets cold.”

Miracle always questioned Devon about living in the small one-bedroom, one bathroom apartment right in the danger zone of Da City. They could easily move out west into a nice quarter of a million dollar home with the income the girls made daily at the clubs. Plus, she knew Devon wasn’t a big spender, so there was money put up somewhere. Sometimes, she would catch herself constantly daydreaming about living in a big house, with a big yard and a big family.

Now, don’t get it twisted, Miracle had no problem living in the murderous, drug-infested hood, since she mainly grew up a few blocks away in Shermville. She was accustomed to the rough life, and so was Devon. But she just feared that either a got-nothing-to-lose baser or a jealous, greedy nigga was going to …

She didn’t like to think that way. She knew Devon generally

steered clear of conflict and was well respected in the county of Palm Beach. But when does the right time come to leave the hood? That was all. She just wanted them to finally enjoy the money somewhere else. Yet, at the end of the day, she loved and trusted Devon, and she would never go against the grain.

Walking into the kitchen, wearing black Dickies and a black wife beater with Dough Boy slippers on, Devon said, "What I told ya 'bout doin' that shit?"

"I know, I know, Daddy," Miracle cooed as she sashayed butt-naked and kissed Devon. "And good mornin' to you, too."

"You can burn ya' self cookin' that shit." Devon sat at the tall, tiny table. On the table was a plate of hot scrambled eggs with cheese, crispy bacon, thick grits and buttered toast. "Y' know I don't want'cha fine ass all burnt up. If ya fuck 'round an' burn ya'self, I'ma find me anotha bitch."

"Don't say that shit, Dee." She frowned. "You and I both know you ain't goin' nowhere. This pussy got you sprung." She bent over and touched her toes for Devon to see. While twirling a nipple between her fingers with one hand, she stuck the other fingers into her moistness, removed them and sucked on the wetness. "You know you'd rather eat this than the food on that plate," she said, giggling and clapping her ass.

You damn right, Devon thought while eating a fork full of eggs.

"So, what'chu an' Rhapsody do in Orlando fo' da Fourth? Y'all make a killin' on da Trail in Leo's?"

"Hell yeah!" Miracle said before sitting on Devon's lap.

"We met two pay-masters in there. They seen how me and Rhapsody were puttin' on our own lil private fireworks show, so they took us both to VIP."

"Is that rite? So did y'all break 'em?" Devon asked while chewing on a piece of bacon.

"Daddy, we tried, but they had so much money. One of them, I think his name was JJ, was all up on Rhapsody. The other one, Bizzy, was real nice to me. We stayed in VIP with them all night, and they kept givin' the money up. Before we finally left to come back home yesterday evenin', Bizzy was tryin' to get us to chill with them all day."

"Huh?" Devon was confused. "How he know what hotel y'all were stayin' at or whateva?"

"Before we left the club, Rhapsody gave JJ her real number." She shrugged. "I asked her why she did that later and she said, 'They got money and they both cute.' So she was talkin' to JJ on the phone while we were in the hotel, and Bizzy wanted to stop by and take us somewhere."

"Where y'all go?"

"You should know me better than that by now," she scoffed. "We didn't go nowhere, even though Rhapsody damn near begged me to death."

"How much y'all make?"

Miracle suddenly got up and ran into the room. She returned shortly with a roll of bills. "We made five hundred in the two hours before we met them. Rhapsody's trick copped our whole pack. So, altogether, we made about ten grand. I think Rhapsody was holdin' out too because of how she was actin'."

"I'll deal wit her triflin' ass later," Devon said after swallowing a bite of toast. "Now, gimmie five hundred of da work y'all sold, an' half of what y'all made from y'all tricks. Then, you keep half of Rhapsody's cut since she think I'ma lame."

Miracle gladly counted out forty-eight hundred and sixty dollars and handed it over, keeping thirty-six hundred and forty-five dollars for herself. "Thank you, Daddy."

With nothing on the plate but the fork, Devon said while standing, "I gotta go pick up this money from these hoes befo' I go re-up. What'chu 'bout ta get into?"

"First, I have to check up on Kamani at my mom's crib." Kamani was Miracle's five-year-old son. He had been living with her mother, Michelle, in Riviera Beach, FL since she began stripping. She loved her son dearly and spent as much time as possible with him. She also spoiled the boy rotten, which her mother didn't approve of one bit. Devon loved Kamani as well and didn't mind if he stayed with them. But Miracle insisted that he stay where he was to keep him out of harm's way. "Then I have an appointment at the salon. You know I must stay fly." She struck a pose. "After that, I'm goin' to the Palm Beach Lakes Mall with Jazzy and Peachez."

"A'ight. Well, I need ya car ta run around, so take my Charger. Don't be goin' places you ain't 'posed ta an' get my shit stolen. An' when ya done, call me. Okay? Cuz I'ma need ya ta retwist my dreads befo' 8:30 tonite," Devon said before walking in the room to get dressed.

***

After five hours of running errands, like collecting money and putting a few hoes in check, especially Rhapsody, Devon stopped by the Downtown Projects to holla at RahRah. RahRah was Devon's older brother. Well, they weren't really siblings, but they were extremely close. They both grew up together without either of their parents in their lives.

Ronell, aka RahRah, was ten years old when he first met five-year-old Devon. RahRah's grandmother, Miss Candace, being the God-fearing, sweet woman that she was, went to Department of Family and Children Services to gain guardianship of Devon, whom she could immediately sense was going to be different but not difficult to raise. Miss Candace did all this only because she knew Devon's mother before she passed away a while back, leaving an emotionally depressed Devon with nothing but the dismal prospect of endless state foster care.

Miss Candace, unfortunately, passed away herself eight years back at the young age of eighty-six. RahRah had his own place by then, so he took in and taught Devon more of the game than he already had, until he went to do a six-year bid for armed robbery.

Left to survive, Devon put all of RahRah's teachings into motion by petty hustling. Having a disadvantage though, caused Devon to come up with a plan that had its advantages; hustling through hoes at various strip clubs. When RahRah got home, he was not at all surprised at Devon's come-up. And since Devon looked up to RahRah so much, they became business partners.

Pulling up to RahRah's building in Miracle's low-key 2007 Chevy Malibu, Devon walked to the first apartment and knocked on the door. *This is a good time to tell RahRah about opening my own club*, Devon thought while waiting.

"C'mon, big bro, it's hot as fuck out here!"

"Who is it?" an unfamiliar voice shouted back.

"Man, it's Devon. Stop bull …"

Devon was tempted to run. But the nigga holding an AK-47 said, "Get'cha bitch-ass in here. Now!" Devon hesitantly walked in with hands up in the air. "Now take yo' ass ta da back room."

Goddammit, I picked a mighty fine time to visit RahRah, Devon thought.

Once in the requested room, Devon was more than happy to see RahRah was still alive, although he was badly bruised and bloody. The jack boy demanded Devon to sit by RahRah on the floor.

Then, out of nowhere, another nigga with a nine-millimeter emerged from the closet toting a backpack. "Who da fuck that is?" the 9mm-wielding nigga said in a high-pitched voice.

The two jackers were your usual product of the hood, misguided young black males with dreads and golds. And the only difference between the two was the one with the chopper was taller.

"This bitch-lookin' nigga was at da door. I only opened it cuz he looked caked-up."

"Man, y'all can have er'thang," Devon nervously pleaded. "Just don't kill me or my brotha."

The shorter one laughed, then said, "Check that nigga an' let's get missin'. I found what we came fo'."

"Take off that big-ass chain, that watch, an' empty ya pockets," the taller one demanded after the other left the room.

Devon inconspicuously looked at RahRah after removing all the jewelry. RahRah stared at Devon until he caught a glimpse of the .380 on Devon's waist, which was within his reach.

Hoping they were on the same page, Devon said, "This is all I got. It's about eight stacks." Devon dropped the wad on the floor with the jewelry. "That's all of it."

"It betta be."

The jack boy took one hand off the chopper to bend down, giving RahRah the second he needed to swiftly clutch the Beretta .380. The first bullet hit the neck, followed by a successful chest and two stomach shots. The jack boy unknowingly pulled the trigger on the fully automatic AK, dispersing the fifty-round clip as he fell.

"What da fuck …" said the other jack boy, running back into the room.

RahRah then emptied the clip into his torso.

When the shots ceased, both jack boys lie dead. Devon was shaken but not hurt. RahRah, on the other hand, was hit in the thigh by a 7.62, and was bleeding profusely.

"RahRah," Devon stammered while placing a blanket over the gushing wound. "Bro, you gonna be aight. Stay wit me. Help on da way."

"Devon ... Dee ... I ain't ... goin' nowhere," he said just above a whisper.

"I know, big bro. You can't go nowhere. Not now. We 'bout ta open up a club, bro. We goin' legit. No mo' hustlin' fo' you an' me. All you gotta do is stay wit me."

"I ... ain't ... goin no ..." is all RahRah mumbled before closing his eyes in Devon's arms.

Flame

CHAPTER SIX

January 12, 2008 2:20 pm

Tallahassee, FL

Fortunate. That was the only word that Demetrius could think of that best described his trial, and tribulations. *I don't know what God has in store for me, he thought, but I'll try to remember his divine intervention.*

Although it was a sunny afternoon, the temperature still had yet to climb above fifty degrees. It really didn't matter what time or day it was, let alone how cold it was, Demetrius was a free man. Yes, after seven months of stressing, and hundreds of thousands of dollars spent on legal fees, he was an unconfined individual again.

And he owed it all to Matthew O'Hare.

In court, Matthew O'Hare's greatness as a lawyer was the equivalent of the greatness of Kobe Bryant on the_court. O'Hare was just phenomenal at what he did. First, he decided to build his case by focusing on Juan Ramirez and Roger "Blaze" Wright, the co-conspirators that were in cahoots with the government. Although Demetrius denied knowing everybody in the indictment that wasn't his blood relative, it was proven that Blaze and he were acquainted. Besides a few pictures of them together at different venues, they were arrested together after an altercation at a gentlemen's club in Pensacola, Florida, a few years back.

Blaze was claiming to be Demetrius' number one go-to man. O'Hare knew his accusations were true and understood the main reason Blaze was cooperating with the government was because he faced life in prison for being a four-time convicted felon. O'Hare ultimately felt it would be feeble talking to him first at that time, so he centered on Juan.

Juan, on the flip side, was a twenty-three-year-old Puerto Rican, who attended the University of Florida in Gainesville. Demetrius informed O'Hare that he never met Juan, nor had he conducted any type of business with Juan in person, or over the phone. And O'Hare took that into consideration when he interviewed Juan.

After relaxing Juan with small talk and learning Juan had never been arrested before and had a three-year-old son, O'Hare then began grilling him about his involvement in the indictment. To his surprise, Juan was not as nervous as a first-time offender should've been. O'Hare also found it interesting how well-versed Juan was in explaining minute details about how he dealt with Demetrius. His gut instincts told him something was fishy immediately after he concluded that interview.

With the knowledge O'Hare had acquired from interviewing Juan for a second time, he began to put together the pieces of the puzzle after he talked to Blaze. He then advised Demetrius it was best to take the case to trial, especially since the government was pursuing a life sentence by enhancing Demetrius with the federal 851 statute for the kingpin title.

Even after hearing what O'Hare had discovered at that time, Demetrius was intimidated by the notion of taking the feds to the door, because leading up to the day of the trial, he remained leery of O'Hare's findings. O'Hare wanted him to trust in what was revealed during the discovery process. But he really doubted everything O'Hare supposedly dug up when Blaze was on the stand spilling his guts. And seeing how the jury was eating up Blaze's testimony only made matters worse. He honestly thought it was all over for him, although Juan had yet to testify.

O'Hare mentally licked his chops when the time came for Juan to take the stand. After a few minutes of insignificant questioning, Juan began telling the truth and nothing but the truth, leaving Demetrius feeling that there was some hope.

According to Juan's testimony, he had never seen or spoken to Demetrius in his life. However, he told how he did purchase nothing more than fourteen grams of powder cocaine at a time from Blaze, which he bought twice a week to use socially. He'd call Blaze on the days that he knew Blaze was in town, and they'd always meet just outside of the UF campus to do business.

From there, Juan began explaining how it came about him testifying against Demetrius. He recalled the first day that he was arrested. Agent John Reid and Agent Ken Brunel, interrogated him for three dismal hours. Not getting anything useful, Agents Reid and Brunel offered him a deal, cooperate for a lesser sentence. He knew the consequences of snitching, but the agents painted a picture so beautiful that he couldn't refuse. And he eventually agreed to testify on Blaze.

Thinking the easy part was over, the agents informed Juan they didn't give two shits about Blaze. Apparently, they wanted him to testify against a man he'd never heard of or seen. He eventually reneged on the deal. But Agent Reid, a twenty-year-veteran with a fiery temper, wasn't taking no for an answer. Reid then pressed Brunel, his young and gullible partner of five years, into coercing Juan with threats of receiving thirty years in a maximum security prison, and arresting his baby's mother for conspiracy.

Juan quickly folded from the weight of the threats. He ultimately agreed, and Reid and Brunel proceeded to coach him over the next few days. They taught him what to say about Demetrius, including details of how they met, when they did business, etc. They made sure he was ready when the time came. But things changed after his second meeting with O'Hare.

The second visit with O'Hare was on a more personal level than anything. O'Hare's way with words caused Juan to open up after getting him to lower his defenses. He was soon telling O'Hare what the agents were doing. O'Hare then instructed him to tell his affluent parents about the shady agents. In the end, his parents contacted Internal Affairs, which began to investigate the accusations against Agents Reid and Brunel.

The I.A. investigations caused a panicky Brunel to confess. Brunel told I.A. that for the last two years, he and Agent Reid had been threatening first-time offenders, in order to make them testify against career criminals of more importance. He also told I.A. about a few other misdeeds Reid had committed, like planting drugs on suspects and performing illegal searches. Brunel did all this just to save as much of his ass as possible.

Then, with Brunel's help, I.A. recorded a session where both Reid and Brunel made sure that Juan had the facts straight for Demetrius' impending trial. All this was done without Agent Reid's knowledge.

After hearing Juan's account, with valid proof from I.A., the judge presiding over the trial instructed the jury to discredit Blaze's testimony, since it too could've been coached. And in return for the information on the crooked agents, the U.S. Attorney was willing to give Juan a plea agreement for sixteen months, and the shady agents were taken into custody.

Now, the only evidence the government had at that time was the single phone conversation. The recording was less than a minute long and was barely capable of being heard. The one sentence heard clearly was someone saying, "Yeah, I got enuff chicken ta feed da whole family this time." Demetrius knew the voice was his brother's, Tyrell. But they didn't.

With only the grainy tape as evidence, the jury deliberated for almost an hour. They ultimately returned with a verdict of not guilty on all counts.

O'Hare pulled it off again, Demetrius thought as he left the courtroom unhindered. *Because beating the feds is like beating Floyd Mayweather Jr; a slim chance to none.* He smiled the entire time as he walked freely out of the building into the fresh air.

When Demetrius saw Chad, Bubba's oldest son, waiting for him outside, his smile faded. His nightmare was over. But Bubba, Obie, and Tyrell were still locked up and facing time. *I got y'all, no matter how much time them crackas give you,* he thought as he got into Chad's 2008 Jaguar XJ full of rage, because I'm my brother's keeper!

***

January 12, 2008 3:00 pm

West Palm Beach, FL. Palm Beach County Jail

"What da lick read, Dee?" RahRah said through the phone behind the glass.

"Ain't nuttin' goin' on," Devon replied. "It's da same shit, just a diff'rent toilet."

Damn, I hate seeing RahRah like this, Devon thought.

RahRah had been locked up ever since that home invasion. Devon was arrested but was released that same day after they both told investigators exactly what went down in the crib.

Rah first spent two weeks in the hospital, almost having to have his leg amputated, before being sent to the county jail with two first-degree murder charges. Although the gun was registered in Devon's name, he was eventually charged with possession of a firearm by a convicted felon and not for the killings, since it was ruled self-defense. And since he saved both Devon and his life that day, Devon visited him faithfully. "I wanna say thanks fo' keepin' my books straight," he said, looking more depressed than usual.

"Miss me wit that, bro." Devon smiled. "I dunno why you keep on wit that shit. Besides, it's da least I can do fo' a nigga that told me where his stash at. So I got'cha, if nobody else does. If it wasn't fo' you, we'd be ... "

"I know, I know." Rah sighed. "Ain't no need ta worry 'bout that no mo'."

"That shit still fuckin' wit'cha, huh?"

"Nah. It ain't that." He shifted in his seat. "I just holla'd at my lawyer befo' ya came, an' … an' he talkin' 'bout I may have ta go up da road fo' three years."

"Shit … look at it this way, you could eitha be dead rite now or facin' mo' time than three years. Rememba now, they ain't charge ya wit da drugs in da crib."

Rah nodded. "Y' know what? You dead rite. I'ma holla at my lawyer an' tell him to run it, only after tryna get it down ta two years."

They both laughed.

For the next fifty minutes, they talked mainly about hoes before switching to discussing future plans. Devon told Rah their money put together was in pocket for the strip club, and the name was going to be StudioX. Devon also promised him that everything was almost legit now, no more hustling. But pimping wasn't going nowhere.

When it was about time to leave, Rah said, "I'm proud of ya, Dee. If they woulda told me back then when you were five that'chu would be who you are, or where you at now, I wouldn't believe 'em." He shrugged. "I dunno. I guess ya was always diff'rent, tho'."

"Look at who I grew up wit. You was a bad influence." Devon smiled. "But you made me da G I am today. Well, you an' O-Dogg from *Menace II Society*."

"Mannnnn, bullshit ain't nuttin' ."

They both laughed before saying their goodbyes.

CHAPTER SEVEN

March 3, 2008 4:20 pm

Coleman, FL

"Damn, I can't wait ta see my dawg," JJ declared as he stopped in front of the building. "Oh, there my nigga go over there." He then began to honk the horn.

Bizzy suspiciously eyed the black 2009 Cadillac Escalade on 28's before spotting JJ behind the wheel, accompanied by a female passenger. He hastily walked to the truck, with his few belongings, and jumped in the back.

"Wassup, lil bruh?" Bizzy excitedly said before reaching up front to give JJ a manly hug.

Quickly breaking the embrace, JJ drove away from the building that he prayed he'd never become a resident of. Then he looked back, and said, "Dawg, you done got all fat an' shit." He shook his head. "You was prolly up in there sleepin' all day, eatin' honey buns an' all type of sweets. But don't worry, Fat Boy, I'ma get'cha back rite on my pussy-robics workout plan."

Boy, I missed my lil bruh, Bizzy thought as he laughed.

It had been almost eight months since Bizzy was on the turf. He turned himself in on July 7, after getting JJ prepared for his absence and attending his eight-year-old son's birthday party in Tally. He pleaded out to ten months and did only sixty-eight days at Coleman's low custody institution.

Although Bizzy didn't have to do hard time, he sure did have a hard time relaxing. During his short bid, he only thought about two things: his pops going to trial, and the money. Once he heard his pops whooped the feds two months ago, he only worried about the money then.

Now that he was out, it was time to lay low and enjoy his share of the money, like JJ was obviously doing.

Focusing on the chocolate brickhouse in the passenger seat, Bizzy said, "Is this my comin' home gift? If so, then she need ta get back here an' give me some—"

"Nah, dawg," JJ cut him off. "This Rhapsody … rememba her from Club Leo's in Orlando?"

It took a second, but Bizzy remembered. "Yeah!" He smiled. "So where ya fine-ass friend at? Her name was ... Mystery."

"Her name is Miracle," Rhapsody retorted. "She stayed in Orlando cuz she didn't wanna come. She strictly 'bout bizness."

"Dawg, just chill. We'll be home in thirty minutes. Wit all da money we got, payin' fo' pussy is just like it's free." He made a gesture towards Rhapsody. "It ain't trickin' if ya got it, an' I'm still gettin' it!"

I can't believe this nigga is flaunting in front of this hoe, Bizzy thought. "About that: What da play lookin' like?"

"We gonna rap when we get ta da crib," JJ said. "Oh, I do gotta surprise fo' ya at da crib."

"Is that rite?"

"You'll see." JJ smiled, showing his now diamond-studded platinum teeth.

Bizzy sat back and finally started to relax for the first time in nine months. *I hope the surprise JJ has for me can suck a mean dick.*

***

March 3, 2008 5:17 pm

Orlando, FL

The bumper-to-bumper rush hour traffic on I-4 turned an ordinary thirty-minute joyride into a fifty-minute headache inducing trip. Overall, the ride was a silent one, as far as conversation. The six, twelve-inch Kickers however, whammed the whole way, causing Bizzy to doze off not even ten minutes after leaving Coleman.

"Biz," JJ said, pulling into the driveway. "Aye, wake up. We here."

Bizzy fluttered his eyes open, then he yawned while stretching.

"C'mon, dawg. Let's go inside an' smoke some of this blueberry."

"I can't do nuttin'," Bizzy said in a sleepy voice, "but work an' fuck cuz of da two years papers I'm on."

JJ and Rhapsody didn't waste any time getting out of the truck. Bizzy, on the other hand, lackadaisically excited. When he finally was on his feet, he had to do a double-take. The immaculate white two-story house he faced had a nice green lawn, as did the other houses in the vicinity. He gazed down the litter-free road and witnessed a group of white and black kids playing hockey in the street. *We must've stopped here to pick up someone*, he thought as he took in the scenery, *because this is too "Beverly Hills" for JJ.* "Lil bruh, who live here? I hope this is one of those spots where da white bitches eat ass, suck toes, an' ... " Just thinking about pussy made his dick jump. "Lil bruh, just get me ta da hoes."

"Nah, this my ... my bad, this is our new crib," JJ replied as he opened the front door, letting Rhapsody in first since she claimed to have to piss badly. Walking into the foyer, he continued, "This bitch has three bedrooms, three bathrooms, a jacuzzi in da master bedroom, which is my room, an' one by da pool. It cost a nigga three hundred grand. But I got it fo' da low cuz it was goin' thru foreclosure. I copped it 'bout five months ago."

As Bizzy looked around, he nodded his head in approval. "What about her?" he asked bluntly. "She live here, too?"

They took a seat in the all-white living room, then JJ answered, "Not really. She stays here mainly on da weekends when she's up here strippin' wit her homegurl. She don't like stayin at da hotel wit her gurl, so she come here. Dawg, da bitch cool as fuck, an' we been vibin' real hard lately. She say she wanna come up here fo' good, but she gotta tell her ... "

"Goddamn, JJ! Why you didn't tell me my boy was home?" Bizzy knew that voice. It could have only been one person.

"Pops, what'chu doin' here?" Bizzy said without delaying.

"I wanted to surprise you."

Bizzy stood up and embraced Demetrius for a long second. It had been close to a year passing without the father and son seeing each other.

"An' I bet'cha thought my surprise was gonna fuck ya ta sleep, huh?" JJ added with a grin.

"I was hopin' so … anyways, I was gonna visit ya sum time this week after I holla'd at my P.O. You still in Tally, rite?"

"Not for long," he said seriously as he took a seat. "I'm about to ... Where is your girl, JJ?"

"Oh, you good," he said. "She know ta stay outta da way when I have company."

"Well," Demetrius continued, "I'm about to relocate to Palm Beach somewhere." He then proceeded to tell Bizzy and JJ how he felt he was constantly being watched, which kind of spooked him from doing any business. The reason for him going to Palm Beach County was to hide out, while Bizzy and JJ quietly kept business afloat until he could come up with a supreme alternative.

Bizzy protested the idea of hustling so early. He had two years' probation, and he wanted to lay low himself. He didn't get a chance to speak his mind, though, because his father wasn't hearing it.

Demetrius was in too deep. All he wanted was to keep his Peruvian connect happy, especially when he was buying a kilo in Peru for eight hundred American dollars! It was already bad enough his connect didn't want to deal with him after he beat trial, because the connect thought he was hot. He got back in good with the connect, though, only after RBF and a few other associates vouched for him by showing how Blaze was the snitch.

The connect was still cautious though, because he wasn't allowed to buy no more than one hundred keys at a time now. Demetrius felt insulted at that time because he was getting five hundred keys fronted to him before he got jammed up. He gradually let it go due to him trying to keep the connect happy until the negotiations were back on the table.

"That shaky muthafucka, Blaze. I knew he was pussy da first time I seen him," JJ angrily said.

"Whateva happen ta that rat?" Bizzy inquired.

"Last I heard, he was trying to tell on everybody and their mothers that he sold dope to," Demetrius responded.

"Punk muthafucka," JJ barked out through clenched jaws. "I pray they don't kill his bitch-ass in there. I'm willin' ta kill him myself!"

"Don't worry," Demetrius said, "I'll take care of him."

"What they doin' wit uncle Ty an' cousins Bubba an' Obie?" Bizzy asked.

Demetrius sighed. "So far, Tyrell facing eighty-eight months, Obie looking at a hundred and fifteen months, and they are trying to give Bubba a hundred and ninety-two months."

Silence filled the room for more than a minute.

"Anyways, back to business," Demetrius said, breaking the silence. "I know I kept you out of RBF business for your safety, but now I need the two of you. I know the two of you are doing good in Savannah, but I'll show you how to get Bill Gates money, son. Just follow my lead, abide by the code, and be wise. So, for now, all you have to do is serve whom I say so only, hear me?" He looked at the two sternly, hoping they understood.

Bizzy and JJ nodded.

"Besides, JJ told me about the stupid but profitable come-up in South Carolina, Byron, so I know the two of you aren't starving. That's good, because that will only make you think wiser. A broke man will result to extreme measures for a dollar, remember that. So you two just keep a foot on the gas until I'm back in the driver seat. Okay?"

Again, Bizzy and JJ nodded in agreement.

"Now what we gonna do?" Bizzy asked. "I know one thing, I need a bust-it baby like JJ's ashy lips need Chapstick." He laughed while looking at JJ. "On da real, tho', tell Rhapsody ta let a nigga ... "

JJ licked his lips, then replied, "Fuck you! Talkin' 'bout my lips ashy. They chapped. An' no, nigga!"

"Ole' lovey-dovey-ass nigga." Bizzy turned to his pops. "Wassup? Don't tell me yo' forty-five-year-old ass need Viagra ta get it up."

"Boy, I'm forty-three. And I'm fucking women you wished you could conversate with." He smiled. "Plus, I can't do nothing this evening. I just wanted to see my boy before heading down to Palm Beach tonight." He then stood up and headed towards the door. "You two just remember what I said. I'll call you later, Byron. And, by the way, you look like you've gained fifty pounds. That's not sexy. You're a Woodson, not a Klump."

JJ laughed hysterically, while Bizzy didn't find it that funny.

When Demetrius finally left, and Rhapsody went for a swim, JJ and Bizzy talked business. JJ informed Bizzy that the clientele in O-Town were plentiful and loyal. In six months, he sold every brick they obtained from the lick. He sold no more than a key at a time, at a price of twenty-one thousand five hundred dollars, in order to stay off everybody's radar. He then told Bizzy his money was in a safe place, and he'd retrieve it whenever Bizzy was ready for it.

After thirty minutes or so of catching up with the times, Bizzy reached the point where pussy was the only thing on his mind. JJ knew this as well, since he would have to continually snap Bizzy out of daydreams, trances, or whatever.

Since Bizzy didn't feel like hunting down new pussy, he decided to holla at his BM. His baby's mother, LaShawn, stayed cross town in an area known as Beirut. It was an ill-bred project on the westside, an unfamiliar face in Beirut most likely wound up in a body bag at any given moment. But the urge to get his dick wet gave him an I-don't-give-a-fuck mentality. He needed some pussy. Now!

Plus, it wouldn't hurt to spend some time with his youngest son. JJ and he were only in O-Town less than three weeks before he had to turn himself in, which pissed his BM off. *Well, we'll fight first and fuck later*, he thought.

"Lemme see ya car keys. I'm goin' ta LaShawn's crib tonite," he finally said.

"You ain't drivin' my Caddy. But'cha can take ya new 2009 Camaro in da garage," JJ said with a smile as he pointed to the key holder in the kitchen. "There's a house key on there fo' ya, too."

Without thanking JJ for the new ride, Bizzy somberly said, "I'ma holla tomorrow, lil bruh." He then walked towards the door. "An' I may need ya ta get that tomorrow. I need ta get caught up!"

"I got'cha, dawg."

***

March 19, 2008 7:07am

Orlando, FL

Phone rings

The morning was definitely not JJ's favorite part of the day. Anything before noon was deemed untimely, especially after going to bed in the wee hours of the morning. An emergency was acceptable for disturbing him. But he even had a few stipulations where an emergency wouldn't make him get up before he was ready.

For example, about six years back, he slept through a homicide. This happened in Seaport, next door to his place in the Fred Cassel Projects. The domestic violence began with yelling, which pissed him off, while the seven shots that followed later caused him to only turn over. He even slept through the police knocking at his door in search of information.

Phone rings

"Keema," JJ said, barely above a whisper. "Yo', KiKi. Get da fuckin' phone."

Phone rings

"Get da damn phone. Shit!" he said louder as he nudged the body next to his.

Disturbing her peace and causing her to stir, Rhapsody muttered, "Why I gotta answer yo' phone? You answer it." She flipped over, found a comfortable position, and proceeded to fall asleep while talking under her breath.

"What? What'chu say?" JJ was furious now. "Damn, I hate y'all lazy-ass ... "

Phone rings

Reaching over the side of the bed, he snatched up his pants and took the phone from the pocket. He was full of rage, ready to cuss out the person calling him. Upon seeing that it was Bizzy calling kind of cooled him down. *Is this nigga calling me about something particularly important*? he wondered.

"Wassup, dawg?" JJ answered, trying to sound sleepy.

"Lil bruh, it's time ta go ta work," Bizzy said without greeting. "We've been workin' hard wit my pops fo' over two weeks now an' ain't got shit in pocket, yet. It's time ta get us a second job. So you need ta get up an' go get that now. I got some B.I. I need ta handle."

JJ rubbed his eyes as he sat up. He looked at the time on the phone and said, "It's still early. Y' know I don't do da mornin'—"

"Nigga, get'cha ass up an' go get that!" Bizzy yelled, causing JJ to take the phone from his ear. "You 'round here flossin', stuntin' an' shit, while I'm broke. Nigga, I ain't gotta fuck thang in my pocket, not even lint. So, go get that an' call me back ASAP!"

Before JJ could say another word, Bizzy hung up.

"Bitch-ass nigga," JJ said to himself. "Who da fuck he think I am?" *That's the last fucking straw*, JJ thought, *I've had enough of his shit.*

JJ been had enough of Bizzy's bossy, ungrateful ways. Ever since Bizzy's father gave them the family's connect, his big homie had changed for the worse. The last two weeks alone was the most running around he ever did in his life, by himself. He was "supposed to be" Bizzy's partner-in-crime, not a do-boy. Whatever they did that involved a come-up they did together and split the proceeds fifty-fifty.

JJ then began to think. *Yeah, Bizzy may have took me under his wing and put me on back in the days. Yeah, Bizzy may be the brains of us two. Yeah, Bizzy was more than a friend he was a brother. But I'm not going to let NO nigga continue to disrespect me time and time again*, he concluded.

As far as JJ was concerned, he performed all the dirty work anyway: the killing, the delivering, the collecting, etc. The only thing Bizzy was good for really was calling the connect to re-up and getting them out of jams. Other than that, he didn't need Bizzy. *Yeah, that's right, I don't need him*, he thought, *because I'll find my own connect with the money ... my money*!

"Yeah, my money," he whispered to himself, smiling at how the words felt great exiting his mouth. "Aye, Keema, wake up." He shook her.

"What now, Javon?" she responded without moving an inch.

There were only a select few that called him by his real name. Being called Javon reminded him of his deadbeat father, Javon Wilkes Sr. He hated having the same name as the junkie that shot his mother, Sadie, the only person in the world that truly loved him. He was five when his father paralyzed his mother from the chest down because she wouldn't give him ten dollars to support his crack addiction. Now, Miss Sadie, lived permanently in a convalescent home; and his father was killed in prison when he was eight, which didn't faze him.

JJ wasn't the only child, either. He had four older brothers, the eldest being twenty-nine, and a sixteen-year-old sister. They were separated after the incident and raised by different family members throughout the southeast region of USA. He was raised by one of his mother's sisters, who was uncaring and an alcoholic. He had no positive male figures in his life, no guidance. He did inherit a fucked-up temper, which led him down a path of destruction. By age ten, he was holding guns and drugs for older niggas on the block, before gradually graduating to shooting and selling them. He dropped out of school in seventh grade and began to steal, rob and hustle. He went in and out of the JDC, Juvenile Detention Center, until he met Bizzy.

"Aye, I'm finna bounce back ta Georgia rite now. So you need ta make up ya mind rite now if you comin'. If ya are, then get'cha ass up." He didn't wait for a response, he jumped out of bed and went into the bathroom.

While freshening up, he found himself thinking about Bizzy and the money again. He really didn't want to fuck over his main man, but Bizzy assumed he had total control over him. He just wanted to show Bizzy he wasn't a bitch by taking the money back to his neck of the woods. And, for all he cared, Bizzy could suck a dick. Bizzy wasn't a killer, Bizzy wasn't much smarter than he was. Bizzy wasn't his real brother, either. *But Bizzy has a father that's the head of the notorious RockBottom Family, and one phone call can get the entire city of Savannah wiped off the map,* he concluded.

"Fuck, Bizzy! He eitha gonna let it go or prepare fo' war!" he professed into the mirror, before exiting the bathroom.

CHAPTER EIGHT

March 20, 2008 10:00 pm

West Palm Beach, FL

The grand opening of StudioX couldn't have come at a better time. First and foremost, it was the beginning of spring. The return of torrid weather was unquestionably going to bring the big-spending tricks out from hibernation. Plus, with spring break and BET's *Spring Bling* generating money in the area, the young vacationing crowd was going to pack every club in Palm Beach County during the first week in April.

The whole StudioX process began with finding and purchasing a building in the correct zone. After that, acquiring the proper licenses and hiring staff came, all of which was the easy part. The most difficult task, nevertheless, was thinking of what direction to take the club. The whole idea was to create a club that was state-of-the-art and one-of-a-kind. That took a few months to accomplish, and the final outcome from limitless brainstorming was astonishing.

The 4,560 square-foot building used to be a family-owned furniture store before it went out of business. It was located in a busy plaza on Palm Beach Lakes Boulevard by I-95. *The location is perfect*, Devon thought at that time.

With an ample amount of space, the club was truly unlike most of the modest and diminutive, hundred-fifty-person maximum capacity gentlemen's clubs. The exterior alone said that the club was classy, with its very large awning over the entrance, the luminous lights and the alluring, lively colors of the building. And that was just the tip of the iceberg. The interior was must-see.

The first few seconds inside, partygoers more than likely would forget there were actually women of all shapes, sizes and colors, strutting around and dancing somewhere in their birthday suits. So, upon entering the club, the elegant gift shop was to the left where just about anything X-rated could be purchased, like the hottest and newest pornos, sex toys, lingerie, etc. From there, there was an electric sliding door to walk through that led to a thirty-seat bar/restaurant with two sixty-inch Vizio flatscreens showing sports at either end, a few poker video game systems on the bar, a pool table and a couple dartboards.

After deciding whether to eat or not, the action itself was beyond yet another electric sliding door to the right, where thumping music could be heard. Entering that door, there was a cashier accompanied by two tall, three-hundred-plus-pound bouncers. Once the twenty dollars was paid, the very first thing that was hard not to notice was the huge stage with three poles towards the rear of the room, flanked by two large exotic fish-filled aquariums. Two smaller stages occupied both sides of the room, as well.

There were comfortable leather couches lining the walls, and La-Z-Boy-style chairs were on the floor, along with a group of ten privacy booths. Another large bar was to the left, which also had a platform for the DJ's booth. Disco balls, strobe lights, neon lights, black lights, and Christmas lights illuminated the room just enough, while a projector showed a fuck flick against the wall of the huge stage. Finally, the restrooms were to the right of the huge stage, and the champagne room was to the left.

The champagne room was sure to be the main attraction. Besides the cheap to expensive bottles of bubbly, this was the anything-goes-for-the-right-price room. The girls arranged their own prices, and every girl in the room was available. Condoms and other products, like aspirin and Alka-Seltzer, were also readily available via vending machines. There were twenty spacious booths, with each booth containing a comfy leather loveseat, a thirty-inch Vizio flatscreen, an iPod radio, a small refrigerator, and lubricants. These booths were specially made for beating pussy, and the beats were made for booty-clapping, thus giving the club the title StudioX.

***

March 21, 2008 6:10 a.m.

West Palm Beach, FL

After a prosperous first night, Devon and Miracle were both burnt out. Once the club closed early at 4 a.m., because every sip of alcohol and most of the food was gone sooner than expected, they both collected money from dancers, counted the night's profit, and ordered things that were needed. The general plan was to turn Studio X into a twenty-four-hour establishment within a month. Hopefully, by then, the club would be prominent and well over-stocked. However, if the club stayed packed to its four-hundred-twenty-person maximum capacity, like it was last night, for the next two upcoming weeks, things could transpire a lot sooner.

To show Miracle appreciation for her hard work, Devon took her to Denny's once all business was conducted and concluded. Devon officially retired Miracle from the pole and hired her as a secretary and treasurer. They both didn't know much about running a legit business, but they vowed to learn together. They were lovers, best friends, and business partners now.

At the nearest Denny's, they found a cozy spot away from everybody. They both promptly ordered the Grand Slam with an OJ.

While waiting for their food, Devon sparked up a conversation. "Where ya wanna move to?"

Miracle was taken aback by the question. "Huh?"

Devon laughed. "Lemme rephrase that then, where would you like to live? What city?"

"What're you talkin' about, Dee?" she said, still confused.

"Damn, girl! I'm askin' ya where would ya like ta live? I'm gonna get us a house soon, an' I wanted ta know what city would ya like ta live in?"

It was at this very moment when Miracle knew her love for Devon was divine. She never owned a house before, let alone lived in a big one. Since she could remember, she and her seven siblings always stayed in an apartment or a tiny house, and they didn't stay in one spot for long. They lived on almost every street in Downtown West Palm Beach, twice! Her parents weren't citizens of the U.S., making it hard to find good-paying jobs. But, no matter how bad the circumstances were, her parents made sure she and her sisters and brothers were well-fed and educated. All the other necessities, though, like clothes and hygiene products, were either hand-me-downs, shared, or off-brand.

Miracle could also remember working since age nine after school with her father at his Jamaican restaurant. She was an ambitious, thankful child, which stuck with her to this day. Once she graduated from Forest Hill High School, she had plans of furthering her education. But lack of resources turned her dream into a wish, that led her to stripping at age nineteen. She fortunately met Devon, the love of her life, at work a year later, whom she was incredibly grateful for being a part of her life.

The stern look on Devon's face let her know how serious the question was. "It doesn't matter, Daddy." She smiled from ear to ear. "As long as I'm with you," she cooed.

"I hear ya. An' you don't have ta call me Daddy no mo'. That's fo' them otha hoes now." Devon paused. "An, if ya want, my lil homie Kamani can live wit us, too. I love ya son, so I'll make sho' da house has a big yard wit a playground or whateva he want." Devon then leaned forward in the chair. "You my girl, an' have been fo' almost four years now. You have really grown on me this last year. You da only person I love an' trust. Hell, you da only person I have strong feelings fo', otha than Kamani an' RahRah."

Those were the words Miracle ... Nope, scratch that.

Those were the words Marie Maxwell was waiting to hear for the longest. She swore she wasn't going to cry if this day ever came. But she couldn't stop the tears from building up in her eyes.

"We'll talk 'bout it mo' later. I don't wanna make ya cry, so I'ma switch da subject," Devon said, reaching across the table and wiping Miracle's tears away. "So, I see yo' ... "

"Here's your breakfast," the wrinkled, cigarette-smelling old white woman said while placing the food on the table. "Would you care for anything else?"

Devon looked at Miracle, then answered, "Not at da moment. If we do, I'll holla fo' ya."

"Well, you do just that, honey," she cheerfully said before walking off.

"Now, what was I sayin' befo' Agatha da Marlboro-smokin' Witch interrupted us?"

Miracle giggled before shrugging.

"Hmmmm ... oh, yeah. I see that'cha invited ya uncle ta da grand openin' last nite. Did he enjoy himself?"

"I didn't invite him, but we talked. He was with some guy he said was his buddy from back in the days that's back in town."

"Oh, okay."

No more was said as they began eating. Ten minutes later, both plates contained only small pieces of pancakes. Seeing the plates empty, Agatha the Witch brought them the check. Some playful debating of who was going to foot the bill ensued before Miracle paid for breakfast, and Devon covered the tip.

They exited Denny's overstuffed, and dog tired. Lazily, they climbed into Devon's newly purchased stock 2009 BMW X6. Miracle drove, upon Devon's request, the ten-minute trip back to Da City.

Finally arriving home, they slowly made their way inside. Surprisingly, only a few jits and older niggas were on the block at the time. *The buck doesn't stop on 20th and Beautiful,* Miracle thought as she shook her head.

"I forgot to tell you, Dee, that Rhapsody called me."

I haven't heard from that stanking bitch since she went to Orlando almost three weeks ago, Devon thought. "What that bitch want?"

"She up in Georgia ... "

"Georgia! What da fuck ... y' know what? I don't even give a fuck. She missin' out."

Miracle was going to tell Devon what else Rhapsody said but decided to wait for a better time.

"I'm sleepier than a newborn fresh off da titty," Devon declared, yawning while unlocking the door.

Miracle walked in first, and said, "I have somethin' that'll knock ya out in five minutes."

"I can't smoke no mo'. I'm smoked out!"

"This better than weed, coke and ecstasy," she teased.

With a raised brow, Devon asked, "What'chu got?"

"This pussy!"

***

March 21, 2008 6:30 pm

Palm Beach, FL

"First, I want to thank you for taking me out last night," Demetrius said as he greeted Virgil with a firm handshake. "I haven't been out since I've returned to town."

"No prahblem," Virgil said in his thick Jamaican accent. "Me hadda gud time meself. Da queens dem in there were blazin'."

"That they were." Demetrius laughed as they sat down in the tasteful room at The Breakers Hotel. "It seemed like you knew one of them personally. She looked as if she should be up on stage."

"That's me niece there," Virgil stiffly retorted. "Me haven't seen her inna long time. She was suhprised ta see me as me was of seein' her. She tole me she ah secretary, not dancer."

"Well ... let's get down to RBF business then," Demetrius said, changing the topic. "You've been holding down PBC since I left here. As I've informed you how things are going to change because of the feds, I'm just glad to have someone out here I can rely on, that didn't get mixed up in the buffoonery." He then patted Virgil on his knee. "So, tell me again, how many kilos you're pushing a week?"

"Befo' da bombaclot govament dem fuck up da money inna economy, me moved forty ah week at twenty-point-five ah piece. Since 2007, me been movin' twenty-five on ah gud week at twenty-four grand."

"That's good, Dread." Demetrius did the numbers in his head while nodding. "But, that's not good enough. I know for a fact that I can sell sixty a week here. It doesn't matter how bad the economy is, it's always going to be money out here! Dope money is always circulating in the streets. The government just wants the ignorant to think that the recession will affect all monies, whereas dope money will always exist. The government will never cease that dope from coming across that water, because they're living off dope money too, in a way. It doesn't matter what happens in this country, whether it be a war, disease epidemic, or recession, they will continue to live the same way ... every day.

"See, I've been in Tallahassee for almost two decades now. Since I've been living there, I've changed the way I speak, dress and look, in order to socialize with politicians and people of their class. Slowly, over time, I've become one of them. I know exactly how they think, and how they think the poor and feeble-minded will settle for anything. Not me, no sir." He shook his head.

"Thanks to Sun Tzu and *The Art of War* I have two mentalities now, theirs and the streets. So, I don't fully blame you, Dread, for being a 'go-fer'. But I do blame you for letting your lack of knowledge affect RBF's business. I knew you were slacking the last few years, but I let it slide since you're my buddy. Shit has hit the fan now, so I have no time for excuses. Now, or in the future."

Virgil tried to take every word with a grain of salt, but he took them to heart instead. He felt embarrassed. He felt like all he did, all the money he made, the hits he set up, the cover-ups he oversaw for

RBF amounted to nothing. And all this he was enduring now was because he wasn't selling as much dope as he used to.

"Virgil," Demetrius continued, "I know you may feel like I'm belittling you. I'm not. I just want you to realize every penny counts now, and your lack of hustle the last few years has cost RBF a helluva lot of copper Lincolns." He then paused to see how well Virgil was taking this. "Now, I'm going to take control of this county because I know its true worth and potential. You, Dread, my old friend, will be doing exactly what I say from here on out, hear me?"

Through clenched teeth, Virgil replied, "Yah, mon, me got'chu."

"Good." Demetrius smiled as he pat Virgil's knee again before standing. "Now, call up all of your people and tell them the new going rate is eighteen-point-five." *It's time to claim my throne and get the money back that I lost from the feds fucking with me,* Demetrius thought while walking to the mini bar. *It's killing season*!

Flame

CHAPTER NINE

April 1, 2008 3:10 pm

Savannah, GA

It had been only a couple weeks now, and Bizzy had yet to track down JJ. His patience was growing thinner than Al Sharpton's permed hair. His father had been trying effortlessly to contact him for a week, but his personal vendetta was number one on the agenda. Plus, he refused to explain to his father how a nigga that he trusted ran off with his cash. *I'll explain everything to him, he thought, once I find and kill this bitch-ass nigga*!

He had been searching all over Seaport for JJ. He'd been shot at multiple times for being in the wrong place, asking the wrong questions. He triple checked motels, associates they knew together, and JJ's honeycomb hideouts. He left no rock unturned, he had no leads. It was as if JJ vanished into thin air!

Nevertheless, he had one last option to exhaust. JJ left him no choice. It was by *all* means necessary now.

He knew precisely how much JJ loved his beloved mother. It was originally a toss-up between Ms. Sadie or JJ's two toddler daughters that JJ swore weren't his. So, choosing beloved Ms. Sadie was a sure way to get his money back. And he knew exactly where to find her, because he occasionally went with JJ to visit Ms. Sadie, a woman he wished was his mother because she was the sweetest woman he ever met. Bizzy was sure he'd catch up with JJ at the expensive convalescent home on White Cliff Road in south Savannah. Not only did he know where her facility was located, he knew the visiting days and hours, and location of Ms. Sadie's room.

"This nigga is goin' ta flip when he finds out this ain't no April Fool's joke," Bizzy said to no one in particular as he sat in the rental car outside of Willow Lake Homes. "Ms. Sadie, I'm sorry fo' what's 'bout ta happen, but'cha coward-ass son is da blame."

He jumped out of the 2009 Ford Taurus, and made his way to visit sweet, old Ms. Sadie. By himself.

***

April 1, 2008 3:32 PM

Macon, GA

Meanwhile, almost three and a half hours west of Seaport, JJ was handling business.

"I want'chu to yell my name," JJ demanded, while thrashing Rhapsody from the back. She began to throw her juicy ass back at him, challenging him to go harder. His onslaught on her forty-four-inch ass sent tidal waves down to her thighs. The melodious sound of balls, pussy and bodies colliding filled the room. "I said … say my name!"

"JJ!"

"Nah, say my real name!" He dug one hand into her fleshy hip and slapped her ass with the other. "Say it!"

The stinging pain combined with a state of gratification caused Rhapsody to sexually erupt. "Ooohhhh … Ja-Ja-Javon!"

He slapped her ass again, then he gripped the small of her back, pushed her face into the bed, and dug deeper into her mushy, hot pussy. And just before he filled her creampie, he pulled out. "Now suck this dick, an' don'tchu spit," he instructed.

Rhapsody was more than willing to bless him with some fire head, especially after he made her nut four times in a half hour. She swiftly flipped over and got on her knees, as JJ stood up with his back pressed against the headboard. She swiped the stray hairs from her face, then she slowly jacked his dick while sucking his balls and staring into his eyes.

She sucked on his balls like they were giant Jawbreakers before placing her full, succulent lips on the crown of his erection. She kissed and licked the crown to tease him, then she gradually took him in her mouth. Inch by inch she swallowed him whole, only stopping when his tool hit the back of her throat. She gagged, but, like Superhead, she removed him from her mouth in a slow manner, leaving his dick covered in spit. She finally sped up the process, sucking and slurping while jacking his wood.

JJ grabbed Rhapsody's head for extra support and balance as his knees started to give out. He stumbled backwards against the headboard, bracing himself for when he was about to explode. And that was going to happen real soon.

"Stop," he suddenly said while pushing her off his dick. Yet, like a true maneater, she continued to devour his manhood like it was the last supper. "I said stop!"

With spittle around her mouth, she aggravatedly murmured, "What's wrong?"

"Nuttin'." He then began to beat his meat. "Open ya mouth. I need sumthin' ta aim at."

Rhapsody readily opened wide with an extended tongue and waited, like how a baby bird waited for momma bird to feed it. By the ugly look on JJ's twisted face, she knew it wouldn't be much longer. Suddenly, when she least expected it, stream after stream of hot man sauce hit her mouth and chin. She thirstily swallowed what she could, leaving the rest to drip down her chin onto her double-Ds, which she politely rubbed into her skin.

JJ collapsed on the bed. "You a cold monsta," was all he could say.

"An' you a pussy pounder," she proclaimed, lying on his heaving chest. "You just beat this good pussy all up. How you fucked me just then, I thought I was bein' punished!"

They both laughed.

"Shit, I was thinkin' da same. An' you ain't got that ordinary head game, eitha. You got that new shit."

"What that is?" she said as she played with her Hershey Kisses-sized nipples.

"You got that Miss Dracula head! You'll suck da life outta nigga." He laughed while running his fingers through her hair. "Bullshit ain't nuttin', I told ya ta stop ta see if ya was drawin' blood from a nigga!"

Rhapsody blushed. "Javon, you crazy."

Some small talk followed before they both eventually dozed off. However, their nap was disturbed by JJ's ringing phone. *Man, it better be someone extremely important*, he thought as he reached across Rhapsody and grabbed his iPhone. To his surprise, it was his mother calling.

"Wassup, Momma? Er'thang al ... "

"I want my money!"

JJ instantly sat up, catapulting Rhapsody across the bed.

"Wha-what's ... wrong?" she said, searching the room with her eyes wide open. “What happened?”

JJ jumped out of bed. “Where my momma at?”

“Where my money at?”

“Nigga, I swear ta God if you—”

“Listen, I dunno where yo’ coward ass at, but you got till midnite ta get my cash up.” There was a pause. “Ms. Sadie is in good hands like Allstate. I love Ms. Sadie, an’ I don’t wanna ... Well, just get that cash up befo’ midnite. If you don’t, then I guess I’ll have ta show ya I’ma coldhearted muthafucka!”

The phone went dead.

“Fuck!” JJ yelled as he punched a hole in the wall. “I’ma kill that nigga!”

Oblivious to what was going on, Rhapsody just sat on the bed mute. She wished that she could help soothe JJ for she never ever seen him so angry. Instead, she just watched as he paced the room back and forth while grinding his teeth.

Before she knew it, JJ had quickly dressed. He grabbed his keys and headed for the door.

“Where you goin’?” she hurriedly asked. “Is everythang okay?” She then got off the bed and began gathering clothes to put on.

“I’ll be back.”

“No,” she said, stepping into her skirt, “I’m comin ... “

JJ slapped Rhapsody so hard she spun out of her skirt and fell. “Bitch, I said I’ll be back! Stay yo’ ass rite here.”

Rhapsody held her aching cheek, crying as she watched JJ walk out of the bedroom.

JJ exited the house like a bat out of hell, angrily hopped into his truck, and backed out of the driveway as fast as he could. While speeding off, he began to think of how dirty Bizzy was playing the game by fucking with his old girl.

Once JJ and Rhapsody departed from Orlando for Savannah, he knew Seaport was the first place Bizzy would search. They only stayed in town a day before they bounced, after he realized his mother was the only person in Seaport he truly cared for. He chose to duck off in Macon, GA, which was close enough to reach his mother in case of an emergency.

The first couple of days in Mac-Town, he and Rhapsody stayed at Comfort Inn on Riverside Drive. He had a few people he conducted business with in town. He found he was still able to network.

And while he did his thing, Rhapsody's solitary assignment was to find a house for them. In less than a week, she found a nice three-bedroom, two-bath brick house on the westside of Mac-Town for a hundred and ninety-five thousand. Shortly after she decorated the house to her liking, JJ bought her a 2008 Lexus LS 460L.

They both were happy, and JJ had no worries. But that was until now.

***

April 1, 2008 11:46 pm

Savannah, GA

"Byron, I'm really starting to worry," Ms. Sadie sadly said. "You said Javon would be here almost eight hours ago."

"He should be callin' real soon," Bizzy replied.

"I really do hope so, because I was supposed to be back at the facility a very long time ago." Ms. Sadie stared woefully out of the passenger window as they sat in the car. "I need my meds, too."

Phone rings

"Here goes our boy now." He answered the phone. "Don't worry, lil bruh ... she's cool ... we're at Lake Meade Park ... y' know da place, rite? ... good, we'll be waitin'."

"Are we getting out?" Ms. Sadie said, turning to look at Bizzy. "If so, then could you get my wheelchair now, please."

"No, ma'am. You won't have ta get out."

"Oh … okay. "

Approximately seven minutes later, the headlights of a vehicle could be seen approaching. The park was well past its closing hours, so it was either JJ, the police, or someone on a late night creep.

"There's your son," Bizzy said once he recognized the truck by the 28's. "I'm goin' ta talk ta Javon first befo' we reveal ta ya our surprise."

"Just hurry, please. I really need my meds."

Bizzy climbed out of the car without responding. He walked and stood in front of the car. JJ stopped some forty feet away directly in front of him. While the headlights were kept on him, JJ got out holding a duffel bag.

"I assume you got my belongings in that bag," Bizzy said loudly. "So, toss it this way an' I'll give up ya momma. Hurry up too, becuz she really needs her meds."

Disinclined to talk, JJ slung the bag. The bag landed within ten feet of Bizzy. Bizzy walked to the bag and peered inside to find his money. He quickly shuffled through the stacks before zipping it shut, satisfied.

"You gotcha money. Now let my momma go!" JJ finally screamed.

"Calm down, lil bruh. You kept ya word, I'ma keep mine." Bizzy toted his money to the car while keeping an eye on JJ. He threw the money on the back seat, then he went to the other side. He removed the wheelchair. Finally, he opened the passenger door for Ms. Sadie and assisted her into the chair.

"I thought you said I wouldn't be getting out," Ms. Sadie said.

"We didn't wanna spoil da surprise," Bizzy replied while pushing Ms. Sadie towards JJ.

"Momma, are you okay?" JJ yelled with tears in his eyes.

Bizzy stopped pushing halfway, and said, "Ms. Sadie, you have a nice nite." He bent down and kissed her on the cheek, then he began to walk backwards to his car. He jumped in his car and left the scene.

JJ ran to his mother. "Momma, I'm sorry."

"What are you sorry for, boy? Why are you crying, Javon? You're scaring me. And what's this surprise you two have for me? Tell me what you and Byron are up to?"

"Nuttin', Momma. I'm just glad that 'chu are okay."

"Yes, I'm fine. I really need my meds, but I'm fine." She sighed. "I would really like to know what's ... "

Phone rings

"Who this?" JJ answered.

"I'm surprised you ain't try nuttin' stupid," Bizzy said before laughing. "I betcha think that was very nice of me ta not harm yo' dear momma, huh? You know yo' momma like da momma I never had, so I didn't wanna drag her into this equation. But you left me no choice. An' I betcha thought I brung RBF peeps fo' back-up an' it was gonna be a big shootout or sumthin', like in da movies, huh?"

"Muthafucka, I'ma kill you!" JJ yelled while walking away from Ms. Sadie.

"Javon, don't use that type of language around me," Ms. Sadie scoffed.

"Yeah, Javon, don't do that," Bizzy mimicked her. "An' by da way, it ain't that easy, Javon. I'm not a nice guy, Javon, I just look this way. I'ma cold-blooded nigga just like you, Javon. I just used you ta do all my dirty work fo' me like da dick-ridin' nigga you are, Javon. So, since you thought I let'chu an' ya momma live … April Fools, bitch-ass nigga!"

JJ dropped the phone, then he turned to face his mother. The look on his face said a million words. Through the darkness he stared into his mother's hazel brown eyes, unable to move or speak.

"What's wrong, Javon?" Ms. Sadie asked, noticing how JJ was acting from afar. She began to roll her wheelchair in JJ's direction as he dashed towards her screaming.

Ka-BOOM!

Ms. Sadie's wheelchair unexpectedly exploded, scattering body parts that all the king's horses and all the king's men couldn't put back together again.

I told you, lil bruh, it's a dawg eat dawg world, Bizzy said to himself as a single tear fell from his eye. He watched the fireball float into the night sky from his rearview mirror as he drove off into the darkness.

CHAPTER TEN

April 11, 2008 3:08 am

Wellington, FL

"Devon, wake up. Baby, wake up," Miracle said, shaking the convulsing body next to her. "C'mon, please, wake up."

Suddenly, Devon awoke hysterically. "Huh? Wha … What's da matter?"

"Damn, Dee, you was havin' a bad dream." She sighed. "It's been almost a year since you had one. I was really beginnin' to think you weren't goin' to have another bad dream."

Drenched in sweat and slightly shivering, Devon sat up in bed. *Shit, I still can't forget that day,* Devon thought, *and it's been many years ago.*

Using her T-shirt, Miracle wiped away most of the sweat. "It was that same dream, wasn't it? Why won't you just tell me so I can help you if I can?"

Devon kicked the covers off and got out of bed. "I need some water."

As Devon walked out of their new bedroom, Miracle sighed again. She laid back down and began to wonder what it could be that was triggering this bad dream.

Today made one week of living in their new home. Devon still had the apartment in Da City, but they purchased a two hundred and sixty-five thousand dollar house out west in Wellington, which was about a thirty-minute commute from Da City. The two-story, stucco-style house in the gated community, Spinnaker Cove, was glamorous. The house contained three bedrooms, three bathrooms, with one of those rooms being Kamani's, who was still at his grandmother's for the time being, at least until school was out for the summer.

So, all in all, everything was good. The club was bringing in mega bucks, and their relationship couldn't have been any better. *Nothing around the house can be triggering this bad dream*, she thought.

Today was also a very special day. It was Devon's twenty-fourth birthday. There was going to be a big bash at StudioX tonight to celebrate. It was going to be a night that became a part of the county's history. The special invites alone took up more than half of the maximum capacity! *Maybe the anxiety of the party not turning out as good as planned is the cause of the bad dream,* she concluded, *or maybe it's just something deeper I may never uncover.*

"I'ma head ta da club ta see how er'thang goin'," Devon said, entering the twenty-five square foot master bedroom. "I wanna make sho' we have mo' than enuff liquor an' food tonite."

In a whiny voice, Miracle said, "But baby, you promised that you and me ... well, never mind." She then crossed her arms over her chest and stuck her bottom lip out. "You're always goin' to do what you want to anyway, so go ahead. I'll be here all alone until you get back." She finally threw the covers over her head. "I'll just sit here and play with myself until you return," she pouted lowly but loud enough to be heard.

Oh, she wants to make me feel guilty, huh? Devon thought with a smile. *So, two can play this game.*

"Well, okay." Devon went into the bathroom and exited in ten minutes. Grabbing the keys, some money, cellphone and .380 off the dresser, Devon said, "I was gonna ask ya ta ride wit me cuz I need my secretary. But since you insist on stayin here an' playin' witcha self, be my guest."

"Give me ten minutes," Miracle suddenly said as she sprung out of bed like Devon said the house was on fire. She dashed into the bathroom and slammed the door. Not even a second later she opened the door, and added, "Give me seven minutes." She then slammed the door again.

Devon laughed and sat on the bed.

***

April 11, 2008 8:30 pm
West Palm Beach, FL

The sun was slowly sinking on the horizon. The clashing of the dark blue of the approaching night and the bright orange of the receding sun was enchanting. The cool breeze that blew off of the Atlantic Ocean made the hot evening bearable. Overall, it was a lovely night to party.

Stepping out of the house in a navy blue, New Era fitted flat brim cap, emblazoned with the Detroit Tigers logo, on top of freshly braided locks, a pair of Louis Vuitton aviator shades, a rainbow-colored Coogi shirt, Coogi jeans with the rainbow-colored back pockets, and Florida Gator colored Air Force Ones, Devon was flyer than all of the Tuskegee Airmen put together. And that didn't include enough ice on the neck, wrist and fingers that was sure to make the Abominable Snowman shiver with jealousy.

Not too far behind Devon was Miracle. She was traffic-stopping gorgeous in her form-fitting black Dolce & Gabbana dress, gold Christian Louboutin peep-toe pumps, and diamond encrusted necklace and rings.

Even the BMW X6 was sparkling with a fresh brandy-wine candy paint and matching color 26-inch Ashanti feet.

They left Wellington ten minutes till eight, and promptly arrived at the club forty minutes later after a few stops. The parking lot was already somewhat full, and it was still early. The club wasn't expected to be jumping until sometime after 10:30 PM. Before then, it was basically an average day. Devon and Miracle only arrived early to welcome guests, to see that everything stayed in order, and to enjoy themselves as much as possible.

"What da bizness is, Dee Baby?" Gudda greeted as Devon entered the restaurant area while holding Miracle's hand. Marcus "Gudda" Mitchell was an agent in Tampa for strippers. He met Devon almost two years ago when Devon visited Tampa to do business. They encountered one another at Gudda's club, and after talking and learning they both were in the same line of work, they became friendly. Since then, they made an oath to call upon each other whenever there was a big event going down in their respective cities. "Happy Birthday!"

"Thanks, Gudda." They embraced. "You must've brung ya girls down early ta get all da bread ya can get, or you scopin' out my hoes. So which one is it?"

Gudda smiled, exposing his white gold with diamond set grill. "On da first part, yes. On da second part, you know me oh so well."

They laughed.

"Well, I hope ya enjoy ya'self tonite. I gotta few celebs that's gonna fall through, like D. Wade, Jackie-O, Kevin Hart, an' Rick Ross da Bawse finna perform."

"Damn, if I woulda known that I woulda brung every hoe I know to get this money, even my grandma!"

Devon laughed. "Nigga, yo' ratchet-ass foul fo' that one."

"Shit, she taught me da game." He shrugged. "So, she know how it go."

"Im'a holla at'cha later, Gudda. I gotta few things ta handle now befo' I start gettin' wasted."

"Cool, Dee Baby."

They promised to link up later. Devon and Miracle walked through the entire building to make their presence known. After doing so, they retreated to the office located by the stripper's dressing room. The office was spacious, with just two desks, and decorated the same as Scarface's business office.

Sitting down in the high-back-leather office chair, Devon said, "Baby, roll us a blunt real quick. Da weed an' Dutches in da safe. An' make sho' you put that Superman in it."

Miracle gathered what was needed, then she rolled a blunt of Purple Haze with a crushed-up bean. She popped beans periodically, but Devon preferred to smoke a bean than to pop one, because it was the same high without the shitty aftereffects. They usually smoke high-grade weed by itself every day, but they smoked a bean every blue moon. It was a full blue moon tonight, so they planned on heading to outer space to walk on it.

Just minutes into the session, they were interrupted by a knock at the door.

"Fuck," Miracle mumbled. "We can never have thirty minutes of privacy when we're here in the office."

"What'chu expect? It's my birthday, an' they know we in da buildin', so they gonna be all up in a nigga face, tryna blow my high." Devon shrugged. "Come in!"

The door opened slowly, and in walked ...

"Hey, y'all?" the person said so pitifully.

Without missing a beat, Devon lashed out. "Oh, so you brang ya funky, triflin' ass back, huh? What happened? Did da nigga get tired of ya trickin', dick-eatin' ass?"

Rhapsody lowered her head to avoid the cold, piercing eyes of them both. She felt ashamed. She knew she was dead wrong for letting money cloud her better judgment. "I'm sooooo sorry, Daddy," she professed while closing the door. "I went to Orlando, as usual, to work at Leo's, but ... but I never told you that while I was up there I had been stayin' wit this buster, to keep from spendin' money at da hotels, becuz I knew you'd be mad."

"I ain[1]t mad." Devon looked at Miracle and smiled. "Are you mad?"

"Uh-uh." Miracle shook her head. "Even though you left me by myself at the hotel, I ain't mad."

"So, how in da fuck you end up in fuckin' Georgia?" Devon snapped.

At first, Rhapsody didn't say nothing. She was contemplating on what story to tell, before finally blurting out the truth.

She started by telling how she fell in love with JJ's money, before gradually falling in love with the man himself. She was so sprung over him, the thought of returning to Palm Beach for the weekdays was depressing. She continued with how JJ and his friend Bizzy must've had an argument about money, because JJ decided to up and leave for Savannah, after just purchasing a new home in Orlando. She briefly went on about the new house they bought in Macon, the Lexus he bought her, etc.

She then told them about the day JJ left the house mad all of a sudden and never returned. She discovered the next day on the morning news that JJ's mother was missing, and the police found an abandoned black SUV and burnt body parts in a park near JJ's mother's residence. She knew right then Bizzy had something to do with JJ and his mother disappearing, so she fled back to West Palm Beach pronto, scared for her life. She ended with gathering the courage to face Devon to apologize after finding a flyer for the birthday bash at StudioX.

Devon looked at Miracle, then back at Rhapsody. "I believe ya. An' I accept ya apology."

"Thank you, Daddy!" Rhapsody happily said. "I swear I won't—"

"But," Devon cut her off, "you owe me. BIG! Now go get'cha ass in da dressin' room an' go get my money. I want four stacks from you tonite. I don't care what'chu gotta do ta get it. You can rob a nigga fo' all I care. If you don't get my money, you might as well go back ta Savannah an' let that nigga kill you, too. If you do get my money, then all is forgotten."

Rhapsody's smile faded as she accepted the ultimatum. *I got four grand and more right now*, she thought. "Thank you, Daddy."

"Now kick rocks, an' get that money wit' cha fine ass."

Miracle snickered loud enough for Rhapsody to hear as she left the office.

"Dee, you so mean," Miracle sarcastically said.

***

April 12, 2008 12:15 am

West Palm Beach, FL

Tonight, StudioX was the place to be. The liquor and food was half price, and the girls were beautiful and plentiful. It was standing room only inside. It was so packed that the bouncer outside was instructed to keep a lookout for the fire marshal, although nobody ever seen the fire marshal.

Devon was white-boy wasted. Cup after cup of Patrón, blunt after blunt of Purp, and bump after bump of paint, did the muthafucking job for Devon. *This is my best birthday bash yet,* Devon thought while chilling in the champagne room with Miracle, Gudda, T-Pain, Missy Elliott, and a few others.

"Excuse me," Solo, the bouncer, said. "Miracle, there's some old nigga out here that claim he yo' uncle. I'm 'bout ready ta smash da nigga cuz he botherin' da shit outta me while I'm tryna keep er'body out as I was told. So what'chu want me ta do?"

Miracle looked at Devon, who was getting a lap dance. She then said, "Go ahead and let him in."

"He got sum one wit him, too," Solo added.

"Well, just ... Fuck, let them both in."

Solo left and quickly returned with her Uncle Virgil. He was accompanied by the same guy that was with him the last time they were here.

"Bloodclot! This fuckin' Yankee mon don't wan' believe ya me niece," Virgil said as he sized the six-foot-eight, three-hundred-and-thirty-pound Solo. Virgil was five-foot-eight, one-hundred-and-eighty pounds, dark-skinned with dreads that reached his calves. He may have been small in stature, but he was feared and well-respected. "So, Marie, introduce me ta ya people dem there." He then nodded at Devon. "Me wan' tell 'im Happy Berthday."

Miracle looked at Devon again to see that the lap dance was becoming intimate. Far from being jealous, she shouted over the commotion. "Dee! Dee, come here for a sec. I have somethin' to tell you."

Looking up with the shades on and the hat pulled down low, Devon arose and staggered over to where Miracle was standing. Devon noticed she was with two dudes, one was her uncle, while the other looked vaguely familiar.

"Wassup, baby," Devon said, palming Miracle's ass while kissing on her neck. "Who this?"

Not embarrassed at all by the gesture, she replied, "This is my Uncle Virgil and his friend ... "

"Kilo," Virgil quickly said.

"Well, actually, my name is Demetrius. Nobody has called me Kilo in a very long time, except for Dread here. So, please, call me Demetrius," he said, while extending a hand.

Devon was stuck, and it wasn't stuck in the zone.

"Yah, me ole' friend here jus' got back inna town not too long ago," Virgil said. "Me haffi show 'im all da hotspots an' all da people dem who make moves in town, know wha' me say? Me know ya boy dem make moves, Marie, so we wanted ta have ah likkle meetin' ta discuss sum tings."

Miracle stared at the silent Devon with a raised brow. "Dee, is that alright with you?"

Devon didn't do nothing but stare at Demetrius from behind the shades.

"Devon, is everythin' okay?" Miracle asked, a little worried.

No response. Just staring.

Demetrius finally took heed to the awkward gazing. He couldn't see Devon's face because, for one, he was about eight inches taller. Secondly, the hat and shades hindered him from getting a good look.

When Demetrius tried to maneuver himself to catch a glimpse of the face under the hat, Devon said, "Yeah, yeah. Set that up fo' me, Miracle. ASAP!"

"Happy Berthday, mon!" Virgil yelled as Devon walked out of the champagne room.

Virgil and Demetrius both looked at Miracle, and all she could do was shrug.

"Don't worry. I'll set it up," she finally said.

"Here's my card," Demetrius said as he admired Miracle. "Call me anytime." He winked. "And I do mean anytime."

Miracle then told Virgil and Demetrius they were more than welcome to stay in the champagne room. They said they would love to chill, then she showed them around first before leaving to locate Devon.

***

Meanwhile, Devon was outside the club talking to Gudda.

"What da beat is, Dee Baby?" Gudda said as they sat in Devon's BMW X6. "Boy, lemme tell ya. It's so much money in there, I had to find a *Yellow Pages* to hire an accountant, just so I won't be audited in da mornin'." Gudda cracked up.

But Devon didn't even smile.

"Yo ... man, I dunno ... I can't ... I'm gonna ... he can't ... I dunno ... " Devon stuttered before suddenly retrieving the .380 from the center console.

Confused at what the hell was going on, Gudda nervously said, "Now, hold on! Calm down, Dee Baby! Don't do nuttin' stupid. This yo' day, yo' birthday!" He slowly reached for the gun and took it from Devon. "Just tell me what's goin' on?"

Devon broke down in tears.

They sat in silence for five minutes before Gudda pulled out an eight-ball of soft. They both began to hit key bumps out of the sandwich bag.

Once the dope was gone some twenty minutes later, Devon slowly said, "Gudda, I need ya ta do a favor fo' me. I mean, this one is ... Dawg, I just need ya rite now. I don't have nobody else."

"What'chu want me to do, Dee Baby? Whateva it is, I got'cha."

"I'ma need ya ta help me handle sumthin'."

CHAPTER ELEVEN

April 13, 2008 8:50 am

Orlando, FL

The explanation was going to be straight to the point. Bizzy was going to inform his father that he was no longer working for him. Well, at least he wasn't until he found another nigga like good ole' JJ. Besides, he really hated hustling hard for little to nothing for his father, when he had stacks on deck himself. "Yeah, it's about time for me to take a vacation," he said to himself, "but I have to break the news to old boy first."

After the phone call to Demetrius, who was in West Palm Beach, Bizzy found it funny how he knew exactly what his "righteous" father was going to say. Whenever he wanted to give up on something that he didn't like, or do something he didn't want to do, his father always recalled the story of how he started off with nothing but a twenty-dollar bag of coke at age twelve.

Demetrius' mother, Louise Anita Woodson, was a single parent and an elementary school teacher. She really tried her hardest to steer her two sons and Sheryl, her only daughter, from the street life, before and after their father was murdered in a gambling house in Georgia when Demetrius was ten, and Sheryl was only a few months old.

But Demetrius had been infatuated with the money, the cars and the clothes his father and the older players had in downtown West Palm Beach. He always possessed an independent way of thinking from his father teaching him to be a man at an early age, so he did everything by himself that was right by him. Going to school full-time and hustling after school part-time eventually became a full-time hustle with overtime. Being one of the youngest, but not smallest guys on the block only prompted him to grind harder.

One day it took him more than twenty hours just to sell twelve dubb sacks. Instead of giving up, though, he knew eventually he'd reap the benefits of an unrelenting hustle, and he'd be the man in the nice cars and fancy clothes with exotic-looking bitches on his arms one day. It took him almost a decade to do so, but he accomplished his goals through vigorous work.

Bizzy surely knew becoming "the man" involved working hard

early on; he just didn't want to. He wanted the world to be given to him on a platinum platter with a side of universe. He knew one reason he felt this way was because of his father pampering him his whole life. Another reason was that he was more than likely going to inherit his father's wealth and gain reign over RBF when the time came, anyway. *So, why do I have to do anything but wait*? he concluded.

Although he clearly understood RBF was a billion-dollar empire his father built from one twenty-dollar sack, he made plans to pack up and head somewhere up north. He needed to getaway, especially after just being released from a federal prison forty-one days ago for his father's mistake. His father may very well disapprove of his decision to take a furlough for R & R when RBF was at a pivotal point, but it was something he was willing to deal with later down the road. *It's time to just relax and be a real family man*, he thought as he played with his youngest son, three-year-old BJ, in the living room of LaShawn's apartment, *so the family business will just have to wait.*

***

April 13, 2008 12:55 pm

West Palm Beach, FL

It was a sweltering ninety degrees outside. Demetrius was somewhat jaded from trying to keep his empire from going under, so he didn't need more to add to his stress. However, the heat, mixed with the latest news of his son taking a leave of absence from the family business so soon, was more than enough to stress him out and aggravate him today -- and the day was really just beginning! *I'm going to need something strong to help me get through the rest of the day*, he thought as he looked in his medicine cabinet.

Knock at door

Since Demetrius had been back in Palm Beach County, only two people knew where his cozy little apartment was, and he'd been patiently waiting for one of those particular people for the last hour. Instead of buying a lavish home out west, or a luxuriant condo by the beach, he leased an apartment in Palm West, which was located in The Villages area of suburban West Palm Beach. Truthfully, though, he didn't even possess the money to buy a nice home or a nice car, yet. That was all soon to change after the meeting with the person knocking at the door.

He opened the door only after peeking through the peephole first.

"What's happ'nin', Big Cuzzo?" Chad greeted as he hugged Demetrius before entering the mellow, under-decorated apartment. "My bad I ain't on time. Da drive from Daytona became hectic on I-95 in every city along the way."

"I'm just glad you've made it here safely."

Chad was Bubba's twenty-nine-year-old son. He looked as if his father spit him out, causing people to refer to Bubba, Obie and him as "the Triplets" whenever they were seen together. He also had the same go-getter mentality as his father. Although he was a hustler, he wasn't a drug dealer.

Demetrius knew Chad had the potential of becoming a good dealer from the stories Bubba always told about Chad when he was a kid. As stated by Bubba, Chad was always trying to sell anything he could get his tiny hands on; candy, his toys, his clothes, other people's belongings, etc. That eventually led him to a life of wholesaling. His get-money strategy for the last ten years was dealing with bootleggers that owned warehouses in Atlanta and New York. He would purchase bundles of knockoff products for the low to sell them individually for the high.

So, Demetrius speculated Chad had to know someone that was into buying narcotics. And, since he wasn't trying to actually touch work himself, leaving just Virgil and a few small-timers to put in work for the family, he'd contacted Chad and arranged to have a meeting in order to exploit Chad's connects and resources up north.

"So, what's da deal wit Cousin Ty?" Chad asked as he took a seat.

"Would you like something to drink first?" Chad shook his head, then Demetrius continued as he sat down. "Well, Tyrell has a good lawyer that's trying to reduce the eighty-eight months he's facing. I wrote him a letter just the other day and instructed him to take a plea agreement, that way he'd accept responsibility, and with his pretty clean record, the government will offer him less time."

"What type of evidence they have on him?"

"They have a few phone conversations and powder cocaine residue at his home, in a room he used for repackaging some dope to distribute to the family, which was a very unintelligent thing to do in the home where he laid his head. Other than that, that's all. No guns were found, so they cannot enhance him with that, which is good.

"Blaze was probably going to testify against him if I didn't win trial, so there's nobody snitching on him, which is great. So, he's more than likely to receive around sixty months."

"My pops is lookin' at fifteen years ... with a plea agreement." Chad sighed. "They caught him wit nine zones an' a pistol. He most likely gonna take da plea like he been tellin' me he was. An' my Unc Obie already took a plea fo' a hun'ed an' eight months. He just waitin' ta be designated ta da prison he goin' to."

"Don't worry. I'll take care of them all as long as I'm breathing. They will not want for nothing."

"Y 'know who I ain't heard from in a long time?" Chad suddenly said. "Cousin Sheryl. What she up to?"

"I haven't spoke to my little sister in ..." Demetrius paused. "Enough of that, I wanted to sit down with you in person, Chad, to run something by you." He then began to try to manipulate Chad into joining his hustling business ventures.

There was no need to manipulate Chad, however, because he'd been waiting to join RBF for the last couple years. Just like Demetrius kept Bizzy out of RBF, Bubba kept Chad out of the business. Yet, unlike Bizzy hustling for himself on the side, Chad was too scared of his father to even think about touching dope.

But now that Demetrius was depending on him, Chad wanted to seize the opportunity to capitalize off the bootleggers that always asked him about purchasing large quantities of all types of narcotics.

The two second cousins chatted for hours, going over as much as possible. They went over the rules and regulations that the family followed, prices, the people they were only to deal with, the places where the business was only to be transacted, etc. Once they agreed upon specific terms, they parted company as new cronies. *It's the beginning of a new order*, Demetrius thought, while preparing to contact his plug's people to place an order, *and the end of a declining RBF empire!*

April 20, 2008 5:41 pm
West Palm Beach, FL

"I'm sorry I'm late y'all," Jazzy said as she walked into the office soaking wet. Already inside the office at StudioX was Devon, Miracle, Peachez, and Gudda. "It's rainin' cats and dogs outside."

"You straight," Devon said. "Now that we're all here, we can get started." Devon leaned forward in the chair and propped up on the birchwood table trimmed with gold. "So, who wants ta go first?"

Devon had organized this meeting for this very day after a week of observing Demetrius. There were numerous questions asked beforehand about why they were spying on Demetrius, but Devon simply told them they could either help or not.

Everybody currently in the office ultimately agreed to play their part, because they knew the task would be extremely lucrative for them all, or was extremely meaningful for Devon. Either way it went, they were game. And after four days of probing, damn near everybody in the office had some substantial intel.

Miracle was the first to tell what she accomplished. She set up the meeting between her Uncle Virgil, Demetrius and Devon, which Devon never did attend, due to an "immediate emergency" that required personal attention. Demetrius and Virgil were highly upset about having to wait. She then summoned a few girls that were working that day to come into the office to entertain them while they hung around for Devon to return. Virgil happily selected Jazzy, who was five-foot-six and one-hundred-and-ninety pounds of breasts, hips, thighs, and ass, from the lineup. Demetrius, on the other hand, didn't see a girl worth his time. Demetrius eventually grew tired of waiting for Devon, while Virgil grew harder and hornier from the appealing, teasing Jazzy. So, they opted to leave, and Miracle didn't protest their decision.

However, on the way out, Demetrius was mesmerized by the six-foot-one, one-hundred-and-thirty-pound, fake-boobed platinum blonde sitting alone in the restaurant. He subtly introduced himself before asking permission to join her, and she said yes. After charming her with intellectual conversation and his gentlemanly ways, they departed together an hour or so later, and Miracle's job was complete once the four left the building together.

Gudda and Peachez had the duty of following Demetrius in his cheap, used 2006 Toyota Camry, to locate where he lived. It didn't even take them fifteen minutes to determine the locale of Demetrius' crib once he and Virgil left the bogus meeting. However, they didn't know the exact apartment that he lived in, which was all good. Ivory was with him, so all they had to do was tell Devon the complex he lived in, while Ivory told what apartment was his. Gudda and Peachez completed their task in less than an hour.

The person with the most vital assignment of them all was Gudda's superstar white stripper named Ivory. Devon's favor was for Gudda to utilize the baddest white bitch in his stable, because Devon figured that a supermodel-looking white woman with blonde hair, blue eyes and a full body makeover would surely draw the attention of a black man of Demetrius' character. The trap worked.

After wooing and servicing Demetrius that same day, Ivory's job afterwards was to gain his trust to the point where he wouldn't suspect her of anything. Her foot was in the door, but there was one exception to her job. She was never to know of Devon, period. She was to do her job through Gudda's instructions from Devon.

Everybody finished explaining their task, and that was when Jazzy decided to put her two cents in. "Daddy, can I ask you somethin'?" Jazzy asked in a squeaky voice. "Why are we going through all this? Now, I know you said either we could help or not, but I would really like to know why this guy is so important to you? He seems like a nice guy."

"Yeah," Gudda added, "what's really happenin', Dee Baby? You know I'ma ride wit'cha till da twenty-eights fall off. So level wit da people who love ya, Dee Baby."

Devon blinked back the tears, and said, "This nigga I got y'all followin' like a dawg trailin' a bitch in heat, is da same nigga that has me wakin' up in a puddle of sweat since I was a jit." Devon then looked at Miracle, who was shocked by the revelation. "Da nigga name was Kilo back in da days. He disappeared fo' years, an' now it's obvious he back. I know it's him, even tho' he changed da way he talk an' carry himself. But he still look da same."

"Why are we exactly followin' this guy?" Miracle asked disappointedly, because she had to learn about the nightmares this way. "What's the real reason you want to get close to this guy? All we know is absolutely nothin'!"

Quietness filled the office as everybody waited for a response.

"What would you do ta da person that raped…" Devon's face was wet with tears now. "…ya four-year-old cousin an' killed ya aunt, while you hid in anotha room scared fo' ya life, huh? What would y'all do?"

CHAPTER TWELVE

September 30, 2008 1:09 pm

Riviera Beach, FL

"Yes, Demetrius," Ivory charmingly said, "fuck me harder. You can do it!"

Demetrius pumped intensely. He was moaning and groaning like a wounded mutt. He tried endlessly to concentrate on lasting as long as possible by tuning out Ivory's seductive demands. But amazingly, she had intriguing methods of making him climax within several minutes. Every time! And today was no different.

"God ... dammit ... I'm .... cum-cum-cumming!" he stammered loudly before releasing his load onto Ivory's golden-tanned thighs. Fatigue instantly set in, causing him to collapse on top of Ivory's fake double-Ds. "I just want you to know you're the only woman I've slept with that makes me feel like I'm getting too old. I say that because you're twenty-six, and I'll be forty-four in less than a month, and you're wearing me out. I cannot seem to last more than ten minutes when I'm inside of you.

"It doesn't even matter if I go fast or take it slow. I don't know if it's the enticing way you instruct me to fuck you harder, your uncanny tactics to get inside of my head, or something else, but I'm really contemplating on whether I need to have a doctor prescribe me Viagra, or something." He laughed. "You're an enigma."

While wrapping her long, lanky legs around his waist, and grinding her Brazilian-waxed pussy into his pelvic region, she said, "Babe, I'm flattered. And you're not too old. You're handsome, intelligent, a gentleman, everything a real woman wants. And, might I add, you're hung like an elephant." She giggled as she continued grinding. "And I'm glad you're not able to last that long, because the time you are up inside of me is more than enough to make me orgasm two or three times. Plus, you ..."

"Oh, shit." Demetrius raised up off the bed. "What time is it? I have to pick up a friend of mine from the airport at a quarter till two."

"It's fifteen after one now, Babe."

Demetrius proceeded to get out of bed, then he walked into the bathroom stark naked. Seconds later, the shower was running. He emerged fifteen minutes later with a towel wrapped around his waist. "Umm, I guess you can stay here until I get back," he said as he dressed. "I'm only going to be gone approximately an hour."

"Okay, if you say I can, I will stay. But hurry back. I have to be at work by five, and I want to have as much chocolate dessert as possible before I leave," she cooed, rubbing a finger around her fat-injected but still thin lips before sticking it in and out of her mouth.

Demetrius cleared his throat. "I'll be right back." He headed for the door before stopping. "And, while I'm gone, DO NOT use my telephone, open my door, or do anything that you think will piss me off! I'll know if you do," he warned as he grabbed a few items off the dresser and left.

Gosh, after five lengthy months, he finally trusts me enough to leave me in his new condo by myself, she thought as she retrieved her phone to call Gudda. *It's the power of this magnificent white pussy that weakens a strong black man's better senses.*

***

September 30, 2008 1:20 pm

West Palm Beach, FL

"Yo', Dee Baby, Ivory just hit me up a few minutes ago an' said she's up in there like swimwear," Gudda said, calling from Tampa. "So what da next play is?"

"Ain't nan rite now," Devon coolly said through the phone.

"What? You mean ta tell me that chu got us doin' all this shit an' you don't got no ..."

"Ya snowflake almost home safe. Now that he finally leavin' her in da crib by herself, means he's comfortable wit her bein' around. He'll let his guard down soon, then I'll be able ta have Ivory do her final task, so I can do my part," Devon explained.

"She don't have ta steal or look fo' sumthin' while he gone?"

"Nope. Don't worry, Gudda, this shit'll be all over shortly."

"I hope fuckin' so, cuz Jackson, Grant an' Franklin have been seen less an' less in my spot since my breadwinner been on this mission of yours." He chuckled. "You betta be lucky I fucks witchu."

"I'ma pay ya whateva ya want once this all over," Devon promised before hanging up.

***

In the meantime, Chad was waiting to be picked up by Demetrius at the Palm Beach International Airport. He just arrived back from New York after stopping in Atlanta first. The two-week trip was crucial for RBF's drug-dealing enterprise. In the last three months, his liaisons in NY and ATL alone had been generating the greenbacks the family was somewhat used to seeing. *Hopefully, my people will hit me back pronto after the sweet deal I proposed to them,* he wished as he waited, *because RBF will definitely be back on its grizzy when they do.*

Nearly ten minutes passed before Demetrius showed up in the pristine 2009 Mercedes-Benz SL 550. As soon as Chad loaded his luggage into the vehicle, and got in himself, Demetrius immediately initiated a conversation about business.

"How did everything go up there?"

"Big Cuzzo, my peeps in ATL will no longer believe Jezzy is Mr. Seventeen-point-five when ya guy 'cross da water tighten up an' trust ya again," Chad proclaimed while adjusting his seat. "An' my peeps in New York will be able ta buy da Yanks in less than a year wit da profit they'll make at da prices we sellin' 'em."

"Although I know you are a bit of an exaggerator, that's great to hear." Demetrius shook his head. "Soon my guy will have no choice but to give me what I need when I need it. Between Virgil, you and myself, we have sold almost four hundred kilos in three months." He nodded at the achievement. "That's good, but not good enough."

"Damn, Cuzzo, what'chu mean that ain't good enuff? At da price one brick goin' fo', we done made …" He began to do the math in his head. "We done made sumwhere 'round three-point-five million dollars. Now tell me how that ain't good enuff?"

"Like I said, that's good. But, if you want to compare that to the seven metric tons of cocaine that Bubba, Obie, Tyrell, Virgil, Blaze, me and a few others sold in one fiscal year, then it's good since it's only three of us. Now, I have other members in the family that can help us sell maybe, two metric tons in a year, but they have their own specific jobs to oversee.

"And don't be perturbed by my guy. I'll handle him when the

time is right. All we have to do is continue to quickly sell the measly one hundred kilos he gives me, that way he'll be forced to extend the leash he has on me. We still have to play by my rules in order to remain off the fed's radar as much as possible, but we will soon be able to quench the thirst of the whole Eastern Coast at a very low price."

"I'm glad that'chu have a master plan ta get'cha guy back on track wit us, cuz we need him like a huntin' dog needs luck. So, I guess I'll tell my peeps in NY an' ATL that my proposition still stands when da time is rite. Until then, da nineteen thou a piece is still good, rite?"

"Right."

They rode without speaking for a while. Demetrius tuned the radio to Contemporary Jazz. The mellow melody of the music instantly relaxed the setting. The sounds of each instrument were so captivating, it made him think he was on an island with a ...

"Yo', Cuzzo," Chad said, breaking Demetrius' tranquil thoughts, "you still fuckin' wit that Hollywood-lookin' bitch?"

"Yes. And why do you ask?"

"I dunno." He shrugged. "It's just that I don't trust that bitch. Fo' some reason, I feel like ... I dunno. I just don't trust her, an' I advise you ta be careful. She look like da type ah bitch ta suck ya dick an' fuck ya wallet."

"It's funny you'd say that when she's in my condo right now by herself for the first time since I've known her." He thought to himself for a second. "There's nothing out in plain sight that's incriminating or worth stealing, but I'll take your admonition seriously and keep an eye on her."

During the remainder of the smooth ride from PBIA to Singer Island, Demetrius enlightened Chad on Bizzy's latest phone call. He hadn't spoken to his son since Bizzy said he was taking a vacation, which was over five months ago. Bizzy only called to check up on him, not to disclose his location. That angered him, and an argument immediately followed.

The main issue was how he felt Bizzy turned his back on RBF, when he needed all the help he could find. He went on by heavily criticizing his son, telling Bizzy it was very essential to get his priorities straight and principles in order. He also went as far as shaming his son by stating Bizzy's overall character lately was unlike that of a real Woodson man. Without even disputing the last comment, Bizzy ended the conversation by hanging up on him. He knew right then, that was most likely the last time he would hear from his beloved, spoiled son, if he really wasn't a real Woodson man.

CHAPTER THIRTEEN

October 1, 2008 11:17 am

West Palm Beach, FL

Horrible. That best described the weather outside. A thunderstorm had been drenching the entire county for the last two hours. It was almost beginning to seem as if the brilliant, continuous lightning followed by the earsplitting, earth-shaking thunder would never cease.

Besides the storm roiling outside, there was another dreadful storm burgeoning. This storm, however, was materializing in the office at StudioX.

"This shit gettin' out of hand, Dee," Miracle said. "You've become obsessed with this guy. We don't do anything no more because you're either not in the mood, or you're too busy tryin' to see what this guy is doin'. You're causin' our relationship to go downhill because of this obsession you created. So you need to do somethin', and do it fast! I ain't goin' to sit here dammit and suffer because you plan on gettin' even with the guy who raped your lil cousin and killed your aunt over twenty years ago. If it matters that much to you then call the police. Let them handle it!"

"Hmph, call da police? Call da punk-ass police fo' what? So they can scare him off? Uh-uh." Devon frowned. "That nigga is gonna feel MY wrath, one way or da otha. One thang fa'sho is I'll be able ta have sweet dreams real soon. In a couple days, Ivory should be close enuff ta him ta carry out her final step, then we all can live happily ever fuckin' after. Until then, nuttin' else matters."

Miracle was stunned by Devon's last remark. She rose from behind her personal desk, gathered her belongings, and headed for the door.

"Where da fuck you goin'?" Devon questioned.

"Since nothin' else matters, I'm goin' home, packin' my shit and goin' to my momma's house." She opened the door to leave and ran into Rhapsody, who was just about to knock on the door.

"Hey, y'all," Rhapsody acknowledged them both before turning her attention to Devon. "Daddy, I was just wonderin' … if … I can go home real quick. I'm not feelin' too good, an' I think it's cuz of da weather. I'll be back later on tonite, tho', to make it up."

"Go 'head," Devon bluntly said, dismissing her with a wave of the hand.

Rhapsody then turned towards Miracle, and said, "An' … ummm … can you give me a ride, Miracle? My mama took my car this mornin'. She 'posed to pick me up later, but I don't wanna wait on her."

"I don't care. Nothin' else matters right now, so c'mon. You can also help me pack my shit," Miracle sneered as she looked back at Devon with a devilish look.

Once Miracle and Rhapsody left together, rather than sitting in the office with nothing to do, Devon decided to go for a drive to get away from the turbulent and ominous atmosphere that had materialized during the last ten minutes. The destination was the streets of Da City. *There's nothing like going back to the familiar pavement of downtown West Palm Beach to chill with my niggas*, Devon thought while aimlessly cruising Da City's streets.

***

October 1, 2008 12:50 pm

Riviera Beach, FL

Since Rhapsody lived near where Miracle's mom, Michelle stayed in Da Raw, it wasn't a hassle for Miracle to drop her off. *Besides, I need somebody to air my feelings out to at the moment,* Miracle thought.

Miracle was furious for several reasons. She was also perplexed and filled with consternation. She really thought that she was performing her role in a cooperative and unselfish manner. Yet, with all the effort she was expending on this Demetrius caper, and the way Devon didn't show any regard for her or the others that were assisting, it compelled her to slowly loathe Devon more and more each passing day. She deeply loved Devon, that was obvious, but she refused to be mistreated mentally for something she had no control over.

During the drive to Wellington, the packing of one week's worth of personal possessions, and the trip to Da Raw, Miracle talked Rhapsody's ear off. Although she knew for a fact that Rhapsody wanted to be in her shoes badly, and was covetous of her relationship with Devon, she felt as if they've been homegirls forever, rather than the couple years that they've known each other. Rhapsody only knew a little about what was going on prior to her revealing the latest details.

"Do you think Devon is gonna kill him?" Rhapsody asked after Miracle finally finished telling the story.

"Ummm, I don't know." She shrugged. "Devon hasn't told anybody, I mean anybody, what the next step is. Once that skinny, renovated, white hoe Ivory do what she's supposed to, which is also this big fuckin' secret, Devon will take over from there. That's all I know."

Still raining, but not as hard, they tried to change the mood by enjoying the sultry sounds of Trey Songz. They were no more than five minutes from reaching Rhapsody's apartment at the intersection of S Avenue and Blue Heron Boulevard, when Miracle suddenly hit something in the road, prompting her to veer hard to the right. Luckily, she was already in the far right lane on Blue Heron Boulevard, making it easy for her to pull over immediately into an abandoned plaza parking lot.

"Damn, girl! What'chu ran over?" Rhapsody finally said, a bit shaken.

"I don't know what that was. It looked like it was a puddle of water, but I guess it wasn't." Miracle cut off the car. "Shit, I don't want to go out there and stand in this rain. I just got my damn hair done, but I must see what's wrong."

"I'ma call Devon, an' …"

"Hell no, you ain't!" Miracle snapped. "As a matter of fact, you're gettin' out with me."

"But …"

"No ifs, ands, or buts about it. Now bring your ass on out here and help me." Miracle angrily opened the door and entered the fine misty rain without as much as thinking about covering herself. "C'mon!"

Rhapsody pouted in the car. However, she knew she'd better get out in order to not risk pissing off Miracle more than she already was. She grabbed her umbrella from the back seat, and reluctantly joined Miracle outside the car.

"Damnit, it looks like I'll have to call my Uncle Virgil because I have a flat tire," Miracle announced as Rhapsody stood by her and held the umbrella over their heads. "Let's get back in the car. There's nothing we can do out here, except catch a cold."

Just as they were about to climb back into the car, a strange vehicle honked its horn while slowly rolling by them on Blue Heron. The dark tints on the windows of the luxury sedan, and the sunless afternoon, made it impossible to see who was in the car.

"Who that is?" Rhapsody asked as the car drove off even slower.

Miracle merely shook her head before they got into the car to get out of the rain.

"Uh-oh," Rhapsody mumbled. "That car turnt around. Ooooh, girl, it's comin' back this way. Ya sho' you dunno who that is?"

"No, girl. Damn!" They attentively watched the silver car as it turned into the parking lot. "I just hope it ain't some nigga that thinks this is the perfect time to holla. If it is, I swear on everythin', whoever it is will wish they kept their happy-ass rollin' down the street."

The sleek car maneuvered so the driver's window was adjacent to Miracle's 2009 Infiniti G37S driver's window. The dark-tinted window rolled down. "I see you two young ladies have a flat tire."

Miracle then rolled down her window. With an inauthentic smile, she said, "Yeah, but we're alright. Thanks, though. The tow truck is on its way right ..."

"I'm sorry to interpose, Miss, but I think I may know you from that club. You're Virgil's niece, aren't you?"

Miracle and Rhapsody simultaneously leaned over to get a look at the driver.

"Girl," Rhapsody whispered into Miracle's ear, "that's Bizzy's father."

"Who?"

"He da father of da nigga that killed da guy I was livin' wit in Georgia, an' his paralyzed mama," she briefly explained after sitting straight up in the seat, trying to hide her face. "Tell him we straight."

Miracle turned her focus back towards the driver, then she realized, after catching a good look at the face, that it was Demetrius. "Oh, shit," she whispered loud enough just so Rhapsody could hear, "that's the guy Devon has us spyin' on."

"Miracle, just tell him we straight. Please."

"Uh, yes. Virgil is my uncle," Miracle confessed. "And he's on his way to help us now."

Demetrius smiled. "I thought you said at first you were waiting on the tow truck?" He raised a brow. "Plus, I just finished speaking with

Virgil, he's down in Miami." He smiled again, only this time he revealed his perfect white teeth. "There is no need to worry about me harming you two ladies. I'm a lover, not a fighter. I just want to be of some assistance, being that you're my right-hand man's niece."

"Umm," Miracle muttered before looking over at Rhapsody, who seemed quite frightened. "It's alright, Mr. ..."

"It's Mr. Woodson. But, please, call me Demetrius."

"Well, Demetrius, we're only a few blocks away from home, sooo ..."

"That's great. I can simply drop you two off then. It's apparent that you were heading east, which is the same direction that I'm heading. I'm on my way home, so it's not like I have anything important to do." He nodded. "Well, I have something to do now, and that's to get you both home safely. So, please, it's the least I can do for two young pretty black women stranded in the rain in the roughest part of Riviera."

Miracle turned towards Rhapsody again.

"Fuck that, Miracle. I'll walk home. Becuz what if Bizzy told him 'bout what happened in Georgia?" Rhapsody was on the verge of crying. "I don't wanna go wit him."

"Hey, JJ's girlfriend?" Demetrius suddenly said. "I almost didn't recognize you over there. Do you remember me? I'm the father of Byron, whom you may know as Bizzy. So, what are you doing down here? And how has JJ been doing? I haven't heard from him in a while."

"See, girl, he don't know nothin'... I think." Miracle shrugged. "Let's just go ahead with him, that way he can leave us alone."

After thinking it over, Rhapsody finally agreed. They gathered their things, locked up the car, and proceeded to get into the Mercedes-Benz.

"You're ridin' up front with him too, since he know you," Miracle demanded as they stood on the passenger side. "And like I said earlier, no ifs, ands, or buts about it."

Rhapsody grimaced. *I hate that bitch,* she thought as she opened the passenger door. To her surprise, though, the passenger seat was already occupied.

What the fuck is going on, Miracle wondered as she climbed into the back seat and seen the hulking, yet familiar, passenger up front.

"What they do, Miracle," said the booming voice. Once Rhapsody was in the back with Miracle, they drove off. "What y'all hit that flattened da tire?"

"I don't know," Miracle confusedly said. "Umm, how do you know Mr. Woodson, Solo?"

"Oh, this my new hussle. Since I left StudioX five months ago, I been Mr. Woodson's personal bodyguard."

"That's why you quit?" she asked, intrigued. "Someone said that you moved to Deerfield with some chick."

"Yeah, I quit da nite after Devon's birthday party. Mr. Woodson offered me a deal I couldn't turn down that same nite. It was bizness, nuttin' personal," Solo explained.

"I know I've probably swiped your best security personnel away from you, and I apologize. It's just that I admired the way he conducted himself in a somewhat hostile environment the night of your boyfriend's party, it was a must that I employed him," Demetrius said.

"What'chu need a bodyguard for?" Rhapsody asked.

"It's not like a requirement." He chuckled. "It's more of just feeling free from harm or risk in a couple cities of lovely Palm Beach County, where the less fortunate people pray upon the well-to-do people, like myself. So, instead of taking matters into my own hands, if something bad was to transpire, my armed security personnel here will handle the situation professionally and to the best of his ability."

"Why he ain't drivin' then?" she continued.

He laughed. "Damn, I just need someone to protect me when necessary. I don't need him to drive for me, or to shake it for me after I've pissed, or even to wipe—"

"We get it," Miracle interjected while nudging Rhapsody. "Shut your big yapper," she then mouthed at her.

Nothing else was said for the rest of the short ride, except for a few "turn-rights" and "turn-lefts." Rather than expose where either one of them stayed, Miracle gave them directions to an apartment building on the next street over from her mother's house; they'd walk from there.

"Thanks for the ride, Mr. Woodson. I mean, Demetrius," Miracle said politely as she and Rhapsody exited the car.

"Anytime, ladies," Demetrius replied after rolling his window down. "You two have a beautiful day. Although, it may be difficult to enjoy this day since it's raining, and because of what happened to your nice car, but make the most of it."

"I'll holla at'cha, Miracle an' Rhapsody. Y'all be easy," Solo said. "Oh, an' if one of y'all see Peachez later, tell her I lost my phone a week ago. I gotta message from her sayin' she need ta holla at me 'bout sumthin' face-to-face. I been busy … an' lazy, lately, so I haven't attempted ta stop by da club ta holla at her."

"We may be able to stop by there tonight," Demetrius said. "Besides, I still would like to sit down with your boyfriend and discuss a few things."

"Okay. We'll see y'all tonight," Miracle quickly responded. "Buh-bye now." She grabbed Rhapsody by the arm and speedily walked up to the apartments.

"What? What's wrong wit'chu, snatchin' me up by my arm?"

Miracle looked back after getting some distance. The car pulled off slowly, then she said, "I have to call Devon, ASAP!"

***

Meanwhile, Demetrius received a phone call just seconds after dropping off Miracle and Rhapsody. The caller was Chad, who was back home in Daytona.

"Yo', Big Cuzzo. I just wanted ta check up on ya an' …"

"Chad, be wise. Think before you speak." Demetrius was hoping Chad continued to show he had good sense by being conscious of what he said over the phone.

"I know, I know. It ain't nuttin' like that, Cuzzo. I was just seein' how ya doin'."

"Well, I'm doing rather good today. How about yourself?"

"I'm straight." There was a pause. "Oh, it ain't nuttin' important, but I just thought I'd tell ya my homeboy bulldog had puppies. You should see da all-white fuckers." He laughed. "Anyway, I wanted ta know if ya wanted one of 'em ta keep ya ole' ass company, cuz he pre-sold all of 'em 'cept one. Dez niggas who buyin' 'em lovin' they lil ass. My boy wish he had mo' ta sell."

The prominent RockBottom Family was an extravagant, and eloquent, money-making organization, owning legit businesses, dealing drugs, racketeering, gambling—you name it, they did it. Of them all, though, drug dealing and gambling were the most profitable.

Aside from hustling, Demetrius was an avid gambler of all sports, and Chad knew this. So, according to the nonsense that Chad was saying, he figured that it was a coded message. It didn't take him long, however, to realize Chad's people in Georgia wanted some more of that work. *Damn, Chad just sold them fifteen kilos two or three days ago,* he thought, *so either the work is A-one, or Chad is a natural-born hustler like I figured he was.*

"Boy, you know damn well I don't have time to raise a mutt. I barely have enough time to take care of myself. But thanks for thinking about me."

"A'ight, since I feel like I'm botherin' ya, I'ma hang up now. Tell er'body down there I said I love 'em. An' tell Eli I said that that giant, sexy red bitch we met at da club when I was down there been blowin' up my phone since we trained her."

Demetrius didn't know an Eli, meaning it was another coded message. He swiftly translated the message: Chad's New York people were also trying to cope some more coke.

"How about you tell him yourself?" Demetrius recited a fake number to Chad. "I have to go now. I have people to call myself. You take care." He hung up. *Boy, my little Peruvian friend is going to have to put all differences aside so we can get this money,* he thought as he dialed Virgil's phone.

CHAPTER FOURTEEN

October 1, 2008 8:25 pm

West Palm Beach, FL

The one thing that was probably better than chilling with the niggas you grew up with, after somewhat neglecting them, was showing love to those same niggas when you came up. It had been a while since Devon threw a block party, held a BBQ, or helped a few people get on their feet. Today, however, those niggas were sort of therapeutic by showing love back when Devon was depressed and stressing. Their presence helped to relieve a lot of stress, and to block out the every-day, fairly-glamorous-life that Devon had been recently living. *Tupac spoke the truth when he said that "You ain't shit without yo' home-boys,"* Devon thought.

Returning to the club feeling slightly better, an intensely hungry Devon decided to grab some hot wings at the bar before going into the office.

"Where you been?" Jazzy shrieked, getting all up in Devon's face. "Everybody been worried 'bout you, Daddy. People been callin' you but your cell goin' straight to voicemail. Miracle in da office cryin' a river 'cause she think somethin' bad done happened to you."

Something bad happened to me, Devon wondered. *Why would she think that something bad happened to me*? "As you can see, I'm straight. I'm hungrier than four fat bitches tryna find a spare rib in a maze, an' you slowin' da process of me tryna order twenty hot wings. But otha than that, I'm good. So run an' tell that!"

Jazzy sucked her teeth and rolled her eyes. She hurriedly disappeared, though, because she didn't want to get snapped on for being impudent. Within two minutes, she'd told every single person that desired to know that Devon was in the building, which caused a crowd to form in the restaurant.

Devon peacefully ignored the hail of questions. The crowd gradually shrunk in size due to the less important, pissed-off, or nosey people walking off. Some ten minutes passed before the food arrived, then Devon politely tipped the server, parted the small crowd, and headed for the office.

"Nobody is to come in, 'cept fo' Miracle. An' y'all leave us alone till I … Matter ah fact, get Big Herb ta come stand guard at da door," Devon ordered. "C'mon, Miracle."

Miracle staggered into the office, with puffy eyes from crying. "I thought you were dead," she said, getting straight to the point. "I've been callin' and callin' you. I had other people call you, too. Why are you doing this to me? I love you, Devon. If somethin' happens to you, I won't … I won't … I'll die! You mean that much to me." She then embraced and cried on Devon's shoulder. "Why are you …?"

"It's okay, Marie. Baby, I ain't goin' nowhere," Devon assured while rubbing her back and kissing her forehead. "Why would ya think I was dead, anyway?"

Miracle began explaining how her tire caught a flat in Da Raw earlier in the day, which coincidentally, led to her and Rhapsody being helped by Demetrius, while Solo was present. She went on telling how they accepted a friendly ride to her mother's house after only being caught in a couple lies. She then explained that when they were saying their goodbyes, Solo said he received a message from Peachez about meeting each other face-to-face. She immediately suspected that Peachez was trying to double cross them all, causing her to fear for Devon's safety.

"I don't know why Peachez needs to talk to Solo for, since he now works for the guy we're spyin' on, but we need to find out."

Devon looked at the dancer's schedule on the wall. "She should be walkin' her funky-ass through da doors in a few. An' I swear I'll kill da bitch if I think she lyin'."

Peachez made an appearance at a quarter till nine. As she was getting ready in the dressing room to start her shift, she was told to report to the office. Not thinking anything of it, she casually strolled to see the boss. Her cool demeanor changed, however, once she walked into the office and instantly received a verbal lashing from Devon.

"What da fuck you got goin' on, huh?" Devon harshly said. "You think I'ma simp, a lame, or sumthin'?"

Peachez looked from Devon to Miracle with a confused expression upon her face. "I-I-I have no clue what you talkin' about, Dee." She fixed her gaze on Miracle, hoping Miracle would give her a sign or fill her in on what was going on. "I just walked …"

"Yeah, you think I'ma lame." Devon untucked the .380 and aimed it at Peachez. "You think I'ma lame still? Do ya?"

Peachez stumbled backwards. She damn near fainted at the sight of the gun. Tears welled up in her eyes as she began to tremble. She still had no clue to what was going on. "Devon, please," she said lowly, "I-I-I don't know what you talkin' about. I-I-I just walked in the door not too long ago." She looked towards Miracle for help. "Miracle, I-I-I don't know what she talkin' about."

"Peachez, what did you have to tell Solo that was so important that y'all had to meet privately or whatever?" Miracle asked.

Peachez looked back at Devon, who was still pointing the gun at her. "I-I-I haven't even seen Solo yet. Every time I call him, he doesn't …"

"Well, what da fuck are y'all 'posed ta be meetin' fo'? What da fuck y'all got goin' on?" Devon demanded.

"Is this what all of this about?" Peachez said. "You have got to be kiddin' me, right?"

"Do it look like I'm fuckin' kiddin', huh? Bitch, you better tell me sumthin', an' it better be what I wanna hear. An' befo' ya start runnin' yo' dick-suckers, if I think ya lyin', I'll just have ta get used ta ya ghost hangin' 'round this bitch!"

Peachez claimed she was meeting Solo for Star. The story was that Star was a few months pregnant, and Star believed Solo was the baby's father. Star was terrified to tell Solo this information, because she loved the adulterous Solo, who was just recently married.

Star eventually told Peachez what was going on last week. Being the rowdy, give-it-to-'em-blood-raw bitch that Peachez was, she told Star she was more than willing to tell Solo. Even after her proposal, Star was still scared, and she even began saying she would raise the baby by herself in order to not ruin Solo's marriage. However, she wasn't trying to hear that bullshit Star was saying, so she pressed Star until she convinced her to let her tell Solo. Star only had one exception: tell Solo face-to-face. That plan changed after she told Star that she was unable to get in touch with Solo, so Star decided to talk to Solo herself the next time they seen each other.

Devon lowered the pistol, then said, "I heard that rumor goin' 'round, so I believe ya. My bad fo' jumpin' ta conclusions. But you gotta undastand that it was a must I did what I did. This shit is startin' ta really fuck wit me." Devon looked at Miracle. "You rite, too. I am obsessed wit this fuck nigga. Still, retaliation is a must. I'll tell ya though, this shit is gonna end tonite!"

"Oh, I forgot to mention that Solo and Demetrius may be stoppin' by here tonight," Miracle blurted out.

"Did they say what time?"

"Nope."

"Fuck! If I want this ta end tonite, I have ta call Gudda now then." Devon began dialing Gudda's cell. "An' I hope he copped da shit I asked him ta get sooner than he was supposed to."

***

October 2, 2008 12:01am

West Palm Beach, FL

The odds are in my favor tonight, Devon thought while watching Gudda pull into the parking lot from the security camera monitor in the office.

Luckily, when Devon called Gudda, he was less than an hour away in Miami, copping "the shit." He had a few errands of his own to take care of before heading to StudioX, though.

"Befo' ya go ta buggin' me," Gudda said as soon as he walked into the office, "yes, I have da shit you been askin' me ta get, Dee Baby." He closed the door and grabbed a seat across from Devon at the desk. "It was hard ta come by … well, it was easy ta get, but I had a hard time pronouncin' that fucked-up name. I still can't say it." He laughed. "Oh, an' Ivory should be here in a few minutes."

"Good."

"So, what made ya change ya mind into goin' through wit this sooner rather than later, Dee Baby?"

"I'm just tired of this shit," Devon declared before sighing. "I'm lettin' this affect my bizness an' my personal life wit my girl Miracle. Fo' da last six months, I've only been focused on gettin' even wit da muthafuckin' child-molestin', pussy-ass nigga Kilo. I'm just ... I can't ... I just can't wait ta get this shit over wit so I can get back on my grown-man an' get money."

"I hear ya, Dee Baby."

Phone rings

"Oh, that's me," Gudda said before answering his cell.

***

Meanwhile, outside in the parking lot of StudioX, Solo was talking to Star.

Since nobody could seem to get in touch with Solo for the last couple days, Star took it upon herself to call his home. She had left a message with his wife, and that message was that Solo needed to be at StudioX sometime tonight for an important meeting with Devon.

When Solo arrived by himself and realized that it was Star who called his house, fury overcame him.

He eventually calmed down, though, and they began to talk sensibly.

Just seconds into the conversation, however, Solo witnessed a cherry red BMW 750Li pull into the parking lot. *Hmmm, I've seen that car, or a car just like it somewhere before,* he thought while paying no attention to Star. Moments later, he spotted a familiar, flashy black male in his late twenties or early thirties approach the red Beemer's driver window. He watched the guy go into his pocket, remove a brown paper bag and hand it through the window. The guy then held a little conversation with the unseen driver of the car. During the convo, the guy began screaming at the driver, causing a scene. Seconds later, the guy finally walked off and went back into the club again, and the red Beemer drove off. *Damn, I know I've seen that car before*, he thought, *but where*?

"Is that okay with you?" Star asked.

No response.

"Solo! Hellllooooo, I said, is that okay with you!?"

"Yeah, yeah," Solo replied, without knowing what the fuck Star was talking about.

She smiled. "Really? Are you sure?"

"Yeah, whateva you say."

"Okay, then I'ma need you to promise me one thing."

"Fuck!" he suddenly yelled. "I knew it."

"What?" Her jaw dropped. "See, you trippin' already. I just asked you to promise me one thing. That's it!"

"Huh? I'm trippin' 'bout what?"

"You know, nigga. One minute you actin' like you care about me and the baby. Then, all of a sudden, you ..."

"Huh? What fuckin' baby???"

"See, Solo! You trippin' hard, nigga. You mean to tell me you haven't listened to a word I was sayin'?"

"Star, I can't talk no mo' rite now. I have ta go handle some bizness real quick," he said as he walked off in the direction of his car. "I'll call you later ta find out what da fuck ya crazy-ass talkin' 'bout!"

"Fuck you, nigga!" Star shouted, burning his back with her fiery stare.

***

October 2, 2008 12:35 am

Riviera Beach, FL

"I'm sorry I'm late, babe," Ivory said as she strutted into Demetrius' condo wearing the tightest, smallest red mini-dress ever made. "I had to make a stop before I came."

"Oh, you're only..." He looked at his custom-made platinum Rolex "...an hour and thirty-five minutes late."

Ivory invaded his space, kissed him, and rubbed his crotch.

"I'll make it up to you tonight. I promise," she whispered into his ear. "And I have a surprise for you, babe."

"I have a great Italian meal for you. And I'm the dessert, your favorite." He smiled before kissing her back. Instead of a night of just straight fucking, he wanted to relax, eat and talk before fucking. Tonight was to be a special occasion.

Just like she was late, though, he was almost unable to make this date himself. A situation came up dealing with his connect in Peru. He'd only had direct contact with the nameless Big Boss in Peru once, and that was to set up the meeting that never took place almost a year and a half ago.

Nonetheless, today, he was told the negotiations were back on the table when he contacted Adrian, the middleman he'd been dealing with for years. It was said that he was contacting Adrian too much to re-up. Even so, until the Big Boss set up a date, time and place for their negotiations, Adrian requested to meet with him in Miami to arrange a separate deal between the two of them.

After close to two hours of deliberating during the private meeting, Adrian finally agreed to give him a deal for six-fifty per kilo after purchasing his normal one hundred kilos at eight hundred apiece. Before he accepted that offer, though, he asked whether his fifteen grand per kilo delivery fees would increase or not after his initial one hundred kilo purchase. Adrian said it wouldn't change the price of the first one hundred, however his fee was twelve thousand, five hundred per kilo. So, he was buying the Big Boss' one hundred keys at fifteen thousand, eight hundred a piece, then each additional kilo after that from Adrian was thirteen thousand, one hundred-fifty apiece. He didn't think twice about placing an order for four hundred of "dem thangs." *Might as well buy as much as I can now,* he thought at that time, *because who knows if I can get this deal next time.*

He was so ecstatic about his new side deal and the rescheduled negotiations that after the meeting he chilled in the sunny, rain-free Miami area until an hour from the present time. He honestly thought he wasn't going to make his eleven o'clock date with Ivory because he lost track of time. But when she informed him via text message that she was running late herself, he had the upper hand again.

When he arrived home finally, he still felt delighted about how things were falling into place, so he ordered Italian cuisine to be delivered to his condo. Not only was he trying to just enjoy the turn of events with Ivory by fucking her brains out, but he also wanted to celebrate his happiness by wining and dining with her first, which was something he rarely did with just any woman.

While he got the meal ready to eat, Ivory was somewhere in one of the rooms. "Heather, would you please join me at the table? This delicious food is going to get cold," he said, preparing the table and opening a bottle of white wine.

"Demetrius, babe, I need your assistance for a second," she hollered from the master bedroom.

"What is it?"

"Just come see, silly. And hurry!"

He sighed.

He then made his way to her. "Heather, the food is going to get cold ..."

Spread-eagled on his king-size pillow-top bed with satin sheets was Ivory. She was wearing red everything: red hair ties, red lipstick, red sheer lingerie, red stockings, and red stilettos. "I don't want food just yet. But..." She sucked on her red-painted manicured nails before tracing her body from the lips on her face to the lips between her thighs. "...I would love to have my yummy chocolate cake. So can I please have my rich, velvety, chocolate cake now. I'm definitely not going to ruin my appetite by enjoying my favorite dessert first."

"Well … I wanted to sit down, eat some great Italian, then have amazing sex. But truthfully, I've been dying to try this little blue diamond-shaped pill that's going to keep me harder than a trigonometry test." He chuckled. "So, I guess, we can have amazing sex first, then eat some great Italian while conversing later, which is something we infrequently do," he said while undressing.

"Babe, we can talk about whatever you want after I have my dessert." She then motioned for him to get on the bed. "Mmm, I'm hungry ... hungry for your loving."

Demetrius stuck the pill in his mouth and swallowed. He then did a little dance as he walked towards the bed, and ...

Phone rings

"Just ignore it, babe. Come and feed me that huge thing between your legs you have the nerve to call a dick."

Phone rings

Shit, I'm not going to answer it, because I know it's bad news, he thought as he continued to undress and approach a sex-crazed Ivory, *but it may be extremely important.*

"Shit! I apologize, but I must answer this. It may be an important call," he said as he walked back into the kitchen to answer his cell phone on the kitchen counter.

He was only gone momentarily before returning to the bedroom. Then, without saying more than a few words, he commenced to having the roughest, kinkiest sex they've ever had. He put Ivory in positions that would have made the Kama Sutra seem like it was a stretching exercise handbook for kindergartners. Instead of her usual teasing moans and seductive demands, he had her screaming in agony and pleading sorrowfully tonight. He was driven by more than the Viagra in his system, and he wasn't hearing none of it. He was a man on a mission right now.

After more than an hour of straight hardcore fucking, they were both too exhausted to move. They lie in silence without even cuddling.

"What was that all about, Demetrius?" Ivory finally gathered the courage to ask. "You just ... fucked me like ... like I did something wrong."

"Did you? Do something wrong, that is."

"No, babe." She moved to rest her head on his shoulder. "Never. I love you, Demetrius."

"Is that so?" He angrily got out of bed and put on his slacks. "I'm thirsty. Are you thirsty?"

"Yes, I am."

"Excuse me," he shouted, "Solo, bring me that bottle of wine please, kind sir."

"Demetrius! What's going on!?!" she frighteningly said, sitting up and covering herself with the wet satin sheets. "Who is Solo? And why is he in your place? I thought we were spending this night alone?"

"I'll explain everything in one second, babe ... as soon as Solo brings us our cold drinks."

The huge shadow that Solo cast made his grand entrance more suspenseful. When he finally came into view, holding a bucket with the bottle of wine in one hand and a small brown paper bag in the other, Ivory gasped in horror.

"Don't be rude, Heather," Demetrius scolded her, "say hello to Solo." He then turned to Solo. "Say hello to Heather." They both acknowledged each other. "Now, Solo, will you please be kind enough to explain why you have blessed us with your hulking presence."

"I'm Mr. Woodson's personal bodyguard, an' I'm here ta stop ya from poisonin' Mr. Woodson." He paused just to savor the facial expressions of Ivory. "I called Mr. Woodson an' told him what'chu are up to.

"I was at StudioX tonite when you pulled up in ya red Beemer. I was talkin' ta sum one at da time but'cha car grabbed my attention. At first, I thought you were a celebrity until that nigga I've seen sumwhere befo' approached ya car. When he gave you this bag..." He presented the small paper bag. "I just thought it was a drug deal goin' down. Then you an' da dude got into an argument. From where I was standin', I could hear buddy say da name Ivory. Afterwards, he walks back into da club an' you pull off, an' that's when I seen ya license plate that said 'INV RED', which is crazy cuz ya car red.

"As soon as ya left it hit me. I rememba my boss man here tellin' me that he had a date wit his girl Ivory tonite. I've never seen ya till now." He tried to catch a peek of some skin. "But I have seen ya car leavin' Mr. Woodson's condo a few times as I was comin' ta pick him up, an' that's how I rememba da tag on ya car.

"Anywayz, I drove, straight here an' found ya car in da lot. I broke into it, an' I happened ta look in da bag I seen buddy give ya at da club. Inside of da bag was this clear, odorless, an' prolly tasteless, liquid in a tiny bottle. Then I called Mr. Woodson, which was almost two hours ago, an' gave him a heads up on ya play. So, that's that."

"Listen, Demetrius, I can explain," Ivory mumbled as tears ran down her pale face, fucking up her makeup even more.

"Please, do."

"Gudda made me do this! He's the one Cee-lo …"

"That's Solo," Solo chided.

"Ummm, he's the one Solo seen me with earlier tonight. I don't know why, but I came from Tampa to set you up. From that day you met me in the restaurant at the club until now has been a set-up."

"Okay, this is a set-up. I understand that part. So, the stuff in the bottle is what exactly?"

"I … I-I don't know, Demetrius. I swear! All I know is that once I put that into your drink I was to call Gudda."

"Well, what are you waiting for? Call this Gudda."

Ivory continued to boo-hoo cry as she got her cellphone. "And just so you know, Demetrius," she said before dialing, "I wasn't going to do it. That's what me and Gudda argued about in the parking lot. I fell in love with you, not your money or personal possessions. That's why the bottle was still in my car. I couldn't do it because you're the man I love. I didn't want to spoil the mood, but I was going to tell you everything in the morning after we enjoyed this special night together. I swear."

Demetrius smiled, then looked at Solo. "Isn't that sweet? That was so sentimental, I almost ... gave a fuck!" He turned back to face Ivory. "You're not the first woman, or third woman, that has tried to set me up. And you're most likely not the last. So, please, call this Gudda fellow ... hmm, never mind. Solo knows how this Gudda looks. I'll have my people take care of him." He turned back to Solo. "By the way, are you hungry, Solo? I have some delicious Italian in the kitchen. I have some yummy rich, velvety white cake, too. And if you are like some people I know, you will probably enjoy having your dessert first."

CHAPTER FIFTEEN

October 3, 2008 9:00 am

Wellington, FL

"Devon, wake up. Baby, wake up," Miracle mumbled while agitating the body in the bed. "Dee, wake up."

Without awareness, Devon awoke frantic. "Huh? Wha ... What's goin' on? Was I havin' anotha bad dream?"

"No." She shook her head as she stood over Devon. "But you need to get up and see this." She then tossed today's issue of *The Palm Beach Post* onto the bed. "Turn to the Local section. It's on the front page."

Devon lazily got into a sitting position and opened the paper to the local section. After briefly scanning the page, Devon discovered what Miracle must have been talking about.

BLACK MAN, WHITE WOMAN
DEAD IN MURDER-SUICIDE
In suburban West Palm Beach, a
26-year-old St. Petersburg woman
was killed sometime October 2nd
by boyfriend, who then shot and
killed himself with the same
weapon, according to the Palm
Beach County Coroner.
Heather Sinclair and her boyfriend, Marcus Mitchell, 33, were
pronounced dead in Sinclair's red
BMW, Palm Beach County Coroner
Charles White said in a statement.
An autopsy is scheduled for today
in West Palm Beach, FL. If you have
any further information, please
contact the County's Sheriff office.

Devon balled the newspaper up and threw it across the room. "I can't believe this fuck shit! Are you serious? How da fuck can da police believe it's a murder-suicide?" Devon hopped out of bed. "It's time ta handle this shit myself. I shoulda neva …"

"No, Dee. You have to think about your safety right now. You don't know if Ivory and Gudda kept their mouths shut. For all we know, this Demetrius guy could be lookin' for you as we speak. So you have to worry about gettin' out of town. That's it!"

"Uh-uh. Ain't nan nigga gonna run me from my city. You got me all da way fucked up!"

"Dee," she screamed, "just listen to me dammit for fuckin' once! You act like you the baddest bitch in this town. You're not! This nigga is serious, and he ain't playin'! He just killed two fuckin' people and made it look like it was a relationship dispute that went fuckin' wrong. So what do you think he will do to you? Or me? "Or…" Miracle began to cry. "…my baby, Kamani?"

Fuck, I didn't even take the time to think about how I was endangering Miracle's life, Devon thought, *and the life of my little nigga, Kamani.* "Once again, Marie, you rite. Call ya mama an' tell her that'chu finna pick up Kamani in an hour, while I call around ta get sumbody ta run da spot fo' me. Da three of us are gonna go away fo' a while."

***

October 3, 2008 4:40 pm

Miami Beach, FL South Beach

Only a few more weeks until the beginning of fall. Although it was the end of summer, today was hot but moderate enough to hold a conference outside of Deep Blue Seafood and Grill on Ocean Drive in South Beach. The public get-together this afternoon was arranged by none other than the man himself.

Demetrius was no longer timid about conducting business while exposed to general view. He very well knew, without a doubt, that the feds didn't just forget about him, and he still could feel their eyes on him at all times. He didn't think he was smarter or more powerful than the federal government, but he knew the key to successfully stay out in front of the Alphabet Boyz was to continue to switch up on them -- and they didn't like that -- because when they think they start to know your every move, they will start plotting on how to take you out of the game. *It's time to switch up on them now*, he thought as he greeted his guests, *because it's about that time to expand.*

The three-man meeting consisted of Virgil, Chad, and Demetrius. The purpose for the meeting was to discuss a number of small things. The main issue, however, was recruiting. Demetrius needed to find a few people that could be trusted outside of RBF and that were worthy of becoming a part of his bigger picture. He needed just a few good men willing to relocate for a greater cause. Florida, Atlanta, and New York's five boroughs were already being serviced by him, which collectively were generating over ten million dollars a month. His new strategy was to recruit at least five dependable, mid-level hustlers that would lockdown a major city in every state from Georgia to New York. And he had a creative way to distribute the drugs from Florida to where it was needed.

As they ate, the three of them deliberated for almost an hour about who would be excellent prospects to bring into RBF's hustling division before finally agreeing upon five guys. Three of the five were from Palm Beach County, one was from Orlando, and the last was from Daytona Beach.

However, before they could put the new plan in motion, they set up five individual meetings between the prospect and whoever selected him for consideration. They chose to do it this way for the possibility of the shit hitting the fan. If one of the prospects was apprehended and folded under pressure, that prospect could only implicate the person who brought him to the table and not the rest, therefore keeping the others in the game to play without interference.

After their meal, and their main issue resolved for now, Demetrius changed the topic.

"By the way, Chad, you were on the money."

"I was on da money 'bout what?"

"Your intuition was right about that white slut I was messing around with. If it wasn't for Solo, I'd probably not be here talking with you gentlemen."

Chad grimaced. "I told ya that hoe was shady! I knew it. So did ya put a handle on that bitch?"

"Yes. The Clean-up Crew took care of her and some want-to-be 'Willie Dynamite' fool name Gudda."

"Yah, mon," Virgil excitedly said, "me hear 'bout dem on da

news. Da police dem found dem shot up inna red Beemer."

"It was a murder-suicide they'd ruled it." Demetrius smiled. "I just wish my Clean-up Crew would've questioned Gudda before killing him. I still feel like they weren't acting alone, because I have no idea why he wanted me dead or whatever." He slightly sighed. "Oh, well, I'll just have to be more mindful of the woman I choose to keep me company. I cannot let a woman be my demise, although my only weakness is a beautiful woman. However, every woman, or person for that matter, that has tried to set me up is no longer breathing. I love women. But I love me even more.

"Enough of that, I'm ready to hit the road. I have some business to tend to in Palm Beach this evening," he added. "I have a small conference with a city official of Riviera Beach about starting or funding a non-profit organization for the black youth in the area."

"Okay, Big Cuzzo. Just lemme know when ya ready ta open up that furniture store," Chad said while standing up. "I got some people that's into wholesalin' furniture fo' da low."

"Oh, I will surely do that. I have my accountant and real estate agent locating the perfect spot for our warehouse, which will be the headquarters, as we speak," Demetrius declared as he too stood up. "I'll call you two later on."

They departed Deep Blue and went their separate ways. *In a few months' time, I will be the man on the streets of the entire East Coast,* Demetrius thought with a Grinch-like grin on his face as he waited for Solo to pick him up. *Kilo is back!*

CHAPTER SIXTEEN

October 7, 2008 6:10 pm

West Palm Beach, FL

Demetrius was in overdrive. Not even a full week had passed, and it seemed like he was the only one putting forth the effort and time to board the money train. At first, he thought that maybe he was high-strung about being back on beat with the connect. But then he realized that it was imperative that everybody got on one accord and got the 'shit' popping. There was a lot of money to be made, and barely enough time in one man's life to get it.

"What it do, Big Cuzzo?" Chad said as he got into the car.

"Did your people decide if they wanted to do business with us or not?" Demetrius asked without greeting Chad back. "I need to know now, because I need to start considering which cities we're going to set up our operation in. So far, my guy and both of Virgil's guys desire to play a part in helping RBF rise to the top."

"Well," Chad sighed, "it seems like we're gonna be one short. My dawg Junebug in Orlando is ready ta bounce rite now. But my nigga in Daytona actin' like he don't wanna get this paper. I can find anotha …"

"Don't worry about it. Four is good." The four new hustlers going to assist in putting RBF in the history books as the first notorious drug empire in the south were Kelly, Junebug, Buckey, and Zooman. Five was the magic number Demetrius was hoping to obtain, yet four would do the job. *Maybe, instead of using five, it's destined for me to utilize the four that's available*, he thought as he drove away from PBIA.

Kelly Kronkite was Demetrius' pick. The two became acquainted about five years back at a social event in Tally. Some small talk ensued before Palm Beach County was brought up during the conversation, and one thing led to another. Kelly was a thirty-year-old white man that owned Kronkite Konstruction with his father, Karl Kronkite. He lived in wealthy Palm Beach Gardens, FL, but he was in no way, shape or form your typical I-can-run-game-on-him cracka, either. He may have not been a product of the hood or subjected to any ghetto influences, but he did possess the same qualities and ambitions as your everyday birdman. He showed good judgment by not serving just anybody, and he mainly dealt with the upper-class.

Demetrius supplied him with ten kilos for a cool two hundred thousand dollars every week, which he promptly sold to his counterparts for twenty-nine thousand per kilo. Between his money-making construction company and lucrative hustling, he had money out the ass. He also owned a few small businesses and houses in different states, making him a perfect prospect. He was a real businessman, meaning that he was only about the Benjamins, nothing else. His favorite motto was "having money isn't everything, it's the only thing!" He knew Demetrius was a pea in the same pod, so he didn't think twice about accepting Demetrius' proposal.

Chad ran with his dawg, Junebug, aka Bug. The two of them grew up together in Orlando as childhood friends, until Chad moved to Daytona Beach, FL, to attend Bethune-Cookman College when they both were eighteen. Bug remained in O-Town, getting himself involved in the street life as a cold lame to the game. However, he knew Chad's father was a big dope boy in O-Town. So, since Bubba treated him like a son, Bug finessed his way into performing little odd jobs for Bubba, like buying large quantities of cut for the coke, weighing small amounts of dope, listening to the police scanners, etc. He never had the opportunity to experience the real grind of block-hustling.

Bubba refused to let him demoralize himself by selling a couple grams at a time. By Bubba's standards, it was do it big or do nothing at all. He eventually jumped from being a do-boy to pushing ounces to moving keys within one year. He ceased his nine-year hustle all together though, after Bubba, his plug, got jammed up with the feds last year. He had enough cash saved up to relax for a long time. But, when Chad told him about the new movement, he couldn't force himself to say no to the money. So, he made a pact with Chad to go hard in the paint.

Buckey and Zooman were selected by Virgil. Buckey and Virgil were friends in Jamaica before they came to the land of the free, home of the brave. Virgil was in the U.S. seven years before Buckey. Buckey chose to live in Delray Beach, FL, after turning down Virgil's plea to move to West Palm Beach. He was forty-one, and a true follower of Haile Selassie I. Besides knowing every trade in the book, he was a connoisseur of marijuana and cocaine. Everyday he'd put in a good eight hours of honest, laborious work before he slung any dope, making him a petty hustler by choice. He also made it well-known he was a loner, only staying in constant contact with his family in Jamaica and Virgil. It took a lot of persuading to get him to deal with Virgil. The large amount of money he could possibly make that would bring his entire family to the States to live a helluva better life than they were in poverty-stricken Jamaica was the only reason he decided to collaborate with Virgil.

Zooman was the most wildly impractical Haitian man that Virgil knew. Well, most Haitians older than forty years of age were already either heavily influenced by or practiced voodoo, making the majority of them mentally impaired by American standards. However, forty-six-year-old Zooman wasn't one of those Haitians. He may have been into blood, chicken bones, zombies, and black magic, but he was also into getting money by the banana boat-load. He was from Lake Worth, FL, which was where Virgil and he encountered each other at a Jamaican/Haitian restaurant about four years ago. And to this day, Virgil still believes that Zooman put "roots' on him, because he has no idea how they became allies that day.

Since then, Virgil has been supplying Zooman with eight bricks a week, which baffled Virgil for a long time, because Zooman looked like the type of immigrant that never had more than a few dollars in his pockets at all times, nor did he own anything that cost more than what it looked like he could afford; simply trying to figure out where his money went was a mystery. Still, one thing was certain, he faithfully bought eight keys a week, at nineteen-point-five a piece, no matter what. Virgil had no intentions of asking him to be a part of the new movement, but a force within Virgil instructed him to invite Zooman, and Zooman happily accepted. Aside from practicing voodoo, he was going to do what he did best: turn powder into paper that was never seen again until it was time to buy more powder.

With the four new hustlers in place, Demetrius could finally get the money train rolling. All he had to do now was figure out who would be the best fit for one of the designated cities he would soon pick.

"What'chu been up to, Cuzzo?"

Snapping back to the present time, Demetrius responded, "Outside of trying to get everything in order for our billion-dollar-a-year profit that's soon to come, I've been up to nothing much." He paused. "Oh, do you recall hearing about a family of gangsters-slash-tyrants that called themselves Possum Boyz? They were highly respected in downtown West Palm Beach until the federal government damn near incarcerated them all in the late eighties, remember?"

Chad rubbed his chin as he refreshed his memory. "I think," he said a minute later. "What about 'em?"

"Well, it has nothing to do with them. But there is a new group of so-called thugs in West Palm Beach that are claiming to be ten times worse than the Possum Boyz, which is damn near impossible to say, let alone do.

"Every few years in West Palm Beach though, a new band of misguided black adolescents declare that they're the new and improved version of the infamous Possum Boyz. They'll terrorize the city until ninety percent of them end up seventy two inches in the dirt, or serving a life sentence for a plethora of reasons."

Demetrius knew first-hand about everything he was telling Chad. RockBottom Family was formed because of what the Possum Boyz had accumulated during the late seventies and early eighties, when he was an up-and-coming young hustler. The Possum Boyz mainly consisted of immediate family. Basically, the crew was run by six brothers, who were the millionaires of the group. The Possum Boyz were the ultimate hood terrorists, and they predominantly conquered Downtown West Palm Beach for a little more than a decade.

Their demise came in 1988 when a corrupt cop allied with the Possum Boyz group was murdered, causing the feds to jump into action and take them off the streets for good by sentencing most of them to life in prison for various charges. Once the hood realized the million-dollar turf was up for grabs, every nigga and their mama tried to pick up where the Possum Boyz dropped the ball. There was a murder or five every day for almost a year because of niggas vying for the foundation of the house that the Possum Boyz built. When the smoke finally cleared though, Demetrius, Bubba, Obie, and a few others, gained total control of the turf, thus beginning RBF's stake in the game.

"Now there's a new squad of hardheads running the streets," Demetrius continued. "According to Virgil, they supposedly call themselves Triple S, which is short for SunSet Syndicate."

"Ha! Triple S should stand fo' Sweet an' Sour Sissies!" Chad laughed hysterically at his own joke. "Shit, wit a name like that, they ain't gonna be 'round that long."

"I hope so," Demetrius added, "because Virgil has informed me that RBF has frequently been mentioned by some of these boys lately."

"Cuzzo, you ain't gotta worry 'bout 'em. They don't want no problems wit da family. Trust me! You an' I both know that one phone call is all it'll take fo' da Clean-up Crew ta come through."

"You're absolutely right. But that's not the route I want to go with a bunch of black boys that're hell-bent and ready to do just about anything to make a name for themselves. I know this personally because that's how RBF was formed." He took a deep breath. "I haven't had a problem since all the blood that was shed in the beginning. RBF made a name for itself early on. I made sure of that. I had a few people try to rub out RBF over the years, but they lacked the manpower. For some reason, though, I feel like this Triple S gang is going to be a future nuisance, because they're openly talking about RBF as if they're not scared like all the rest.

"I have Solo for protection, but he's not with me twenty-four seven. I employ him when I mainly travel to other cities, not my own hometown. I may need him now just to walk outside. Who knows what the hood has discovered about me since my return? I may be known as Demetrius now, but back then, I was the heartless, unflinching killer and the greedy, back-stabbing hustler called Kilo. Kilo was loved by none and hated by all. I left for Tallahassee in September of '88 when I felt that RBF was grounded, yet the hood still remembers Kilo to this day. The hood probably thinks that Kilo is dead, and that's how I plan to keep it."

"How do ya think Triple S know 'bout RBF now? Ya think Virgil has opened his big curry-goat-eatin' mouth?"

"I wouldn't put it passed him. He does have the tendency to lie and run off at the mouth, which I'm ready to close any day now. He's just lucky that I need him right now to get this thing up and running. I'll take care of him once we're established." He inhaled deeply again and exhaled before continuing. "You know, I've grown accustomed to not having to look over my shoulder all the time. Hopefully, whatever is being said about RBF in the hood will die down or pass over soon. Only time will tell, though."

Absent of music or noise, they rode for approximately thirty minutes before arriving at their destination, an industrial area on the outskirts of West Palm Beach full of light manufacturing facilities and warehouses.

The building Demetrius finally stopped in front of had to be no less than fifty thousand square feet. A fleet of brand new white trucks of various sizes were stationed on both sides of the warehouse's huge door. They both exited the vehicle and admired the discreet area.

"Is this da spot ya been talkin' 'bout?" Chad asked as they stood side by side in front of a small door that led into the massive structure.

"Yes, this is where the big bucks will start rolling in." He smiled. "This is where it's better to receive than it is to give."

"I'm feelin' that," Chad replied, rubbing his hands together in a greedy manner.

Demetrius unlocked the door, and they stepped into the darkness. He walked a few feet over to a panel on the wall and flicked about eight switches. The overhead fluorescent lights slowly lit up. After several minutes, the lights were bright enough to reveal the voluminous empty interior. He then proceeded to the far right of the building to a metal staircase that led to the building's office.

Once inside the big office, which was already furnished with posh desks, ergonomic chairs, high-tech computers, gleaming file cabinets, etc., Demetrius entered the largest of several rooms. It was obvious the decked-out room was his. Sitting down in the exquisite Gunlocke Washington high-backed office chair behind the most expensive-looking burnished hardwood desk money could buy, he motioned for Chad to take a seat opposite him.

"Well, from da looks of thangs, this is gonna be a legitimate bizness. Exactly what are we gonna use dis place fo' again?"

Demetrius leaned forward in the chair with an earnest look upon his face, folded his hands together, and replied, "This is a legitimate business. I'll never run a business unless it's legitimate." He displayed his signature grin. "Now, what I need for you to do is to call your people that you said sold furniture. I need to purchase all the furniture that they have. I'm hoping to have this place full to the max well before my birthday this month. Can you handle that?"

"Umm, I got'cha. I guess you really serious 'bout sellin' furniture, huh? I thought we were focusin' on sellin' da dope. But hey, it's evident that'cha know sumthin' I don't." He shrugged. "That's why you da man."

Demetrius laughed heartily before shaking his head at his protege. "Chad, I may know a lot more than you because of my age, but knowing how to make money is the most important thing I know. Believe me when I tell you I'd rather be uneducated and know how to make a ton of money to live well, than to be book smart and just barely getting by."

"I'm feelin' that philosophical shit, Big Cuzz."

***

On the other side of town, Miracle was handling a few things in the office at StudioX. Since her arrival a couple hours ago, she had one simple demand, to be left alone. Yet, a knock at the door clearly let her know it could only be one of two people. She knew who it was before she instructed the person to enter.

"Hey, Miracle," the person shyly greeted after closing the door lightly as if walking into a room of sleeping infants.

Miracle agitatedly stopped what she was doing, and responded, "What's up, Rhapsody?" There was no use for stalling, because she knew Rhapsody was only in the office right now for one thing. Although Rhapsody wasn't the type to run and tell everything to everybody, she still didn't want to be bothered answering all of Rhapsody's intrusive questions. "I'm quite busy now, Rhapsody. If what you have to say ain't important, can you please wait until I'm finished doin' what I have to do? I will be done shortly."

"Oh … okay." Rhapsody frowned, then turned around slowly to leave. She was in the motion of opening the door to exit before she suddenly stopped. She did an about face, and continued, "Miracle, I know somethin' bad happened to Dee. You can come here an' tell everybody that Dee is on vacation, but I ain't believin' that. I know it got somethin' to do wit Gudda an' that white girl he was wit gettin' killed. Everybody out there spreadin' rumors and tellin' lies 'bout where Dee really at, 'specially Jazzy.

"I know that'chu … love Devon to death, Miracle. Well … well, so do I." She cleared her throat. "All I wanna do is help. Lemme help y'all do whateva it is y'all plannin' to do. I got plenty money put up from when JJ was killed in Georgia, so I'll give y'all whateva ya need, as long as I can help." The tears that were welled-up in her eyes began to roll down her baby-doll face. "Please, Miracle, lemme help," she begged sincerely.

Miracle took every single word Rhapsody spoke into consideration. She and Devon did need some form of help from at least one person. It was simply a shame how Devon couldn't find someone responsible enough to run StudioX, so she ultimately chose to stay behind, after heavy protesting from Devon first, to make sure the club would remain open while Devon took Kamani to hideout in Cocoa Beach, FL.

Little did she know that the task she took on was overwhelming. Her hands were extremely full. She kept a fresh bottle of aspirins close by for the never-ending headaches. She determinedly tried though, to juggle the duties she and Devon usually did together, which was too much work for two people, let alone a single person. She also had to endure unnecessary stress, like being interrogated daily about stuff that had nothing to do with business. And, on top of all that, she had to remain mindful of perhaps being killed by somebody that was possibly looking for Devon. *Well, my momma did tell me that I'd have days like this,* she thought as she rubbed her temples sturdily, *so I can most definitely use Rhapsody's help, but I'd have to consult with Devon first, of course.*

She was fairly sure though, that Rhapsody was the helping hand she desperately needed. She could have Rhapsody take the trip up to Cocoa Beach and help take care of Kamani, while also assisting Devon with the whole "identity change" thing, instead of her driving nearly four hours up to Cocoa Beach to do what she needed to do before driving another four hours back down to West Palm Beach. Indeed, it was exhausting enough that in the last four days she had already made that round trip three times, therefore it was no military secret that she was extremely burnt out. The dark bags under her eyes and lack of energy were evident, so there was no doubt at all that she needed a long period of rest from working nearly nonstop. And Rhapsody was just the person to lift some of the weight off her shoulders.

The extra help should also result to things getting handled much faster, which was essential for Devon's arrangement to return to West Palm Beach sooner than expected to put an end to Demetrius' existence on earth. *Rhapsody's adulation and devotion to Devon is exactly what we need to accomplish just that*, she concluded.

"Alright," Miracle finally said, "I'll have to convince Devon into lettin' you help us, which is no big deal." She then stared into Rhapsody's soul before continuing through clenched teeth, "But mark my muthafuckin' words when I say you better not fuck up our plans by flappin' your dick-suckers. 'Cause if you do, I'll make you wish you had died before my wrath could fall upon you. You understand me, Miss Keema Langston?"

Rhapsody simply nodded.

CHAPTER SEVENTEEN

October 25, 2008 10:20 pm

Lake Worth, FL

Forty-four years. Demetrius never imagined that he would live to see age forty-four. Being subjected to the street life at an early age caused him to see how real and malevolent the world actually was, so it was hard to fathom how he made it this far. After forty-four years of existing, his testimony of "been there, done that" couldn't have been any truer. He'd done so many terrifying, inhumane things in the past thirty years, he really doubted God worked in mysterious ways. To him, God was just an entity he was taught to believe in as a youngster. Over the years, everything he achieved came from his own desire to get it. His opinion was he had total control over his destiny during his lifetime, not God. *I'll be the Almighty One that people worship and look to for comfort and help*, he thought with a demonic grin, *very soon*!

Utilizing *The Art of War,* Demetrius had *learned* (listened), *foresaw* (aimed), *marched* (moved), and now he was *forming* (claiming). The blueprint he had laid out for dominating the east coast was looking mighty good. All was going accordingly, the rise of RBF was imminent. Not only was he prepared financially and physically, but he was also prepared mentally to set things in motion. Since the second day of this month, neither did he relax nor deviate from his supreme "come-up." Now it was time to reap the benefits of a well-conceived and processed plan. *The wait is finally over,* he concluded.

But before he was to make the call to get the ball rolling, it was about that time to lounge for one night, and party!

He was talked into celebrating his birthday at The Palace Gentlemen's Club by Virgil, who was told by Miracle that it was a nice spot to party besides StudioX. He had been all work and no play for the last six months, so clubbing with Virgil and Chad on his special day was exactly what he needed.

Upon arrival at The Palace, around 10:25 pm, they immediately sought refuge in the VIP lounge. Virgil didn't hesitate to announce loudly over the mic in the DJ's booth that it was Demetrius' birthday, and they had plenty of money to blow. However, it took Virgil and

Chad to flash wads of money before they garnered the attention they yearned for from the ladies.

Soon enough, they were having a jolly good time throwing Benjamins, drinking Rémy Martin, and enjoying the service of the ghetto-fabulous, super-thick dancers.

Yet, of all the money-hungry hoes in the VIP, there was one PYT that caught Demetrius' eye, sitting with some buster on the opposite side of the room. He directly became intrigued by the dancer's aloof looks, and, unlike every other bitch in the building, she didn't seem at all interested in the activity that was taking place around his table.

As the big booty strippers focused on sucking their money up any way they could, Demetrius remained focused on the trim figure that sipped on something clear, like vodka or Patrón, while holding a conversation with a guy that wore old-fashioned nerdy glasses, dull-colored casual clothes, and had the attributes of a stalker or pedophile. *Boy*, he began to say to himself, *she reminds me of …*

"Yo', Big Cuzzo," Chad yelled, "why ya ain't enjoyin' da show these hoes puttin' on fo' ya over here? Ya been muggin' that one bitch over there fo' da longest."

"Chad, I must correct you on one assumption you've made. That female over there," he inconspicuously pointed in her direction, "is hardly comparable to these leeches over here, shaking their … their derrieres for a single dollar bill." He shook his head slightly in disgust. "That female is what I classify as a woman with morals, although she may have a few issues that have called for her to be placed in a dubious situation like this. What are those issues? I have no idea." He shrugged. "But I will find out for myself before the night ends."

Chad couldn't hold it any longer. He burst into laughter. "Ha!" He continued laughing as he clutched the nearest dancer by the waist, forcing her onto his lap. "That was some GQ Smooth type of shit ya said, but I'ma keep it real witchu an' tell ya that'cha really sound like ya 'bout ta be Captain Sav-A-Hoe." He laughed some more. "Well, you can't get ta know ya woman over there from over here, Captain. So, while ya fantasizin', me an' Dread finna get ta know these freak bitches over here." He then commenced to rubbing all over the dancer's body as she grinded in his lap. "I know these hoes have issues, but that ain't none of my bizness. I just want da pussy. That's da only issue I want from 'em all! Ain't that rite, Dread?"

"Yah, mon," Virgil agreed as he fondled the ass of one dancer and the pussy of another. "Me wan' jus' fuck."

Demetrius just shook his head.

"See there," Chad said. "So loosen up an' cherish this moment. It's ya forty-fourth birthday, Cuzzo, an' we tryna have a good time. Fa'get that high-class foot-dragger over there an' get wit da program over here. Besides, she rappin' wit a lame anyway, so ya can get at her anytime ya want. But rite now, it's time ta celebrate!"

After thinking for a bit, Demetrius took Chad's proposal into consideration. "I'm finally going to take your advice for a change." He shrugged. "So, if we're going to party, then we're going to need the most expensive liquor and a case of their most expensive bubbly. And, to top it all off, I'm purchasing the entire bar. Everything is on me tonight."

"Uh-uh, Cuzzo, me an' Dread gonna put a handle on all that. All I want'chu ta do is party yo' ole' ass off!"

Demetrius should've had his name on the front of the building for how things were going down inside. At first, the tension in the air was thick enough to cut with a butter knife. Every nigga in the main area and in the VIP became envious of not being able to get any action from the dancers that were flocked around Demetrius and company, causing some to mean-mug. However, Demetrius sensed the tension, and he didn't want the broke-ass, jealous niggas to ruin his night of celebration, so he brought the party from VIP to the main area. This tactic relieved a lot of pressure that was building up.

From that point on, the party became even wilder. The liquor and bubbly flowed freely. The best part, though, was the girl-on-girl action that was taking place on the main stage. *Man, I don't know if I'm going to be able to top this one next year*, Demetrius thought, *because this party here is on the verge of giving my ass a damn heart attack*!

As the night dwindled to the wee hours of the morning, Demetrius was heavily intoxicated, and burnt out. Chad and Virgil, however, were the Energizer Bunny twins; they were still going hard. The Palace itself was still somewhat crowded with people for it to be well after four in the am. It was almost like nobody wanted to go home, except for Demetrius. He'd had enough.

"Ummm … Chad," Demetrius slurred while slouching on a sofa with his eyes barely open. "I'm about … I'm ready to go home now. Oh, boy." He slowly sat upright. "I have to call … What's his name? Ummm … I have to call … Solo! That's it. I have to call Solo and tell him to … What is it I have to tell him?"

Chad laughed at his bumbling cousin. "I got'cha, Cuzzo. Where ya phone at?" He patted Demetrius' pockets until he found the phone. "I'll call Solo ta come pick ya up." He then shook his head while smiling. "I'm glad ya had a good time."

"Never again," Demetrius mumbled as he slouched back down. "Oh, before it slips my mind, I'm going to need to talk with you and … What's his face? I need to talk to you and … Virgil! Yes, that's it. Tomorrow. It's very important … I think." He rubbed his whole head. "Boy, never again. You two will not have me like this … ever again!"

Demetrius smiled before passing out.

***

October 26, 2008 4:56 pm

West Palm Beach, FL

"Why, Demetrius?" The familiar voice resonated throughout the pitch-black room. "Why did you do it? I thought you loved me?"

"I did love you, Mel," Demetrius aimlessly replied, "but ..."

"If you loved me," the voice softly said, "then why did you ... KILL ME!"

The last two words echoed repeatedly, getting louder and louder every time it was said. It became so loud in the chamber, or whatever it was he was in, that he thought his ears were literally bleeding.

Without warning, and to his delight, the echoing stopped. There was absolute silence for a few seconds before the voice shouted, "You're a fucking murderer, Kilo, and soon you'll pay!"

Demetrius awakened fully dressed, sweating and shaking like a reckless gigolo waiting in the free clinic for his blood test results. He fervently wiped at the sweat covering his face, before he worked on correcting his fast and abnormal breathing. Using a method he learned on a tv show, he dropped his anxiety attack to a level where he was almost back to normal.

Once calmed, he finally took in the strange environment in which he found himself. Unable to recognize anything in the room slowly caused his anxiety to return. In a panicked manner, he leapt from the saturated sheets and searched the suite for the presence of another person. When he discovered he was alone, he hurried to the door. Quickly, he opened the door and stepped into an empty hallway. Stopping dead in his tracks, he immediately realized he had to be in some fancy hotel because of the plush carpet, the immaculate decor and costly fixtures in the hallway. *How in the hell did I end up in a hotel*? he wondered as he stepped back into the room.

He phoned the front desk to find out where in the hell he was. The woman informed him that he was in the Crowne Plaza Hotel by PBIA under Chad's name. He then called Chad immediately, because he needed to know why he was in a hotel instead of the safety of his home.

Chad answered his cell on the second ring, and Demetrius planned on scolding his cousin over the phone until finding out that Chad was just one room away. He instructed Chad to come to his room … pronto!

Chad, with his happy-go-lucky self, walked through Demetrius' hotel door without knocking, and said, "Damn, I thought you'd never get'cha ass up, Big Cuzzo. So, what da lick read? Ya ready ta have da meetin' finally?"

Somewhat mystified, Demetrius replied, "What meeting are you referring to?"

With a slightly raised brow, Chad began to scan the place. "Where's Virgil? Ya said last nite at da club that'chu wanted ta meet wit us an' talk 'bout da bizness." He took a seat in the living room. "Well, actually, you passed out first. But when ya came to, ya said that'chu wanted ta go ta da hotel instead of ya crib, that was after I couldn't get in touch wit Solo, an' that's also when ya said that'chu wanted ta discuss sumthin' wit me an' Virgil sumtime today. So, instead of goin' back ta Daytona, I gotta room here too just so I can attend this meetin' of yours befo' I burnt up da road."

"Well, ummm …" Demetrius jogged his memory bank. He couldn't remember none of what Chad just told him. *What in the world did I have to tell Chad and Virgil?* he wondered. "Honestly, Chad, I … I'm in need of something to deal with this hangover I have right now." He massaged his temples. "I cannot recollect a single event that took place last night. I'm pretty sure, though, that whatever it is I had to tell Virgil and you wasn't that important. But, if it was important, I'll let you know as soon as I can remember."

Demetrius looked at his Rolex. "Boy, I had no idea it was this late in the day." He gathered his few belongings. "Please, take me home now. I'm in desperate need of aspirin, a cold shower, and fresh clothes."

Rather than waiting for Chad to gather his belongings in his room, Demetrius rode the elevator down to the lobby alone with intentions of getting some much-needed fresh air.

He sluggishly made way for the exit once he reached the first floor. Then, just a few feet from the exit, he caught a glimpse of a female standing at the front desk. The powder blue halter top and ass-hugging jeans wasn't the only reason he had to do a double-take. It was also the familiar, yet extraordinarily tall, solid frame that popped into his mind. *I've seen a lot of women of all shapes, sizes, and colors in my day, but I have yet to see a woman built like that,* he thought as he walked …

WHAM!

Demetrius was so busy gazing at the lovely lady that he totally forgot about the door, which he promptly walked into face-first. The collision produced a loud bang that caused everybody in the vicinity to look in his direction. He grabbed his face and stumbled backwards.

"Sir, are you alright?" a young white man asked sincerely as he ran up and took hold of Demetrius' arm to support him. "Do you need medical attention?"

"No, I'm fine. Just fine." The headache he had already intensified. "I guess I can say it looked and sounded worse than it actually was. But, honestly, I'm fine." He forced himself to smile. "It isn't nothing a handful of aspirins cannot fix."

When the young white man left his side, everything returned to normal in the lobby, almost. When he looked back, he noticed the female he was ogling at the front desk was no longer there. Mad for being so distracted by the honey that he humiliated himself, he surveyed the lobby quickly yet thoroughly. Unable to pinpoint her, he sighed as if he lost his dream girl. Accepting defeat, he turned around to exit the hotel once again.

"Whoa, Mr. Smooth Operator," a female shrieked in an odd but sexy low tone. "You just bumpin' into everythin' an' everybody, aren't ya?"

"Pardon me. I'm sorry …" Demetrius was awestruck to have run into, or damn near run over, the lovely lady that captured his full attention just moments ago. From afar she was astonishing, but up close and personal, she was the breath of fresh air he needed. His six-foot-four solid physique eclipsed the statuesque honey bun. She was at least five-foot-seven. "I apologize, Miss. Or is it Missus?"

"It's Miss."

Once he realized she wasn't giving up her name easily, he continued, "Well, Miss, I'm having one of those days, as you can tell."

"Don't we all," the golden-brown-skinned, heart-stealer mumbled. "Well, just be mindful of where you goin' next time, okay? You have a nice day." She spun around with her Coach tote bag and started to walk away from him.

Demetrius, however, wasn't going to let her leave without at least obtaining her name. *Hell no, she isn't getting away that easy*, he concluded. "Excuse me, Miss ..."

"I heard that old song way too many times," she retorted without as much as looking back. "Da funny thing is I woulda thought you were gonna be more original instead of tryna copy Luther Vandross' style."

"Huh?" He was puzzled and had no clue of what she was talking about. "You've completely lost me."

Rolling her eyes, she said, "Luther Vandross once sung, 'Excuse me, Miss/What's your name?' I know that's what you were about ta say, right?" She stopped walking and turned to face him. "So, ta beat you to it, my name is Beauti. An' I do not associate with wanna-be baller old men who act an' talk like they're highly educated, but throw away money, even if it was their birthday," she concluded before walking away again.

"Excuse me, but what did you just say?" He began to jog behind her as they entered the cool evening's air outside. "How did you know my birthday had recently passed?"

She sucked her teeth and rolled her neck. "I seen you an' your two goons buyin' up all da liquor, throwin' money like it was confetti, an', as you would say, acquiring' da services of all those bit ... of those strippers."

"Oh, so you were in attendance of my birthday party last night?"

"Hell no!" she snapped. "Unfortunately, I was at work."

That was when it hit him like a .50 caliber to the sternum. The one and only thing or person he could remember during last night's party was the slim, attractive stripper that was preoccupied with the Ivy League-looking chump. However, he noticed Beauti's natural beauty didn't match her ugly and arrogant manner. *Maybe she's just fronting,* he wondered, *or maybe she's just the one woman I want so bad, that she really isn't meant for me to have.*

"Yes, I can recall seeing you with a moderately nice-looking gentleman. It was almost as if you could have cared less about all the money that we gave away," he professed while walking by her side at a fairly fast pace. "So, if you aren't dancing to make money, what are you…" He cleared his throat. "…stripping for? I apologize if it seems like I'm intruding into your personal life, but I'm somewhat curious."

"Haven't you heard curiosity killed da cat? You're probably old enough ta have coined da phrase," Beauti declared, approaching a pearl white 2009 Nissan Sentra on twenty-two-inch Davin spinners. "If you not familiar with da phrase, then I'll have ta ask you nicely ta mind your damn business."

Demetrius anticipated her attitude, and he liked how she accentuated most of her words, so he couldn't help but laugh as he opened the door for her to get in. Before closing the door for her, he said, "I just hate knowing that a woman, especially a fine woman like yourself, expresses extreme hostility towards me for an unknown reason. There is absolutely nothing in the world that hurts me more than being hated by a ravishing woman."

"I-I don't … uh, I don't hate you," she stammered under her breath while diverting her gaze to her steering wheel. "I … I don't … know you, so how can I hate you." She paused briefly. "I don't like you cuz you da type—"

"Good," he cut her off before smiling. "Well, it's apparent I've misread you and jumped to conclusions. It's nice to know that you can one day like me, so you should get to know me. And I guarantee that you will like … no , let me rephrase that, I guarantee that you'll love me!"

"I bet," she sighed. "I'm too busy ta be bothered by…"

"No need to worry, Ms. Beauti." He had already pulled out one of his cards with his personal information on it and placed it on her dashboard. "You can call me whenever you have time. Just, please, do not make me wait a long time to hear from you again, because I'll begin to worry about your well-being. Now, you have a pleasant evening," he said, closing her door and walking back towards the hotel.

Chad stood in front of the hotel's entrance, searching in both directions for Demetrius. Demetrius wasn't at all troubled by the worried look upon Chad's face, yet he was troubled by Beauti's face. "Hmph, I just cannot seem to put my finger on it, but her facial features and her body structure resembles that of someone I once knew," he spoke aloud as he walked up on Chad.

"But who?" he mumbled.

"Who? Who's who?" Chad asked. "Never mind that, where ya been? I been lookin' all ..."

"I'm alright. Let's just go," Demetrius demanded. While strolling towards Chad's Jag, he suddenly added, "Oh, I just remembered what it was I had to discuss with Virgil and you. I'm still very tired, and very hungover, so I'll tell you two first thing tomorrow."

CHAPTER EIGHTEEN

January 5, 2009 11:15 am

West Palm Beach, FL

"I hope the two of you have gotten a chance to relax and enjoy your vacation, because it's time to get back to this money," Demetrius announced as he entered the office. Being the "extremely nice" guy that he was, Demetrius decided to discontinue all future business ventures until after the holiday season. Since he very well knew he was light-years away from even being considered a "family man," didn't mean he would deprive his associates from spending quality time with their respective families on Thanksgiving, Christmas and New Year's.

Doing so made it the first time in many years that he'd halted his operations for a holiday, let alone three holidays, because holidays had no sentimental value to him. He was an adamant businessman year-round, and now it was time to get back to business. "But, before we go any further," he added as he took a seat in his comfy chair, "I would love to know how your break was."

"Big Cuzzo," Chad began, "y'know it's been hard fo' me ta enjoy myself wit my pops an' uncle…" He sighed. "…behind bars. Since I ain't been approved ta see nan one of 'em, I just sent 'em da money ya gave me, along wit mines. But, otha than that, my break was alrite. I mainly just kicked it wit my lil ones an' my homies in Daytona."

Just knowing that his cousins and baby brother were still incarcerated was depressing, so rather than talking about them, Demetrius replied, "That's good." He then turned to Virgil. "And what about you, my Jamaican friend?"

"Me don't have too much family dem over here, so me took 'pon meself ta relax wit bad bitches dem an' smoke some fiyah ganja."

"Well, I didn't do much myself," Demetrius chimed in. "Now that that's out of the way, it's time to tell you two the job that's at hand." He looked from Virgil to Chad. "If we fail to plan, then we plan to fail! And I'm not accepting failure, not on this one. I'm going to make sure you two are ready, then we will make sure our new guys are ready."

"Big Cuzzo, stop bullshittin' already an' tell us what da lick read. I been on pins an' needles since ya told us that'cha was gonna wait 'till after da holidays ta holla at us."

Demetrius nodded. It took him a few seconds to gather his thoughts before he began to give them the game.

From beginning to end, approximately a half-hour passed for him to lay it all out for Chad and Virgil. They attentively soaked up all the information, only asking a couple questions each, once he was done talking. He answered their questions clearly and thoroughly to such a degree that there were absolutely no misunderstandings. He finally concluded the business after going over a few minor details, like what prospect would best fit what city and how much dope to start them off with.

"I know this may seem as if I'm placing a large amount of pressure upon us as a whole, however just know that pressure either busts pipes or makes diamonds. I can assure you I have no skills whatsoever when it pertains to plumbing, but I do know how to shine like DeBeers finest. So, if you have any further questions in the near future, please do not hesitate to phone me. It's a must that we're all on one accord. I'll promise you that if you do as I say, and don't stray from my plans, we will be multi-millionaires in less than a year.

"And do not fret one bit, we will not run this scheme any longer than it is needed. This is just to solidify RBF as an elite in such a manner that the government won't know how we did it. This will also make the head honcho in Peru take heed and conduct business with me on a much larger scale. When that happens, I plan on laying low while thinking of my next big scheme."

Chad nodded, then said, "I really have faith in da plan, Big Cuzzo. I know it's gonna work, altho' we ain't da first ta try da shit. But after ya explained everythin', I know it'll work. At first, tho', I thought da shit sounded im-impl-implasible."

"The word you're looking for is im-plau-si-ble." Demetrius laughed. "It's good to hear that you're working on broadening your vocabulary. Now, if only I can get my broken-English-speaking, illiterate Jamaican buddy over here to work on his verbiage, and ridding himself of his accent, then I could take you two to some nice places to meet people that're worthwhile. *Do y'all feel me*?" he said sarcastically before shaking his head with a smirk on his face.

"Mon, me hadda stop go ta school be'caw da politics friction was breakin' out inna school in Jamaica. Even teacher was shot dead in school compound, so me drop out in me youth an' tote gun. Guns was swingin' 'round like crazy. It's not that me go ta rude boy school an' groom ta become rude boy. Rude boy ting come ta me inna geto!"

Silence overcame the office.

"Ooookay," Demetrius finally said. "This meeting is adjourned." He rose from his chair. "Now, if you would excuse me, I have a lunch date with a young lady that I'm in the process of grooming to become a full-fledged woman."

Chad shook his head in disappointment. "Big Cuzzo, you gon' learn da hard way. One of these days, one of those dirty bitches outta da hood, or one of those preppy hoes from da 'burbs, gon' be ya downfall. Watch what I say. An' when it go down, I ain't even gonna say I told ya so."

That was the final statement before everybody exited the office, leaving to go their own way.

***

January 5, 2009 12:20 pm

Lake Worth, FL

It had only been a little over a month, but Demetrius finally gained some ground. He had never imagined in a million years that he would militantly pursue one particular woman. Nevertheless, it was well worth it in his eyes.

Beauti was her name. Initially, he thought she was playing hard-to-get. But, after voluntarily going through the obstacles that he had, it eventually dawned on him that she wasn't playing at all. It was just something about her though, that intrigued him to a point where he felt like an exuberant creep, chasing behind a woman that was clearly not interested in him, or his money. Despite the fact that she really reminded him of somebody in his past, somebody he actually had feelings for, he liked how she gave him a sensation that he hadn't felt in a long time.

The much-anticipated lunch date was a humongous step in making progress with Beauti. It began with her not calling him in the time frame he desired, causing him to take it upon himself to find a way to contact her. Tracking her down was the real reason why he chose to give everybody a vacation for the holidays. He would frequent The

Palace strip club in hopes of running across Beauti on the job. After she was a no-show for an entire week, his patience grew thin, and he began feeling like an imbecile. Ultimately, he decided to give up.

It just so happened that on his way out of The Palace, for what he considered to be his final day of trying to get in touch with her, he bumped into his Beauti again. Some awkward small talk followed, before she reluctantly gave him her cell phone number.

They scarcely talked from that day on, and they didn't talk long or about much when they did. During the last month or so, they'd spoken over the phone no more than five times, yet he recently decided to ask her to join him for an innocent date. She accepted without delay, surprisingly, but she had a condition. She would call him and meet up with him at the spot she picked on the day and time she chose. He had no problems at all, of course, with any of the stipulations she proposed. At that time, he couldn't believe how thrilled he was to actually be hooking up with the mystical being; it was as if he had never been on a date before.

Today was the critical day of trying to make a better first impression than his first encounter in the club, and the catastrophic second meeting in the hotel lobby. *I've got to approach this girl in a way that I haven't done with another woman since my teenage days,* he thought as he parked and made way for Bonnie's on the Beach. *I just have to find a way to get past her high level defenses so I can woo her.*

The somewhat aromatic smell of salt lingered in the air as he casually strolled into the busy restaurant that overlooked the Atlantic Ocean. Once he was greeted by the hostess, he covertly handed her a crispy Grant and requested a booth for two that faced the entrance and was "out of the way."

He lazily scanned the crowded eating place while the hostess located his seat, which only took a minute. *It seems that I've beaten her here,* he thought as he trailed the hostess, *that's a good thing.*

Then, right there in the midst of everybody, he noticed Beauti sitting alone at a table. He looked at his watch, which read twenty-five minutes after twelve, and said, "I do apologize if I'm late." He looked down at the empty seat at the table that would put his back to the entrance. "But, if I'm not mistaken, I recall you saying you'd meet me here at a quarter till one."

"I know," she replied snippily. "I had ta stop by work ta handle a few things. I finished what I had ta do early over there, so I came straight here since I was in da area. Now, would you please sit down?"

"Ummm … I-I-I," he stuttered as he looked uneasily at the chair. "How about this? How about we relocate to a booth that's a little more secluded and not amongst everybody? The hostess was kind enough to find a nice booth over there in the corner. I bet that we could actually hear ourselves talk without yelling at one another. So, how about it?"

"What's really wrong?" She sat up straight and folded her arms. "You too rich ta sit with me an' da rest of us? Or do you have a problem with sittin' with your back ta da entrance? I mean, if you have ta watch your back everywhere you go, then I don't need ta be around you," she said before gathering her things and standing up to leave.

Demetrius then did something he hadn't done in over twenty years. He succumbed to a woman.

Jumping in her path, hindering her from leaving, he said while shaking his head, "Please, pardon me. I've been very rude to you. Instead of greeting you, or complimenting you on your appearance, I've started this date off the wrong way by complaining. It's just that I have soooo much on my mind right now that I ... just, please, accept my apology and stay for lunch."

With her hands on her thirty-six-inch hips, she slightly rolled her eyes before grunting and taking a seat.

"Thank you," he added as he looked around and slowly sat down himself. "And just so you'd know, you're always safe around me. I have absolutely no reason for anybody to harm me, and I won't hurt a soul. Trust me, okay?"

Beauti laughed, then said, "Sure."

Once he was done complimenting her on her casual attire, which consisted of a snug white shirt that showcased her B-cups and the designer jeans that embraced her small but luscious ass, he moved forward with getting the formalities out of the way while they waited for their meals. It took a tad bit of effort on his part of trying to get her to open up, and she eventually did. *Damn, it seems easier to squeeze water from a rock than it is to get this chick to lighten up,* he thought, *or maybe she just has something against older men ... with money.*

By the time his lemon-peppered fish and shrimp platter arrived, along with Beauti's Caesar salad and tuna melt on wheat, he learned more than he thought he would. For instance, he managed to unveil her real name, which was Tamara Carter.

As told to him, she was a twenty-one-year-old student currently enrolled at Palm Beach Community College (PBCC), majoring in Psychology. Her birthplace was Boynton Beach, FL., and her place of residence was currently in Lake Worth. Unfortunately, both of her parents perished in a fatal car accident a few years back. She had no kids, which was another shocker to him, and she wasn't looking to get involved in a serious relationship, for she considered all black men "unfaithful and egotistic assholes" after being cheated on by her last four, money-hungry, dog-ass boyfriends.

As Beauti continued to speak, Demetrius did not once interrupt her. It was evident he was fascinated by her short life story, because he didn't touch his plate of food until she was completely finished. He was all ears. Plus, during the brief time they'd known each other, if he could've recorded every single word she'd spoken prior to this conversation, this was the most she had ever said, hands down.

He was sensing that she was warming up to him. He was also certain that Miss Carter's ferocious attitude and slightly improper English weren't the only things she acquired from the hood. He simply watched her body language closely and actually paid attention to what she said, for it was beneficial in unraveling her. He perceived she was street smart, she wasn't for any bullshit, she wasn't just about making a dollar, and she was what he genuinely believed to be his type of woman! *Trying to buy this girl's mind, body and soul is futile,* he thought as time seemed to be at a standstill while looking into her emphatic eyes, *so I must think of a method that will keep me on her good side without making it seem like I'm extremely interested in her.*

As soon as he concluded the brief account about himself, he didn't wait a second before offering Beauti a job. Once he asked her, and before she could reply, he said, "Before you give me your final answer, just think about the so-called job you have now." He paused. "What I'm offering is to remove you from a dishonorable, unsympathetic workplace and place you in a position where you can set up a schedule that best fits your personal life. I'm already convinced that you're prepared emotionally, mentally, and physically, to handle the toughest of jobs. You'll get to work in a peaceful office setting while earning a decent salary, so this job will be a walk in the park for you. And, about your salary, I'm willing to consider whatever you think is reasonable for you.

"I'm inclined to do all I've presented to you because I would love to see a lovely, young, intelligent woman with aspirations, in a much better situation than the one you're currently in. So, please, Ms. Carter, let me help you fulfill your dreams by transforming you into the successful businesswoman I can clearly sense within you. Would you do that? Let me help you, that is."

Beauti took a very deep breath and exhaled. She then began to run his elaborate proposal through her head. Nevertheless, the longer it took her to answer, the more troubled she saw Demetrius become.

She proceeded to sip from her glass of water, then she said, "I must admit that you got game. You obviously know that no female in their right mind likes takin' off their clothes fo' a bunch of wanna-be ballers an' broke niggaz that think they gonna get some ass at da end of da night."

"So I'll take that as a yes," he quickly said while trying not to sound too enthusiastic.

"Wait a minute," she retorted sternly before sipping from her glass again. "First of all, how am I ta know if your intentions are good or not? How do I know if you really have my best interests at heart? An' why me? Why are you willing to do all that you said fo' me, huh? Why?"

After a few seconds of thinking, he said, "See, I'm a philanthropist, so I gladly give back to the community. It may not seem like it now, but I once was a misguided adolescent that had no positive role models or father figures, besides my mother, to keep me out of the streets. Luckily, I was fortunate to remove myself from the hood and provide a better life for my family and me through entrepreneurship, instead of waiting for someone to rescue me." He smiled.

"Now that I own multiple lucrative businesses, I'm ... quite wealthy ... enough to give back to the streets that took a lot from me. I don't blame the streets, however, nor do I resent my city, so I donate money to local charities, pay for black kids to go to college that meet my standards, build and renovate recreation centers in the hood, and so on. So, it's not just you that I'm willing to help, I try my hardest to help as many people that I can, because I know firsthand how it is. I really wish that I could help all of the struggling redeemable people in the hood, but I'm only one man."

Although Beauti tried her best to dismiss what he just said, she couldn't help but be impressed by the man's philanthropy since she knew what he said was true.

"What's gonna be da name of your chain of stores?" she asked without commenting on his last remarks.

Demetrius smiled childishly as if she asked to go home with him. "After much deliberation, you've actually inspired me in the naming process. The name I'm going with is Timeless Treasures Furniture. Ageless pieces of art, just like yourself, is what we offer."

"How nice of you," she responded with a slight grin.

"Well, let me know your final answer as soon as possible." He let out a deep breath. "And for clarification, you'd be working at one of the three furniture stores that I'm opening soon. I have yet to find a desired location in Dade County, but the other two stores are in Fort Lauderdale and West Palm Beach. The store in West Palm is where I would like to employ you as a clerk or manager, or whatever position you think is best for you."

"I'll really consider it. Well, I have ta go now. Thanks for lunchin' with me. I had a nice time." She pulled two twenty-dollar bills from her purse, placed them under her glass of water, and rose from the table. "I'll definitely call you 'bout da job, okay?"

He didn't even make an attempt to stop her from footing the bill for both of their meals, because he knew already that that was one way of her flaunting her independence; he was actually starting to figure her out more and more as time progressed.

"Okay. And thank you for having me for lunch." He, too, rose from the table. "If it's no problem, may I walk you to your car?"

"No disrespect, but I'm okay. Now you have a nice day." She then waved and left the restaurant in a hurry.

Hmph, this free-living young lady is really something else, he thought with a smirk as he headed out of the restaurant while retrieving his vibrating personal cell phone from his pocket, *but I can say she's a rare jewel in this world of scandalous, gold-digging women.*

***

January 5, 2009 1:02 pm

West Palm Beach, FL

During the intervening time, Miracle was in the office at StudioX with Rhapsody, who drove down from Cocoa Beach with Kamani to visit her, and she was at the end of a long awaited important phone call.

"Okay. I understand," she said over the phone. "You be careful ... I miss and love you ... Buh-bye."

Once she hung up the office phone, Rhapsody eagerly asked, "Is that da call ya been waitin' on?"

"Yeah, that was Devon." The look on her face transformed from worried to serious. "And it sounds like the two of us will have a mission to start preparin' for."

CHAPTER NINETEEN

January 21, 2009 2:32 pm

Miami, FL

In the most up-to-date dictionary, there was not a single word in it that could have described how Demetrius felt. Saying that he was filled with joy would definitely be a major understatement. What he personally witnessed yesterday was not only the most memorable historical event that occurred in his short life. He considered it the most memorable historical event that occurred in the United States of America.

January 20, 2009, in Washington, D.C., the U.S.A. made history with the inauguration of the first African-American president. Demetrius, along with hundreds of thousands of excited people of all races, was in attendance at the inaugural ceremony, and they all enchantedly watched Barack Obama become the forty-fourth Commander-in-Chief of this country.

Once President Obama was officially sworn into office, Demetrius' favorite slogan became, "Yes I can." The symbolic nature of the ceremony inflamed a passion in him that was once lost, and it reminded him, and blacks in general, that all plans and goals were capable of being achieved, even if the plan or goal looked or sounded far-fetched. Mr. Obama was unquestionably the sole factor for him having a new look at life and becoming a diverse man. He would no longer inhibit himself from what he believed was achievable as a black man in this "so-called" white man's world. *Thank you, Barack Obama*, he thought as the Presidential inauguration ended that day, *now I know the sky is not the limit!*

Now, since his return from the monumental milestone, it was time to mash the gas. He was presently down in cool but always sunny Miami for two reasons. First, he was looking to purchase a mansion. And secondly, he was meeting with Adrian Mendoza about "pushing it to the limit."

While his real estate agent located a mansion that was no less than ten thousand square feet, in the price range of ten to thirteen million dollars, and had a dock, he was busy lunching with Adrian, the middleman, at a Cuban restaurant in the Little Havana section of Miami. The pair were engaged in small talk, lightening up the mood before business was to be conducted.

"How is business?" asked Adrian while shifting the aura from relaxed to humorless. Adrian was your typical Hispanic that had major money. He was a modern-day Tony Montana, although he had a barely noticeable accent, but he was also both civilized and chic. He was in his mid-to-late thirties, extremely handsome, and he surrounded himself with nothing but the best life had to offer. His entire wardrobe was custom-made in South America out of the finest fabrics and materials that man could buy. His jewelry was costly but subtle. His cars were foreign, just like his many ravishing women. And his large imposing villas came straight off the pages of a travel brochure.

Demetrius admired Adrian's lifestyle a lot, and he periodically imagined himself enjoying all the perks in life like Adrian. Yet, he knew that reckless way of living drew too much attention on a black man with too many goals to fulfill in one lifetime. *In the next life, maybe, I'll enjoy all the finer things that life has to offer,* he thought as he grinned at the idea of being reincarnated as a Hispanic man of Adrian's caliber.

"Business is good," Demetrius replied. He then paused momentarily. "But it can be better."

Adrian nodded. "Well, my friend, business is about to become a lot better for you."

"Oh, really?"

"Yes, my boss has informed me that he would like to meet with you … in Peru. He says that out of all his clientele in the States, your organization being just one of a handful of blacks my boss does business with, you are the most prosperous. He also says that he never once doubted your integrity when you had a problem with the federal government, he just wanted to be safe. See, when there's large sums of money involved, it's advisable to trust nobody, so that's why he put a limit on what you could purchase from us. It wasn't because he thought you were a cock-a-roach, it was just him playing it safe. So, since you weathered the storm, he's ready to see you face-to-face, which is an honor, and do major business."

Demetrius was overjoyed on the inside because the negotiations were back on the table after almost a year and a half of waiting, but he appeared unfazed by the news on the outside. "When is this meeting going to take place?" he asked nonchalantly.

"The specific date and time has yet to be set. However, I do know that it will take place sometime in the month of April. You just make sure you're free to leave the country when it's time. Trust me when I tell you, you'll never get another opportunity if you blow him off. No exceptions!"

"I'll be there when the time comes."

"Before we go any further," Adrian said while picking up a menu, "we might as well order some food. This place has the best Cuban sandwiches. I grew up eating them and I still cannot seem to get enough, so I'd suggest you try one."

Although Demetrius didn't have much of an appetite, he decided to try the Frita Cuban sandwich.

When their orders were taken, Adrian continued by saying, "Soon, you won't be needing me anymore. So, before it's time to turn the page and close the book on our side deal, I have an even better deal than before."

"Is that so?" Demetrius said with a raised brow.

"Now that we have only two months left to do business, and you're definitely the most successful businessman I've dealt with in the States, I have some new impressive numbers to run by you that're too good to turn down. I'm doing this because I'm profiting either way it goes. But you should triple your money.

"As you know, a kilo of pure Peruvian yayo sells for no less than twenty-four grand in the streets of Miami. But once that same kilo leaves Dade County, it's cut with so much shit I'm surprised it's still coke, and the price jumps to damn near thirty grand. I don't know how much you're selling your kilos for…" He winked at Demetrius. "…but I do know that ten-k for a kilo, which is the price I'm charging you, will certainly put a little something extra in your pocket. What do you say about that, my friend?"

Hell fucking yes, that's what I say, Demetrius thought as he shifted slowly in his seat.

However, calmly and casually, Demetrius lowly replied, "And what about the mandatory hundred blocks that I purchase from your boss before our deal?"

Adrian smiled. "They're all going for ten grand flat." His smile faded. "However, the only requirement is that you must purchase a metric ton or more for the deal."

"Ten million dollars," Demetrius replied hastily. He relaxed his posture, then continued, "How soon can you deliver?"

"I'll have it for you faster than a Mexican evading Border Patrol, my friend," Adrian said before laughing throatily. I'll contact you ASAP with the details on where to pick up your package, okay?"

"I'll be waiting."

Adrian paid the bill, and the two men concluded their meeting with a firm handshake without even receiving their food.

Other than Demetrius still trying to overlook the fact that the reliable, but susceptible, Virgil was the only one managing two of the four new hustlers, everything was finally ready. The new hustlers had been situated in the cities he chose since the first week of January. They were just waiting for their individual packages now.

Luckily, Demetrius had associates in damn near all of the continental states, because a few phone calls was all it took for "his" new hustlers to have a couple loyal customers already locked in with them. After that, word of mouth about the quality, and low prices, would gradually cause an increase in consumers. It was just a matter of hours now before the money train began moving.

After some deliberation, he decided to station his new hustlers in New Orleans, Nashville Charlotte, and Philadelphia. Since Zooman was heavily into voodoo, it was a no-brainer to place him in Nawlins, a city that had Creole roots and also believed heavily in black magic. He would fit right in with the locals. Being that Tennessee touched several different states, it was obvious to set up shop in the capital Nashville -- the city was almost in the center of the state -- and let the young energetic Junebug take helm of Cashville, the city of country music and the home of the mythical "ten-a-key."

Picking Charlotte, North Crackalack as one of the spots was easy, but, with the rising gang violence going down in Queen City, it was undetermined if appointing Kelly Kronkite to work the treacherous city was a good or bad idea, even if his second largest business office was located there. Only time would tell if he would make it out of the demon's ass once entering the belly of the beast. And Philly, aka the city of brotherly love, was the city Buckey would have to try to conquer without the love from the brothers in that city. Now, the south and northeast were sewed up by RBF, making at least half of the fifty states in North America prepared to be serviced.

The prospects had already acquired their modest homes to reside in, along with a separate small house or shop to "work" out of, which were totally paid in full by Demetrius. And since Demetrius was fronting everything, including the dope, he had a few conditions for his new team to abide by.

First, all of them, except for Kelly, had to find a part- or full-time legit job so they could "appear" as normal businessmen. Secondly, they could entertain company, but they had to live alone, meaning no live-in girlfriends or homeboys. Thirdly, they couldn't sell nothing less than half a kilo at a time. Lastly, and most importantly, other than hustling, they had to avoid doing anything that would cause the police to take interest in them, so there was no stunting, flossing, flaunting, or splurging allowed! If word were to ever get back to him that any of his requisites were broken, he would send out the Clean-up Crew immediately to sanitize the mess. Too much time was invested, and too much money was involved, for his master plan to be compromised by an incompetent fool. *I have a lot riding on this, he said to himself while removing the ringing phone from his pocket, and I'm going to do everything I can to assure that the ride is smooth, short and lucrative.*

Phone rings

"Hello?" he said as he approached Solo, who was holding the rear car door open for him. "May I ask who's calling?"

"What it do, Pops?"

Taken aback by the voice, Demetrius said, "Byron? Is that you, son?"

"Damn, who else gonna call ya Pops? Of course, it's me," Byron replied with happiness in his voice.

There were so many heartless things that he wanted to say to his beloved son at the moment. He just stood outside of the car speechless.

"Boss," Solo said, "everythin' straight?"

Without saying a word, Demetrius climbed into the car. Solo then promptly shut the door, got behind the wheel, and drove off.

"Hello? Pops, are ya there?" Bizzy said over the open line. "Fuck! I knew his ass couldn't …"

"I'm here … unfortunately," Demetrius replied just in the nick of time before Bizzy hung up. "But I will not be on the phone much longer. So say whatever it is that you have to say before it's too late."

Demetrius could hear Bizzy laugh lowly.

"That's how ya treatin' me now, Pops?"

"Listen!" Just like the average person occasionally lost self-control, Demetrius proved that he too, was an average person by losing his cool. "I don't have time for your fucking games, boy. Spit the shit out and be the fuck on your way!"

Silence.

"Well … I was just hittin' ya up ta see if everythin' is good. I only got one pops, so I gotta check up on ya. I gotta call ya every blue…"

"Hahaaa!"

"What's so funny?"

"I haven't heard one fucking word from you in almost four months. Then I haven't seen you in ten months. Ten fucking months! Now, all of a sudden you decide to call to check up on me! Boy, I suggest you find someone else to play with, because you're wasting my valuable minutes." Just as he was on the verge of hanging up, he heard Bizzy say something. "What was that you just said, boy?"

"I said, I apologize." There was a pause. "I was dead wrong fo' doin' you like that, outta all people. It's … I-I-I had so much ... I wasn't ready ta go in like that, 'specially after I just got outta prison fo' sumthin' ... fo sumthin' I didn't do!

"I got kids ta take care of, an' I wanna be there fo' 'em, unlike you, who wasn't always there fo' me when I needed ya ta be. Doin' that lil bid made me realize that I must be there fo' my kids. But you ain't try ta put ya'self in my shoes. You just asassinated my character, becuz I ain't do what da hell ya wanted me ta do when ya wanted me ta do it. I know ya needed my help, but I wasn't …"

"I understand, Byron." Demetrius became compassionate. "I duly apologize for the unwise actions that caused you to be taken away from your children. That wasn't intentional. You very well know that I'm not family-oriented, but I know how much your kids, my grandkids, mean to you.

"However, I still cannot believe how you left without an explanation as to why you were going away, and where you were going. I swore that we were better than that. To my knowledge, we have no secrets. The bond we had, and hopefully we still have, is more complex than just any regular father and son. You're my ... How can I put it so you'll understand? You're my ... my dawg, my pot'nah, my ace-boon-coon, and the only person that I can fully trust out here."

Once the soulful, sappy part of the conversation was over, the father and son began catching up with the times. Demetrius learned that Bizzy had been living in a town just outside of Charlotte, NC, called

Mint Hill, just enjoying the money he had obtained with JJ. Demetrius then curiously asked if JJ was with him in Mint Hill since they were almost inseparable, and Bizzy told him JJ was in Savannah taking care of his mom and holding down the city until he returned.

"So ... I heard that'cha got a few new stores up an' runnin'," Bizzy declared, changing the topic suddenly.

I just knew there was a real reason behind this call, Demetrius thought as he shook his head disappointedly. "Yes, I'm always exploring my options when it comes to business, and opening up a few stores is always beneficial," he replied, choosing his words carefully.

"That's just like da ole' man." Bizzy laughed. "Well, do you, by any chance, need a ... salesman? If so ..."

"Byron," he cut Bizzy short, "may I ask who you've attained this information from?"

"I have my sources." Bizzy paused. "But since ya asked, I got it from Virgil."

"Virgil, huh?" *Virgil is beginning to become a real nuisance by running his big fucking mouth,* he thought as he switched the phone from one ear to the other, *and I just might have to put a handle on him before the snake in the grass finally bites me.* "Well ... I'm sorry. All the salesmen positions are full. But I do have an office job for you that's available whenever you decide to come home."

"Hmmmm ... I'm gonna pass on ya offer, Pops. I ain't an office guy. So, I'm 'bout ta bounce now. Just call me when ya need me an' I'm there quicker than a dyke at a all you can eat pussy party."

They both laughed.

"Okay, son. You remain safe up there. Call me if you need anything, and I do mean anything. I will also keep you in mind on that position, because I'm almost positive that I'm going to have to fire one of my best before the store even opens."

"By da way, when is da grand openin'?"

"Very soon. Maybe tomorrow, depending on certain people."

"Okay. Well, I'm gone. Holla."

"I'll talk to you soon, son."

During the remainder of the trip from Miami to West Palm Beach, Demetrius slipped into deep thought. All he could think about were ways of making sure that his plans were flawless. He had only one chance at this, and the one chance he had at taking over the entire East Coast would have to be executed flawlessly.

I got this, he concluded as he mentally hyped himself up. *There's nobody or nothing that can stop me!*

CHAPTER TWENTY

January 23, 2009 6: 49 am

West Palm Beach, FL

The grand opening was well underway, and all was going accordingly. The "package" was received and prepared for shipping yesterday, and the fleet of delivery trucks, at that very moment, were burning up the highways and byways. Deliverance ranged from twelve to sixty hours, depending on where the recipient lived -- the least distant being Atlanta and the furthest being New York.

Demetrius was unconsciously worn out. He hadn't had a good night of rest in over forty-eight hours. He'd been strenuously planning and supervising all operations, conducting business, and planning on planning some more. Since meeting with Adrian, he was certain his scheme was foolproof. All he wanted to do right now was sit back and watch his master plan blossom, although he knew that considering some relaxation was just illogical thinking. He would just have to settle for a few sporadic naps and get the rest he needed once he was informed that everybody secured their "furniture."

Being that it was still early morning, he wanted nothing more than to alleviate his mind and body of the stress that he endured while getting everything ready for takeoff, so he decided to call upon Beauti. *I hope it's not too early to call,* he wondered as he scrolled through his phone and highlighted her number, *but I just want to know if she's up for having breakfast with me this morning.*

"Hello?" Beauti answered on the second ring.

"Good morning, Sunshine."

"Good mornin', Demetrius."

"I'm truly sorry for calling at such an inconvenient time, but it sounds to me that you've been up a while now."

"Yeah, y'know what they say, da early bird gets da worm. Plus, I haven't slept much lately, cuz I been havin' bad ... headaches. Anyways, what's up?"

"First, I want to thank you for helping me the last few days with my stores. Your valuable input and ideas have led to things running a lot smoother than I thought." He paused. "Honestly, I'd have thought that you've owned a business before because of your knowledge about certain things. You are really amazing, so I would love to show my gratitude for your assistance and for accepting my offer to work for me."

Beauti cleared her throat. "What ... what do you got in mind?"

"What I have in mind is breakfast, just the two of us. Then, later tonight, I want to take you to a classy restaurant across the bridge in Palm Beach. How does that sound?"

"Ummm ... I don't think ..."

"Please, Ms. Carter. It's not like I plan on proposing to you." He sighed. "I've had a grueling forty-eight hours, with all of the ... You've seen a little of what I've had to deal with. That wasn't even a tenth of all the work that I have to tend to lately.

"Is it a sin that I just want to unwind and kick back finally? I hope not, especially since I would like to unwind while also becoming more acquainted with my new sexy and intelligent employee. So, breakfast followed by dinner, is that too much for a hardworking man to ask for?"

"Okay," she mumbled. "Where do you want ta meet at?"

"Is there a problem with me picking you up?"

"Yes."

"Well ... When and where do you wish to meet?"

"In a hour, meet me at da IHOP on Okeechobee."

"Will do, Ms. Carter."

***

Later that day, Demetrius was pacing back and forth outside of Majestic Provisions, waiting for Beauti to arrive for their eight o'clock dinner date. It was five minutes till that time now, and there was no sign of her. He tried calling her, but she didn't answer. *I hope that everything is alright and she arrives soon,* he thought as he looked at his pink gold Patek Philippe watch for the umpteenth time since his arrival twenty minutes ago, *because it has cost me a pretty penny to get reservations here on such a short notice.*

Their breakfast date earlier in the day was satisfactory. Over scrambled eggs, hash browns, sausage and pancakes, the two of them chatted almost like high school sweethearts. It was amazing to him how much Beauti began to lighten up more and more. Her true beauty was starting to materialize with every meeting and conversation. They talked about some of everything. However, there were certain subjects which seemed to cause her to withdraw from the conversation until the topic was changed. Nonetheless, the nearly two hours they'd spent together this morning was great. *So I'm sure there has to be another reason for her absence,* he concluded as he looked at his watch which read two minutes till eight. *Or she at least would've called and told me something.*

Refusing to stand there any longer, he gave up. He finally instructed valet to retrieve his Benz. He sadly waited for valet, then, out of nowhere, Beauti pulled up in front of him in her eccentric Sentra on spinning rims.

Enraged by her tardiness, Demetrius fixed his gaze elsewhere as she got out and handed her keys over to a second valet. Initially, he was going to tell her the date was off. But he had a sudden change of heart when he saw how marvelous she looked. He didn't believe a woman so hood yet beautiful existed until the moment he saw her strutting towards him.

The elegant fuchsia, slim-fitting sheath conformed to the outline of her five-foot-eight body, accentuating every one-hundred-forty-five-pound curve that a man lusted after on a woman. Her toned calves were worthy of praise due to the red bottomed black platform pumps that she wore. Her hair was fashionably styled, and not "ghetto fabulous." The makeup she put on her golden-brown skin was perfect, as if the world's greatest makeup artist applied it themselves. And the perfume that she wore was so tantalizing that it tempted him to grab her and devour her like the mysterious fruit that she smelled of. Overall, in his eyes, she was the most fascinating creature that God created in the hoods throughout the world.

"I'm sorry I'm late," she proclaimed. "It's weird how I lived in this county all my life an' I only been in da city of Palm Beach two or three times, an' that was when I went on field trips ta da Flagler Museum." She giggled. "I had a hard time findin' this place. I'm just surprised I actually made it here though, without gettin' pulled by one-time."

"Yes, this majority white, rich and subtle city isn't accustomed to outlandish things, like your car on spinners with the outrageous paint job." He smiled. "However, there's no need to apologize. No harm has been committed. If anything, I should apologize to you for not asking if you knew how to get here."

“It’s cool.”

“All is forgotten then,” he said as he stuck his arm out for her to take. She slowly took his arm, then he added, “Let’s go inside now before they give away our table.”

Before entering the actual restaurant, the grandeur of the outside of the place left Beauti awestricken. She was completely focused on looking at the magnificent decorations like a young child walking through an amusement park. When she and Demetrius approached the restaurant’s doors, Demetrius, being the gentleman that he was, courteously let her walk ahead of him after holding the door open for her. And, upon entering the restaurant, that was when it went down ... literally.

When Demetrius moved from Beauti’s side momentarily to hold the door for her before he followed behind her, she lost her balance, stumbled forward, and fell face first. Both the maître d’ and Demetrius hurried to help her to her feet.

“Oh, my God, Tamara, are you okay?” Demetrius asked, full of concern.

“I’m sorry, ma’am,” the maître d’ professed with a look of pure horror on his face. “Are you hurt? Can I get you anything? I don’t know what happened. Did you trip over something? Or did you ...?”

“She’s fine, sir. Thanks,” Demetrius declared stiffly, ceasing the headwaiter’s barrage of questions. “I have everything under control from here.” He then turned his full attention to Beauti’s potential injuries. “Honey, are you okay?”

Beauti’s pretty face was flushed red and contorted with a mixture of pain and embarrassment. She then looked around and saw how the upper-class snobs in the vicinity were staring at her conspicuously. “I’m fine,” she announced in an attempt to deter the rubberneckers.

“I know that you’re fine,” he said trying to make her smile, “but are you hurt?”

“I’m not seriously hurt. My ankle hurts a lil bit from rollin’ it.” She bent down and rubbed her sore right ankle. The tall pumps on her feet were problematic, and she knew they were an accident just waiting to happen when she first saw them. She truly felt like she was walking on stilts the first time she put them on. “I knew I was gonna bust my ass wearin’ these damn pumps.”

“Do you want to leave?”

“Hell no! Uh-uh, we stayin’,” she snapped. “I’m not gonna give these rich assholes da satisfaction of talkin' 'bout da Negro that fell an' left. Besides, that was my grand entrance."

They both laughed as they were escorted to their table.

"Now you know exactly how I felt that day in the hotel lobby," he said, recalling the time when he first interacted with Beauti. "I was so embarrassed that day that I wished that I could've went invisible and ran until I couldn't run no further. However, I'm glad that I didn't disappear and run away, because then my other wish wouldn't have come true."

"An' what was that?" she asked as he pulled her chair out from under the table so that she could sit.

After he assisted her with her chair, and took a seat himself, while staring into her comforting eyes, he answered, "My wish to meet an angel."

Not knowing how to respond, she just simply changed the subject by complimenting him on his formal attire. In return, he gave her multiple flattering remarks. She then began explaining how her wardrobe, makeup and hair were the reasons for her running behind schedule. She playfully took a stab at pronouncing all the weird designer names she saw while shopping, but she ended up only making them both laugh, so she stopped.

When the maître d' returned to take their drink orders, Demetrius instructed the headwaiter to bring them a bottle of white wine of his choice. Beauti strongly objected to drinking, but Demetrius advised her that the wine was exclusively for the enjoyment of the meal, not for getting drunk. She vowed to only sip some wine with the meal, and he didn't protest.

They dined on fish, pasta and salad, and they drank not one but two bottles of Brewer-Clifton chardonnay in less than an hour. They began the meal with their usual exchange. However, once the wine kicked in, their conversation became filled with good-natured witty joking. From the moment the wine's effects began, they laughed amongst themselves about a little bit of everything. Eventually, she had made the "hood" come out of him, and he was genuinely having a good time with her. It was one of the best times either one of them had had in a long time.

When they finally agreed it was time to call it a night, because they both wound up more than a little bit tipsy, Demetrius paid the sizable tab, while Beauti left a tip. Then, for Beauti's sake, they *care-*

fully made their way outside to the valet, who promptly retrieved their cars, respectively.

"You know, I've been wondering," Demetrius started saying when the valet brought Beauti's car, "if those spinning wheels of yours have been spinning the entire time we were inside." He then laughed. "If so, the mileage on your car has to be extremely high."

While rubbing her throbbing head, Beauti said, "You're silly."

Thereafter, they stood in awkward silence for a few seconds.

"Well, it's time ta go home an' take this expensive shit off so I can return it in da mornin' fo' a refund."

"Are you seriously going to return that sensational dress?"

"Yup. No need ta keep it unless you want it. It ain't like I'm ever gonna wear it again. I know I ain't wearin' them damn shoes ever again." She yawned. "I was really surprised ta see da tag was hidden when I bought da dress." She then displayed the price bag on the inside collar by the back of her neck. "Da shit been itchin' me all night!"

Shaking his head, he said, "You're very outspoken. Yet, I must admit I love the fact that you are ... you. Now, don't misconstrue what I just said, you are as real as they come. Plus, you're business-minded and street-smart, and you're a woman that quickly adapts to her surroundings, meaning you know exactly when it's appropriate to be lady-like and when it's time to be, as they say, a hood chick. BUT, at all times, you're the same person internally, so ... I hope you understand what I'm trying to say, because I'm starting to believe that I don't know what I'm trying to say."

"I think I got'cha." She eloquently looked into his ambiguous eyes for the first time ever. "An' I wish I could say da same' bout you'."

"What do you mean by that?" he inquired.

She frowned. "I'm just ready ta go. I'm really startin' ta feel … woozy. I never drank wine befo' an' I think I drank ... I did drink too much."

"Are you sure you're capable of driving?" he asked as he took a hold of her arm.

"I .... don't …"

Talking to Demetrius was the last thing Beauti remembered before she blacked out.

***

January 24, 2009 9:03 am

Riviera Beach, FL

Brought back to consciousness due to an uneasy feeling, Beauti fluttered her eyes open as a result of the sunshine flooding into the room. Unable to remember a thing at the time, she routinely climbed out of bed.

When she finally realized she was wearing the dress from last night, and that she was by herself in an unknown room, was the moment shock overcame her. The revelation temporarily paralyzed her, and caused her heart to pound up against her chest so hard, it sounded like SWAT banging on the door with a battering ram.

Snapping out of the daze, she swiftly got up. For reasons unbeknown to her, her right ankle was sore and slightly swollen. But that didn't stop her from peeking out of the closed door. When she saw nobody was in what seemed to be a living room, she swung the door open and began searching for an exit.

"Good morning, Sunshine."

Startled by the voice, she turned and saw Demetrius perched on a stool at the bar.

"Where da fuck I'm at?" she snapped. "An' how did I get here?"

Getting up from the bar with a small tumbler glass in hand filled with a few ice cubes and a brownish liquid, he said, "Calm down, Tamara. You're in my condo in Riviera Beach. You were too inebriated to drive, and I didn't know what to do at that time, besides bring you here to sleep it off once you passed out. What else was I supposed to do?" He then shrugged. "I don't know where you live because you have no form of identification in your purse or car, and your phone was locked. I honestly think I did a noble thing by …"

"So you brung me here, huh? Where's my car then?"

"It's downstairs. I had it towed here. Your keys and belongings are over there," he said, pointing to the table by the door.

She saw her stuff on the table that he pointed at, then she proceeded to limp over to retrieve her things. She wildly rifled through her purse to see if anything was missing.

"Is it all there?" he sarcastically asked.

While rifling through her belongings still, she suddenly blurted out, "Did you touch me?"

A puzzled look spread across his face before he laughed.

Through clenched teeth, she shouted, "Did you fuck me?!"

Hearing the seriousness in her voice and seeing the fire in her eyes let him know that she was not playing. "If you honestly think that I'm that type …"

"I don't think, I know you're a lotta things. So just answer da fuckin' question!"

"No. I don't take advantage of drunk ... women. I just brought you here out of generosity, but, apparently, that was a huge mistake, because I'm being accused of rape." He paused. "Now, since I answered your question, answer this question before you go."

"I don't have ta answer nothin'."

"Do you know Melina Herrera?"

The question caught Beauti off guard, but she calmly and promptly said, "Who?"

"Melina Herrera."

"Is there a reason I need ta know her," she retorted with attitude. "Who is she? She must be one of your side chicks. See, I knew your old ass was nothin' but a playa. All you niggaz with money are da same, y'all think y'all got all da fuckin' sense." She then furiously gathered her stuff and stormed towards the door. "I can't believe …"

"Tamara, I apologize ... again. I only asked you if you knew her because I realized last night as I watched you sleep that you resemble ... you reminded me of a female named Melina I knew over twenty years ago. She ... passed away."

With her back to him, and tears in her eyes, she said, "I'm gone. I'll talk ta you later, meanin' I'll call you."

As she walked bare-footed out of his condo with her shoes and purse in her hands, Demetrius couldn't help but feel like the biggest asshole ever. *I should've known better than asking a female about another female, let alone telling her that she looked like a female that's dead*, he thought as he swigged the scotch on the rocks.

CHAPTER TWENTY-ONE

February 26, 2009 3:30 pm

Coral Gables, FL

Based upon various accounts from multiple reliable sources, such as the *USA Today's* newspaper and *CNN*, Demetrius learned that the crime rate in a half dozen major cities throughout the south and north-east regions of the U.S. had simultaneously increased dramatically by twenty percent or more than the previous years on record. The cause of the escalating violence was relatively unknown to the officials in those affected cities, but the locals in those areas blame an abundant amount of drugs flooding the streets for the rise in crime.

Damn, word about the high-quality, reasonably-priced kilos has reached those bottom-feeding thugs out there, causing them to rob and kill for my coke, thought Demetrius as he cut off his large plasma flatscreen. "Well, I have no choice but to inform everybody the price is no longer twenty-four grand, its twenty-seven now," he said to him-self. "That should cause the crime rate to drop ... a little."

Initially, "business" was sort of slow. But once Demetrius' few loyal customers were handed over to his new crew, and the snow cir-culated in the streets, the business started bringing in the money faster than he expected. The fast cash RBF was accumulating was quite alarming, therefore it was a good thing that he couldn't be linked to the executive duties pertaining to his legitimate businesses. His lack of involvement with his legit businesses made it easier to conceal the true origin of his cash by laundering the dope money through his own stores. Ninety percent of his stores were yielding a handsome profit all by themselves anyway, so slowly washing the millions of dollars through his stores should slip by unnoticed.

Now, since everybody disposed of majority of their one hundred and thirty keys in somewhat of an untimely fashion, Demetrius was holding on to his two hundred and twenty keys for a rainy day. An-other phone call to Adrian was imminent.

Instead of using his cellphone, he opted to call Adrian from a payphone because of how soon he was calling Adrian again. How *is Adrian going to react when I inform him that I need to re-up already?* he wondered as he left the house to call.

Leaving his newly purchased 11,500 square foot, twelve and a half million dollar estate in his newly purchased three-hundred-sixty-thousand dollar English white 2010 Rolls-Royce Drophead Coupe, with light creme leather, he drove the fifteen minutes it took to reach South Beach and called Adrian.

"Hello?" Adrian finally answered after two attempts.

"Hello, Adrian. This is Demetrius."

"Oh, hello, my friend." He laughed. "I usually don't answer unknown numbers."

"I apologize, and I apologize for disturbing you. But can you meet me in ... let's say, an hour or less. It's urgent."

"Yes, I can ... I have free time until my daughter's recital at six this evening. Where would you like to meet?"

Demetrius instructed that they were to meet at Deep Blue Seafood and Grill.

Adrian arrived in approximately forty minutes, and he wasn't expecting Demetrius to be there so soon. "Once again, hello," Adrian greeted as he sat with Demetrius outside of Deep Blue. "So what brings you back to Miami so soon?"

"Besides residing in Coral Gables now, I'm here for business."

"And what type of business are we talking about here?"

"Twenty-million-dollar business," Demetrius softly said.

Adrian laughed. "You're kidding right?" The smile on his face then slowly vanished when he realized that Demetrius was serious like a venereal disease. "How do you do it, my friend? Seriously. How is it that you've sold out already?"

"I'm the black Houdini. Hocus pocus, abracadabra." He shrugged. "Plμs, it's income tax time."

Adrian laughed again. "Houdini. Income Taxes. I like you, my friend." He then paused. "But, I'm sorry to tell you that I cannot sell you no more."

"Huh?"

"Yes, I know. But the Big Boss says not to sell you no more if you contact me for more ... "business" ... in less than three months. It has only been a month and you're ..."

"Wait ... wait a minute." Demetrius sat upright. "Let me try to comprehend what you're telling me. So, since—" He slyly looked around to see if anybody was listening to them, "—since I sold my narcotics too quick, you refuse to sell me anymore. Is that what you're saying? If so, then I think you are …"

"Whoa, my friend. I'm not the one responsible for what's going on, I'm just the middleman. Besides, the Boss was only testing you."

"Testing me?" Demetrius frowned. "Testing me, how?" he inquisitively asked.

"We both knew you would sell that with no problem. We figured you out, my friend. We knew the pack was sold before you even got it." He winked. "Plus, I read the papers, I watch the news, and I have my own set of eyes and ears out there, too."

"Since you both know so much about me, what now?"

"There has been a change of plans. The Boss wants to see you ASAP, like the first of March."

"That's in three days!"

"No exceptions, remember? Either you go to Peru and get blessed with so much coke that you'd be the black Escobar rather than the black Houdini, or stay in the states on March first and find yourself another supplier during a time where cock-a-roaches are everywhere."

***

February 27, 2009 7:10 pm

Riviera Beach, FL

Demetrius and Beauti shared a strange "friendship," if that was what it was called. Ever since that day she flipped out after awakening in his condo, she basically acted as if that eventful day never took place; and he too never mentioned that day again. Since then, they became closer associates, but they remained detached in so many ways.

Although he undeniably felt that they were still somewhat compatible, and he still couldn't help being infatuated with Beauti for being Beauti, he ultimately chose to keep it strictly business by reducing his pursuit at stealing her heart. Besides, he was actually beginning to like that she kept her guard up at all times, and that her personality and morality were unchangeable. *She just might become the official First Lady of RBF*, he thought while waiting for Beauti to arrive at his condo to discuss a few things before he left for Peru, *that's if she sticks around long enough.*

So far, everything about Beauti as one of his employees was superb, from her always being on time to her dedication to the dreary job. Her job was rather simple. She was the head clerk, so she was responsible for correspondence, records, and accounts, while also selling furniture when she wasn't behind the desk. She was paid a generous twenty-five dollars an hour and given a commission of thirty percent of the furniture she sold.

Other than her work performance in the store, the thing that Demetrius appreciated most was that she freely did "reasonable" tasks and ran errands for him outside of the store. That was enough to show him she was unselfish and spontaneous, while remaining independent and hard-nosed. He really wished all of his workers possessed her mentality and work ethics. And for that reason alone, while he was absent for the next few days, he was going to ask her to supervise the store in West Palm Beach, along with the stores in Fort Lauderdale and Homestead, which was the northernmost populated city in Miami-Dade County before the Florida Keys. It was his test to see if she could handle the pressure.

When Beauti arrived approximately five minutes before the suggested time, he welcomed her into his place and offered her something to drink. After she simply declined, instead of engaging in their usual small talk, he began telling her about his abrupt vacation to Peru. He then asked her if she would tend to all three furniture stores until his return on March 3, and she insouciantly told him that she didn't mind.

"So … when ya leavin'?"

"My departure is ten o'clock tonight."

"Are you takin' some America's Next Top Model chick with you?" she curiously asked as she walked over to his ready-to-go luggage and other belongings by the door.

The question caused him to freeze. *Is she jealous?* he wondered while staring at her. "No," he replied a few seconds later. "I'm going alone. It's a vacation, mixed with a little bit of business. But, why did you ask? Would you like to join me?"

"No ... I mean, I would love ta go, but I can't. I-I-I have ta stay here an' … an' help you with da stores."

"Oh, okay," he said without making any further attempts at convincing her to go. "Maybe next time?"

"Maybe." She shrugged. She then picked up his passport and a few other items, observed them quickly, and put them down. "I guess I'll be goin' now . You have a good trip, an' you don't worry 'bout a thang. I got this."

"Okay. Well, all the information and things that you need to handle your business are already on your desk at work. And I also took the liberty of renting you a car so that you can use it to run from one store to the other while I'm gone. The keys, along with a credit card, are at work, as well. Now that you're set, I'm set, so I'll see you March 3rd."

They said their friendly goodbyes with their normal wave, and she left.

Once she was gone, he picked up his phone and began to call Chad. Chad should have been in the area already since he told him earlier that they, too, needed to discuss something face-to-face sometime today. He would've had Chad stop by while Beauti was there, so that he could introduce them for the first time, but her insolent demeanor would've surely caused Chad to judge her without as much as getting to actually know her. So, instead of hearing Chad bitch about his choice of women again, he had decided to introduce them at a later time.

Still, he wanted to tell Chad the reason for his trip, and to inform him on what he was to do while he wasn't present, like keeping a close eye on the problematic Virgil. *Hopefully, when I return, it'll be like I never left,* he thought as he waited for Chad to answer, *and I hope that I come back with so much coke that I'll have to start figuring out how I'm going to conquer the west coast!*

CHAPTER TWENTY-TWO

March 2, 2009 11:30 am

Lima, Peru

Breathtaking.

Surreal.

Paradise.

These were the best words that described Peru, the third largest country in South America that extended along the Pacific Ocean -- only Brazil and Argentina covered a greater area. The capital Lima, which was also the largest, busiest and most modern Peruvian city, and the neighboring city Callao, Peru's chief international port, made up Greater Lima. The six million people that populated Greater Lima were almost all lower class Indians and Mestizos (people of mixed blood) while the small upper class consisted almost entirely of whites that spoke Spanish, seldomly mixed with people outside their class, and lived in fashionable sections of Lima. Overall, though, the country was famous for its grass-covered plateaus, crystal-clear air, and sparkling sunshine.

Just about everything in tropical Peru, so far, was lovely to Demetrius. From the cordial, western-dressed locals, to the delightfully warm coastal weather, to the Peruvian coca plants that produced the narcotic that he needed to take over. *I never respected material things that I could purchase,* he thought as he looked out the window of Lima's most luxurious hotel Casa Loma and observed the boisterous streets that resembled a low-class version of New York City, *but I have always respected cocaine, because you'd be a damn fool to believe the hype about the quality of coke and where it's from until you've seen how fast it flipped your money*!

Demetrius had been in the alluring country one full day now. Yesterday, as soon as he claimed his baggage, he was promptly escorted by two of the Big Boss's men to the hotel that he was currently in. He was informed then that he should enjoy the vibrant city, because he wasn't due to meet the man himself until sometime today. To kill time, he decided to go sight-seeing and shopping not too far from the hotel for a few hours. He finally returned to the hotel and began mentally preparing for the face-to-face with one of the world's largest cocaine manufacturers, and he hadn't left the hotel room since.

He'd had a good night's rest, woke up just before dawn, and he was currently anticipating to be called for at any moment. He watched television for a while -- the best shows he wasn't able to comprehend much due to the program being in Spanish, before finally receiving the phone call. The unknown person on the line simply instructed him to be in front of the hotel in an hour. He quickly contemplated on whether it was appropriate to ask the person where he was going. But he decided to say nothing, only because he knew that he was in no position at all to ask any questions. He then looked at his watch and confirmed the time to be picked up before hanging up.

Exactly half an hour later, he was on his way to somewhere. From the very moment he pulled away from the hotel in the backseat of a five-year-old black Benz, along with two different burly South American men up front, he imagined that the trip would begin with them leaving the populated area. Busy streets would eventually thin out and lead them somewhere on an unpaved road in a rain forest near the rugged Andes Mountains. Soon enough, they'd have to ditch the comfort of a vehicle and travel by boat on one of the country's many rivers, maybe the Amazon, through an impenetrable jungle until they reached an invisible-from-the-air plantation. He would then meet some cigar-smoking, modestly dressed guy that would explain his operation while giving him a tour of the "factory", in which they'd have to walk on planks set on swamp land. From there, they'd relocate to another spot that was more in the open and sit down by a pool to conduct business as beautiful bikini-clad women and guards toting assault rifles paraded around them.

However, not one to usually stereotype, he was completely wrong.

The approximately eight-mile trip west on the Pan American Highway from Lima to the severely earthquake-damaged city Callao (pronounced Kah-yah-oh) took no more than fifteen minutes. *Damn, those big-time drug-dealing movie producers and directors just show what they think the overseas connect's lifestyle looks like*, he thought while shaking his head as they pulled up to a villa that overlooked the Pacific Ocean, *and I'm the idiot for actually believing that what I saw on TV all these years about the "big man" was somewhat true.*

Once the Benz came to a complete stop, the henchman in the passenger seat turned his head slightly and ordered Demetrius to exit the vehicle. Demetrius, however, couldn't fully understand what was being said due to the heavy Spanish accent. The henchman then turned around completely after Demetrius didn't budge and rudely gestured for him to get out of the vehicle.

"Thank you," Demetrius said as he climbed out of the backseat. "Muchas gracias."

Neither of the two men said a word. They just sat there like two crash-test dummies waiting for impact.

"Mr. Woodson," a female voice called out. It took Demetrius a second or three to pinpoint where the voice was coming from. Standing in the massive doorway of the villa was a cute petite Spanish woman in her early thirties. She was wearing a gray women's business suit, and she was motioning for him to follow her. "Right this way, sir," she added as he approached.

After walking through the noble foyer, she guided him through the glorious villa. He undeniably found himself marveled by the regal interior design. Every single piece of furniture, including all of the statues, in the first room was sparkling white. As they moved on, he childishly observed the colorful abstract paintings moderately displayed on the walls, and the multicolored vegetation and tropical trees strewn stylishly throughout the rooms he encountered. Gold and crystal fixtures complimented everything, creating an extraordinary aura. And for a split second, the elegant place caused him to vehemently feel like a mere pawn in the intrinsic drug game.

Nonetheless, he instantly realized he probably made others feel the same way back home in the states, which made him feel a lot better. *I'm more than positive if I was born and raised over here, I would be in these very shoes,* he assured himself.

After almost three minutes of entering and exiting several contiguous rooms, with each room being better than the previous one, the woman finally said, "Please, wait here."

She then disappeared, leaving him standing alone in a room full of stuffed and mounted game.

He stood in place for a few seconds. He eventually began strolling around the room, examining the various stuffed animals. Of all the animals, the most intriguing animal he saw was the seven-foot grizzly bear in a corner, fixed in an attack position with razor sharp claws and menacing teeth displayed. *Did he shoot this beast himself, or did he buy this*? he wondered.

"I see you like my prize pet ... Yogi."

Turning around rather quickly, Demetrius was startled to find a man standing right off his left shoulder. A quick analysis revealed this was the man himself, the Big Boss. The man was almost the same height and weight as him, although he could see this man regularly worked out, unlike him. He knew the man to be ten to fifteen years his senior, but he didn't look a day over forty. The man's sun-tanned skin glowed in the dimly lit room, his jet black hair was cropped quite close on the sides while curly on the top, and his tweed blazer, light blue dress shirt, cream-colored slacks and mahogany cowboy boots all appeared to be fabricated by the finest hand.

"Yes ... Yogi is a fine ... specimen," Demetrius replied.

"Please, have a seat," the man politely said in a smooth, gentle voice, without the slightest hint of an accent. "I'm sure you'll find the settee there is highly comfortable, especially since it's made from the fur of Peru's indigenous chinchilla."

Demetrius slowly sank into the plush, pearl-gray sofa. "Yes this is amazingly soft."

When the man himself took a seat across from him in a similar sofa, the only thing separating them at the time was an ivory-based table with a quartz top. The man then called for "Rosa," a young, chubby servant that appeared out of thin air and took their drink orders before disappearing as fast as she came.

Soon after Rosa left the man leaned back, crossed his legs and said, "Now, since I know virtually all about you, it is only polite that I tell you a little about myself."

Demetrius was ready to ask how the man knew virtually all about him. But, once again, he knew he was in no position to ask any questions. Besides, the man had mucho power, so he more than likely did know his entire background.

"First and foremost," the man continued, "let me introduce myself. I am the Cesar Vargas DePalma, a fluent businessman. And what type of businessman am I exactly, you might ask? Firstly, business is an art to me. I like to think of it as extracting money from another man's pocket without resorting to violence. I hate violence, although violence is necessary ... at times.

"With my businesses, I really try to help all my people by giving them jobs and offering them other opportunities, because I'm ... living good. So, since I'm living good, everyone around me should too. Are you a man of a similar principle, Mr. Woodson?"

"I must say I am, Mr. DePalma."

"Good, good. And you can call me Cesar." He paused as if he was waiting for Demetrius to suggest it was okay to be addressed by his first name. When Demetrius said nothing, he continued, "Well, moving right along. The United States has long been Peru's chief trading partner, because Peru is one of the world's leading producers of copper, lead, silver, zinc, and fishing. It's also one of the leading producers of cocaine. And by this country being one of the leading producers of cocaine, farming is the preeminent occupation in Peru. Oh, by the way, did you know Peru's officers rank among the best-trained and -educated in the world?"

"No, I did not."

Looking into Demetrius' eyes, Cesar said, "As you probably know from past experience, even the best of the best contain corrupt, money-hungry individuals, so my least of worries are the police. But, that's besides the point.

"Since most of the large cities, commercial farms, and factories lie along Peru's coast, the remote rainforests and jungles are up for grabs. However, I've managed to grab majority, if not, all of that valuable, unexplored land and claimed it as mines some twenty years ago. This is my country now, you could say. So, how do you like my country thus far?"

Demetrius smiled.

Demetrius wasn't smiling because he was thinking about how wonderful Peru was, he was smiling because he was thinking about how Cesar wouldn't stop running his mouth about his country. Cesar was basically giving him a history lesson about Peru, so he really hoped that there was a reason for the nonstop facts. *This guy has got to be the world's friendliest kingpin*, he thought.

"I've only been here a full day," Demetrius said, "and since this is strictly a business trip, I won't be able to enjoy ... your country ... as much as I would like. However, from what I've seen so far, Peru is simply indescribable." He took a deep breath. "And maybe, in the near future, once we start extracting money from other men's pockets without resorting to violence, I'll return to Peru, purchase a nice estate and become your neighbor. Then, I could really enjoy ... your country."

"Ha-ha," Cesar laughed solemnly. "I like you already. Adrian was right when he said you were a valiant man. My father once told me a long time ago that when I encounter a man like you, I'd learn many great things. But he also said that a man that knows a lot won't tell because a man who tells doesn't know a thing."

"Your father was surely a knowledgeable man."

"Hmph, my father was an insolent, self-centered pig and a woman beater. He only cared about himself, so I stabbed him to death as he , when I was twelve years old." Cesar nonchalantly shrugged. "Before we continue, there is one thing I must know."

"What is it you don't know about me already? You claimed a few minutes ago that you knew everything about me."

"Well," Cesar grinned, "let's just say I'd like to know, for my pleasure, how you're moving your cocaine after the federal government indicted you once already? Although I already know how, I just want you to explain to me, including all the details of how you're distributing your yayo, if you wouldn't mind."

Willingly and confidently, Demetrius began from the top of his most elaborate scheme.

It all started with Demetrius trying to discover a way to move large quantities of coke from state to state in a rather subtle, legitimate manner. It took him months of contemplating before finally recalling the time when his cousins Obie and Bubba would occasionally take a trip to California to visit family. During those visits, his cousins always stumbled upon some cheap, high-grade weed. Instead of taking the chance of stashing the marijuana in their luggage and catching a flight, or riding the highways, they'd buy a few microwaves, put up to two pounds in each, and overnight the package through UPS to an anonymous address or recipient back home.

Their simple plan worked every time, thus giving him an idea to do the same but in a different way, and on a much larger scale. He then took the idea to the drawing board and came up with the perfect plan a few months later.

Once all the little details and aspects were in check, he proceeded. First, he purchased land in specific areas. Soon after that, he built the stores and the warehouse. After that, he bought the furniture and a fleet of trucks and cars before hiring the right people for the job at hand.

His beloved master plan was to open up a chain of furniture stores and use them to clandestinely move his cocaine. He'd thought of a way to gut and reinforce large couches to hold up to one hundred and fifty kilos. While the stores would actually sell and deliver furniture at a cheap price to everyday people, it was all just a front.

His trusted "employees" in the various cities he set them up in would receive their "package" via delivery truck, and they knew what to do from there. Out of the last metric ton of Peruvian coke he received and sold, he took a risk by supplying his six employees with one hundred and thirty kilos each, setting a base price of twenty-four thousand dollars per brick. In the end, he demanded three million dollars from each employee, leaving them with no less than a hundred and twenty grand in their respective pockets. Their cut may have been more, depending on if they sold their kilos for more than twenty-four grand a piece.

Cesar switched positions, and unexpectedly switched subjects by saying, "I want to share some interesting facts with you, if you don't mind. Did you know coca is a large group of tropical shrubs that grows between three to twelve feet in height?"

Somewhat perplexed by the sudden change of topic, Demetrius simply answered, "No, I did not know that."

"Yes, there are only two species of the coca plant that are cultivated as drug plants. The two types are considered the Bolivian and Colombian plants. The Bolivian plants are greenish-brown with shiny, thick stems, while the Colombian plants are pale green with smaller leaves. I said all that to say this…" He uncrossed his legs and leaned forward a bit "Ninety-nine percent of all drug dealers in North America claiming to be connoisseurs of cocaine believe that there is such a thing as Peruvian coke." Cesar then laughed. "Unless there are scientists in a lab creating a Peruvian coca plant, there's no such thing. But, as long as the unwise think there is such a thing as Peruvian coke, I'll remain a major boss in this industry. Well, I'll remain a major boss no matter what now."

Is he trying to belittle me with his interesting facts? Demetrius wondered as Cesar continued to laugh, *or is he just messing with me*? "Well, like my father once told me a long time ago, an intelligent person can play stupid, but a stupid person can never play intelligent," he retorted sternly.

The two faced-off in silence.

Shaking a finger at Demetrius, Cesar finally said, "I really like you." He then stood up. "Now that I'm done scrutinizing you, let's go to a more professional setting to conduct our business. You've passed what I like to call the 'Intimidation Room.' This room is full of death, and although they're animals, it still has an effect on one's psyche."

As they left the Intimidation Room, Cesar began talking about American sports. They trekked through the house before eventually entering into the seventy-six degree Fahrenheit weather outside, while Cesar went on pleading his case of how the Yankees were better than both the Florida Marlins and the Tampa Bay Rays.

Seizing the opportunity to cut Cesar off and change the topic, Demetrius said, "If you want to small talk about something, then please tell me about this snorkel semi-submersible I've read about."

Cesar stopped walking and said, "That's the work of Colombian cartels. See, after the false-paneled pickups and tractor-trailers began attracting suspicion at the U.S. checkpoints in the last ten to twelve years, the Colombians and their Mexican comrades built intricate tunnels under the United States – Mexico border. That worked for a while, until Border Patrol agents rounded up too many squealing human mules. Their next scheme was surgically implanting drugs into purebred puppies, and that is still going on today. But the Colombians' most persistently productive system is semi-submersible vessels, which are dubbed drug subs by the American press. In fact, the vessels are nothing but cigarette boats encased in wood and fiberglass, that are sunk after a single mission."

"So, technically, they're not real subs?"

"Correct. These subs are incapable of diving and maneuvering like real subs. They simply cruise, or are towed by fishing trawlers, just below the ocean's surface." Using a hand as a shield, Cesar looked up at the sun. "They cost around a half-million dollars to build and around ten thousand dollars per crew member. I only use them when I want to move a few tons of cocaine from here to Mexico."

"So is it true the U.S. and South American officials estimate the cartels have used them to ship hundreds of tons of cocaine over the past five years?"

"Yes, it is. Despite the sub's limitations, they're notoriously difficult to track, due to the material it's made of. But that's the Colombians' method. I have my own method, though, and it has yet to be unveiled." Cesar removed a handkerchief from the inside pocket of his blazer and wiped his brow. "Let's go now. It is hot out here."

They finally reached an adjacent house that was smaller but

equally appealing as the first. They entered and walked a short distance, before settling in an undecorated room that had just an office desk and a few chairs.

"How long have you been doing business with Adrian?" Cesar asked.

"Since July of 2002."

Cesar took a seat behind the desk, and Demetrius sat opposite him.

"Since this is the first time we've actually spoken, I will—"

"Pardon the interruption," Demetrius intruded, "but this is the second time that we've spoken. This is the first time that we've met, however."

"When was it that we apparently spoke?" Cesar curiously asked.

"I'd have to say it was around June 2007. We were supposed to negotiate then. But unfortunately, I was going through legal matters with the federal government at the time ... as you may already know."

"Hmmm," Cesar muttered while rubbing his bare chin. "Oh, I remember. You spoke to a representative, not me. I didn't know what type of man you were at that time. All I knew was that you accumulated money quickly and you were a consistent buyer. Other than that, you couldn't be trusted to meet me face-to-face."

With a raised brow, Demetrius asked, "You trust me now?"

"I don't trust my own mother. I just admire how you faced the federal government like a man with grande huevos, and you were acquitted of all charges the federal government presumably had against you. I knew right then that you weren't a chivato."

"Listen carefully, Cesar, because I'm going to make this very clear." Demetrius leaned forward and stared fiercely into Cesar's eyes. "No disrespect, but unlike you, I'm a man first and foremost, then I'm a businessman. You will never hear or have to worry about me doing things a boy or a bitch would do," he said seriously, making sure Cesar clearly understood that what he was saying was sincere. "I'd rather die broke than to live with an invisible skirt on."

Cesar rhythmically tapped his fingers on the metal desk. He also nodded his head slightly with an inconsiderable frown upon his face.

"Okay, Mr. Woodson," Cesar finally said after a moment of silence which seemed like an eternity. "I'm going to disregard what I feel like was a snide remark towards me and get straight to business. No more bullshitting around. So, it's time for you to listen carefully,

Mr. Woodson, because I'm going to make this crystal clear." He then returned the same fierce gaze at Demetrius, except his eyes were fiery. "Ten metric tons. Ninety million dollars. Fifty million up front. Forty million owed. And since I really like you, three million to assure you the package will be safely delivered wherever you wish."

Instead of asking Cesar how it was possible he could manufacture that large amount of cocaine from now to delivery time, Demetrius quickly replied, "Deal."

"Now, there's only one condition."

"And what is that?"

"You are not to contact Adrian for twenty-four months. Before you say anything, I just want you to know that North America is a lot different than the majority of the other countries. Quitting while you're ahead isn't the same as simply quitting. I suggest strongly that you do what you have to do, then lay low and enjoy your riches. Live the so-called American Dream before your egotistic ass has a second rude awakening by the federal government. I don't believe in luck, but you were lucky once already. I've dealt with many men from North America somewhat like you that're currently serving lengthy sentences in your country's federal prisons. I just ..."

"Thank you, Cesar, for the advice. I'll surely keep what you've said in mind. But this is my philosophy. Instead of putting money in a bank, I'm trying to be the bank."

Cesar nodded.

The two men then went over a few details, like the time to expect payments and a few places suitable for the package to be picked up at. Afterwards, they concluded the meeting with friendly parting remarks.

Back at the hotel, Demetrius excitedly gathered his belongings. Once he was finished packing his luggage, he decided to make a few phone calls home so that certain tasks were done or in the process of being handled, before his arrival.

After minutes of rambling through his packed bags though, he had difficulty locating his treasured black book, which contained numbers and information about all his legit and illegal dealings. *I must've left it in the safe at the condo*, he concluded as he repacked his things and headed down to the lobby for his departure.

"I'll just have my hands full when I get back," he said to himself during the lonely elevator ride.

CHAPTER TWENTY-THREE

March 4, 2009 8:27 pm

West Palm Beach, FL

Phone rings

"Hello?"

"What it do, baby?"

"Damn! I was wonderin' if you were ever goin' to call, Dee." Miracle sighed. "Is everythin' alright? Where are you? Do I need to hop in my car and come check on—"

"I'm fifty-four. An' don't worry 'bout where I am right now. Did you handle that fo' me?"

"Yes," she said after sucking her teeth. "Skat just left here not too long ago."

"Is he down?"

Miracle unexpectedly burst into laughter.

"What's so funny?"

"I still can't get over how you sound .... different."

"Marie, just answer da question."

Still giggling, she responded, "Yup. He didn't even think twice about it, once I told him how much he was gettin' up front, and what he could possibly get, if everythin' is like you said."

"Shit lookin' sweeter than that ... than that juice box 'tween your legs." Devon moaned. "I'll be headin' down there soon, only if I feel like me seein' you won't fuck up this lick. So, hit up Skat as soon as I hang up, an' tell him I'll have that bread fo' him ..."

"Rhapsody already gave it to him."

"She what?"

"I hope you're not mad, but she had the money. And she claims she not trippin' on whether you pay her back or not. You know what that's about, right?"

"Yeah. That ratchet-ass bitch still want a nigga, an' she willin' ta do whateva ta take your spot."

"Can she take my spot?"

Devon chuckled. "Baby, if you don't know by now that no bitch can replace you, then ..."

"I know. I just like to hear you tell me every now and then." She sighed again. "Ughhh, I can't wait until all this bullshit is done and over with. I really miss you, Daddy. And so does this fat pussy."

"Hmph, it's been a hot minute since anybody called me Daddy. That there took me back ta my hardcore pimpin' days just that fast." Devon paused. "Anyway, don't worry, Miracle. This'll all be behind us shortly, if everythang goes accordin' ta plan. I pretty much got my end sewed up."

"So, he really has no clue whatsoever that—"

"Aye, I have ta go. This phone has a dead battery an' I don't got no access to a charger right now. I love an' miss you."

Before Miracle could respond to her lover's gesture, the line went dead. "I love and miss you, too, Devon," she said out loud in the lonely office as she laid her head down on the desk, "you be safe."

***

March 4, 2009 10:55 pm

Homestead, FL

It was a rather quiet, cool night. The unusual quietness and coolness caused Chad to be a bit jittery. Shit, it wasn't every day he had to help orchestrate the distribution of ten thousand kilos! And on top of that, Demetrius chose him, along with the Clean-up Crew, to assist in unloading the insanely large shipment when it arrived in two days. *Boy, we're likely to receive the death penalty by the feds if we get jammed with this*, he thought as images of his incarcerated father ran through his mind.

"Are you okay, Chad?" Demetrius asked, evaluating his cousin's condition as they sat across from one another in the store's office. "You're sweating profusely."

"Y'know …" Chad let out a deep breath. "I'd be tellin' a fat lie ta ya, Big Cuzzo, if I said I was straight. Da weight we 'bout ta get is a lotta ... weight on a nigga. feel me? I-I-I ain't never think a nigga would be movin' Scarface an' Pablo Escobar work. Shit, da most work I've dealt wit was da one hundred and thirty birds ya dropped on me not too long ago. Now we're talkin' 'bout ten thousand of dem white squares!"

"Don't lose self-control now, Chad. This pending shipment is what we've been hustling for. There's absolutely no turning back, so remain focused. I need you more than ever. If I lose you now, then all we have accomplished in the past would've been for nothing." Demetrius paused. "I know it is hard not to worry. I'm a little uneasy myself. But, all we're doing now is planning on how much of the coke can everybody move in a timely fashion, without causing any suspicions, that's it. We'll worry about the shipment when it's that time."

"That's easier said than done."

Demetrius laughed at Chad's last remark.

The Timeless Treasures Furniture Store they were presently in was home base, for now at least. Although the property was purchased for twice the fair market price, it was always in Demetrius' mind that this very store would eventually become the main pickup/dropoff store, since the beginning of his intricate planning. And for that reason, out of the three stores, this store's storage was designed twice as big than the others, and the security system was state-of-the-art.

Once the shipment was delivered, Demetrius would gradually funnel the coke needed at the time, from this store to the warehouse in West Palm Beach, which was where the coke was being inserted into the special couches and delivered to the out-of-state hustlers.

"Are you capable of handling more than one hundred and thirty kilos?" Demetrius questioned Chad. "And, if so, I do not want you to feel like it is essential you sell them quickly, drawing unnecessary attention upon yourself. There's no rush to get rid of the coke. But, I do not want to sit on it longer than I have to." He then smiled. "The situation is sort of ironic, for me."

"Hmmm ... Since I'm da only one workin' two states, two hundred keys of that good Peruvian shit like da last load'll be gone in ... let's say, it'll be gone in a lil under two months."

"Okay. So, instead of giving out one hundred and thirty kilos this time, if everybody, including myself and not including you, moved a meager one hundred kilos at twenty-five grand per unit, that would be approximately eight hundred kilos sold every two months." Demetrius massaged his chin. "I really think that's a reasonable pace." He then nodded. "So, since I have to wait two years before I'm able to purchase more from my trusty connect, we should be out of coke between ... twenty and twenty-five months from the day we get the load."

"Or way befo' then."

"Either way it goes, this will be an extremely perilous task, so we must do whatever it takes to sell this coke in a rather fast manner, while remaining five steps ahead of the Feds. See, I very well know that they're still out there in the shadows, just waiting for me to ... slip, as you would say."

"Slippers count, bet that."

"Right. I've been toeing the line lately, seeing if the feds will come out of hiding. But I know they're not taking a chance of letting me get away next time, so they're trying to get some concrete evidence. They have nothing, so far. I'm sure of that. And they'll continue to have nothing, as long as you and everybody else follows my lead, by doing exactly what I say when I say. If we can manage to stay on one accord, we'll ride the money train until I reach my goal."

Seeing the wicked grin on his cousin's face, Chad reluctantly asked, "An' what goal is that?"

"To reach one billion dollars!" Demetrius paused. "I know it sounds far-fetched, but I'm already a little more than halfway to my mark now. Once these ten metric tons are gone, I'll need just one more shipment like this to solidify my name as a prestigious businessman, not a second-rate drug dealer. And then, I'll retire."

This nigga sound like Dr. Evil from the Austin Powers movies, Chad thought as he inconspicuously shook his head, *and the crazy part about it is that I know he's dead serious and willing to risk his freedom to get his 'billi'.*

Demetrius looked at his Audemar Piguet watch, which read 11:37 pm, and said, "It's getting late. For the time being, I'm going back to my condo in Riviera Beach…" An immediate thought of seeing Beauti for the first time since his return from Peru entered his mind "…until the shipment arrives in a few days. I firmly advise that you remain in the vicinity, because I have yet to be informed of the exact time and location the coke will be delivered. All I know is that Adrian is going to call me sometime that day and fill me in on all the particulars. So, please, do not stray too far."

"I got'cha, Big Cuzzo. I'll prolly just swing by O-Town or Daytona an' fuck wit a few of my dawgs an' a couple hoes till then."

"It doesn't matter. Just answer your phone, okay?"

They casually stood and shook hands to end the night.

Once outside the store, just before they went their separate ways, Chad said, "I almost fa'got ta tell ya how Virgil been actin' strange while ya were gone."

CHAPTER TWENTY-FOUR

March 7, 2009 6:58 am

West Palm Beach, FL

"Whatta gwan, Big Mon?" Virgil said to Solo once the behemoth opened the side door of the warehouse. "Kilo ah send fa' me an' Buckey this mornin'. So, where me brutha at, mon?" Virgil then noticed something odd about Solo. "Whatta happen wit'cha arm, Big Mon? Everyting irie?"

"Where da Haitian?" Solo asked abruptly, ignoring the question about why his left arm was in a sling.

"Yah, Zooman no make it, caw 'im say 'im haffi ..." Virgil suddenly started laughing, then he continued, "Zooman say some bad man wan' take 'im bread, so''im haffi defend it. Voodoo drive da man crazy!"

Instead of replying to him, Solo simply pointed into the crate-filled, furniture-laden warehouse. When Virgil and Buckey both entered the building, Solo secured the door, then he instructed the two men to head towards the back of the warehouse, as he trailed closely behind.

The trio zig-zagged through the desolate warehouse before eventually reaching a twenty square foot void. Directly in the middle of the encircled section were three foldable chairs.

Solo then said, "Take a seat. I'm gonna get Demetrius."

"Yo', Big Mon," Virgil said loud enough to create an echo, "while ya gon', bring sumting ta drink an' ah bumbaclot cigar fa' me gunja."

Solo just continued walking away as if he didn't hear Virgil's orders.

"Battee boy," Buckey exclaimed shrewdly.

A couple minutes passed before Demetrius stealthily appeared from behind a wall of crates, and he was accompanied by Chad and four other goons with unusual suitcases. Fury was clearly seen on Demetrius' face as he walked slower than normal and stopped a few yards from the seated pair.

The very second he stopped, as if choreographed, two of the goons, one of which resembled the wrestler Mark Henry, stood next to

Virgil, while a dark-skinned tall, muscular guy and a short, stocky fellow posted up by Buckey. Chad stood behind his cousin. Virgil personally knew the four goons. The physical presence of the men standing over Virgil and Buckey, along with their cold-blooded countenances, caused both of them to begin perspiring in the frigid building.

"Since Virgil is well acquainted with these fine gentlemen, I want you, Bucket, to meet the Clean-up Crew," Demetrius said matter-of-factly before nodding his head.

Virgil's and Buckey's eyes instantly began bulging out of their heads. Their eyes weren't about to shoot from their sockets because of Demetrius' appalling introduction of the Clean-up Crew. No, it was the extreme pressure being applied simultaneously to their necks by huge, well-muscled arms. They determinedly struggled. Although they were fighting a battle that couldn't be won, just as they were at the point of passing out, an abundant amount of cool, refreshing air overwhelmed their dilapidated lungs. Still, they reflexively thrashed around. But their thrashing was in an effort to catch their breath. They harmoniously coughed and wheezed until their breathing practically returned to normal, then they realized they were now barefoot and bound to the chairs with duct tape.

Demetrius was unable to determine whether Virgil was crying or not, because of him also sweating like a snitch in the United States' worst federal penitentiary, until he said distressfully, "What da bloodclot up wit this fuckery, Kilo? W-w-why ya brutalize we?"

"Because you dead, mon! Death soon come!" Demetrius cried out sharply, imitating Virgil's patois. "But first, I must ask you a few questions. You can choose to remain silent, or you can run your big fucking mouth like you usually do. Either way though, I don't think your answers are going to save you." He then paused. "Or, I can be wrong and the right answers just may help you and your brethren next to you, in some type of way."

"Me ah talk, mon. Jus' let we go first."

Demetrius paced back and forth briefly before stopping between the two. He then bent down, leaned within inches of Virgil's face and eerily said, "I know you, your friend here and the Haitian were secretly meeting while I was away, because I had Chad keep an eye on you. I don't give a fuck about the meetings, but I would like to know, where's my coke you kept that didn't catch on fire. So, where's the coke?"

The expression on Virgil's face was as if Demetrius asked him where he was hiding Sasquatch. "Chad mon, dunno whatta gwan, Kilo. We jus' come togetha ta talk 'bout how we finna send fa' we family dem inna Jamaica an' Haiti. Yunno me ... "

Bam!

The hideous sound of a sledgehammer obliterating Virgil's left foot was followed by a shrill, unmanly cry.

As Virgil wailed and sobbed, Demetrius went over and leaned towards a petrified, convulsing Buckey, and rephrased the question. "I hope that you have better sense than to lie to me since you now know what lying will get you." Demetrius nodded towards Virgil's foot. "So. . . where's my coke? The coke you ... Well, maybe, just maybe, Kunta Kinte over here acted alone, but you have been found guilty by association. So, where's the coke? You know something, don't you? I know about the secret meetings, *Bucket*. Save yourself, *Bucket*, or you won't have the chance to kick the bucket naturally. Do you understand?"

Buckey was emotionally and physically disturbed by Demetrius, whom he never seen or heard of before today, for he found it impossible to utter a syllable. All he was able to do was look from Demetrius' piercing gaze to Virgil's mangled foot.

"Irie," Demetrius sarcastically said before nodding at the goon with the sledgehammer.

Wham!

"Ooooooowwwwwwwwww, ya pussy dem!"

After Demetrius shook both of his legs to rid his slacks of the splattered blood, flesh and bones, he leaned back towards a whimpering Virgil, who was hunched over in his seat and mumbling to himself, and said, "It sounds to me like you're saying what I want to hear. However, it's too bad that you'll have to repeat it, because I cannot ... Hear you! Speak up. Tell the truth. The truth just might set you free."

"Kilo," Virgil sniffled, "me nevah ... Virgil nevah betray ya. Since youths, da same streets we come from, mon. All da time da police dem fuck wit we ... we fa' each otha. We friends, mon!"

Demetrius stepped away from Virgil and took a slow lap around the void while rubbing his chin. He quickly but thoroughly ran what Virgil had just said in his head, reevaluating the thirty-plus year friendship they had, before he resumed his position between the mauled Jamaicans. His reply to Virgil's statement was, "You're right.

We are friends, Virgil, which is why I'd rather kill my friend in error than to let my enemy live."

Phone rings

Virgil began whining even louder as Demetrius removed the cell-phone from his pocket. The caller was Adrian.

"Would you all excuse me for a minute, please," Demetrius said. "And while I take this call, continue to try to make those fuckers talk." He then began to walk off. Just as he was about to exit the void, he unexpectedly spun around like he forgot something, and added, "do not … and I repeat, *do not* kill them. Just torment them until my return."

Demetrius answered the phone. Yet, he didn't say a word into the receiver until he was out of earshot. "Adrian," he finally said, "what seems to be the problem early this …"

"I'm out back," Adrian said straightforwardly. "We need to talk. And leave those seven other guys behind."

The call ended.

Taking only a split second to gather and compose himself, Demetrius lionhearted made his way outside of the building. *It was just a matter of time before Adrian heard about my misfortune*, he thought as he approached the rear door of the 2010 black Mercedez-Benz S63 AMG, *especially since it was on every news channel and frontpage in America this morning*!

"What happened, my friend?" Adrian inquired not a second later after Demetrius climbed in the back alongside him and shut the door. "Well, you should know by now that we know what happened. Maybe there's something you know that we don't. Personally, this is really a matter you have to resolve on your own, which I know you're capable of doing. However, it is personal for us because we want to know when we'll be expecting that forty-three million dollars cash you owe."

"Cesar will get his money. He'll just have to give me a few months to gather it up, because it's not like I have it in a piggy bank on my dresser. I have monies tied up in so many …"

"Three days from now. That's all you have."

"Three days! Seventy-two fucking hours is all he's giving me! It's impossible for me to obtain that amount of money in three days!" Demetrius paused and lowered his voice after seeing the frown on Adrian's face. "Listen, it took me almost two months to collect the money I had to pay Cesar up front. Beforehand, it was rather difficult housing, safeguarding and constantly relocating those bills until it was time to deal with Cesar, so I need at least ... one week."

"I'm sorry, Demetrius, my friend, but you have just three days." Adrian proceeded to remove a tin case from the inside of his blazer, then he opened the case, took out one of the four cigars inside, and lit the cigar with a match. He finally cracked his window, puffed on the redolent cigar a few times, and continued talking. "Initially, Cesar wanted to kill you. But, since I know you're one helluva businessman, I persuaded Cesar to give you a little time. Now, since I did you that favor, there shouldn't be any problems getting that money out of you. We would love to continue what we have, because you're no good to us dead.

"Hopefully, you can understand why Cesar wants his money as soon as possible. It's just that ... he was generous enough to give you three days. There's simply no telling if, or when, the Federales are looking to pick you up after the debacle that occurred yesterday. Somebody is going down for that, and we don't want to take a chance of the feds apprehending you before we get paid. So, after three days and you still have yet to pay us, you're dead. Simple as that. Or, if you get locked up before the three days, we'll just have someone take care of you on the inside. Either way, you're dead if you don't pay up. Understand?"

"I'll have Cesar's money in three days," Demetrius said defeatedly.

"Good, my friend. Very good." Adrian puffed on the smelly cigar again. "Now, tell me what happened? How'd you manage to let a bunch of little nappy-headed niggers rob you?"

Dismissing Adrian's derogatory remark, Demetrius began to divulge all that was told to him.

According to Solo, his security personnel present that night, who was extremely fortunate to survive the onslaught and escape afterwards with only a single gunshot wound to his shoulder, the robbery transpired as so.

Just before midnight on March 5, Solo was instructed by Demetrius to show up for extra duty at the Timeless Treasures Furniture Store in Homestead. While in the company of ten other guys he'd never seen before, he was to guard the store until sunrise, which was when Demetrius said that he would arrive from West Palm Beach. He knew very well the store was recently loaded with a shipment of cocaine not too long ago before his arrival. He thought he was looking over a few hundred keys like he had done in the past, but he also knew it was an assignment that paid very well.

Being that this was his fourth time having to guard something for Demetrius, his standard routine was to check the perimeter of both the store and the store's warehouse every thirty minutes. During his routine checks, which he performed by himself, he constantly wished someone would be dumb enough to blitz the store while he made his boring rounds. However, nobody ever did.

A little after his perimeter check at two in the morning, he searched for and found a comfy, quiet space in the store that was secluded from the others, and it was there that he decided to nap until the alarm on his phone woke him up when it was time to check the perimeter again.

POW

No more than ten seconds into his planned thirty-minute snooze, he was jolted awake by the sound of a single gunshot. He determined though, the shot had nothing to do with the store shortly thereafter, because no more shots followed. And he closed his eyes again.

Sprat Spratatatat

When his heart returned from the pit of his stomach to its normal position, he found the courage to leave the safety of his resting place. He rose and promptly drew his registered Smith & Wesson .45. The booming incessant gunfire persisted as he followed the shooting, which gradually led him to the back of the store. Once he swung open the back door, he claimed it was as if he were in a realistic first-person shooter video game, with dozens of muzzles flashing, bullets whirring past and ricocheting off of everything, glass shattering, men yelling in pain.

He then claimed images of his wife and kids flashed through his head, causing him to totally freeze up. He snapped out of the daze however, when a perpetrator wearing a black T-shirt as a makeshift mask—he said that the way the guy wore the mask reminded him of a ninja—ran by the door and stopped as soon as they saw one another. They momentarily stood staring at each other, until the Mini-14-toting masked man flinched. He reacted quickly by upping his .45. He landed two chest shots, dropping the perp for good.

His adrenaline was really pumping then, so he darted a few yards from the door and took cover next to a badly bleeding guard that was leaning against a vehicle in the parking lot/loading dock. From where he was, he could see a few other severely wounded guards ducking behind whatever they were able to. The dying guard next to him briefly filled him in on what was going down as high-powered rifle rounds continued to rattle and demolish everything at the opposite end of their barrels.

The dying guard told him that approximately twenty men jumped out of four caravans and stormed the store's warehouse, which was less than a hundred yards behind the store and separated by the space where the warfare was taking place. The jack boys had to have been casing the warehouse for their window of opportunity earlier, because they rushed the warehouse as all the guards gathered and talked by the store's back door. As the jackers ransacked the massive building, they basically kept the guards at bay and away from the warehouse by constantly firing rounds at them.

He then declared that what seemed like an hour was actually four agonizing minutes. The robbers must have found the cocaine because he witnessed them load all four caravans with at least three large duffle bags in each vehicle. As he watched them all hurriedly pile into the vans, leaving the bloodied scene, they steadily fired shots while hanging out of the sliding side door.

When the jack boys were finally gone for good, he began to hear the faint sirens of the police approaching the scene. He stood up from the spot that he was taking cover at and realized three things: one, the warehouse was smoking; two, there were eight guards dead in the parking lot with just one of the robbers, of which he shot; and three, he was shot in the left shoulder. He finally managed to get to his vehicle, and fled the scene before the police arrived.

"It sounds to me that someone in your organization that wasn't supposed to know, knew about your load and plotted against you, my friend," Adrian proposed.

"That's logical, which is why I'm in the process of getting down to the bottom of it as we speak. So, if you would please, I have a lot of unfinished business to tend to now." Demetrius reached for the door handle. "Oh, and I'll call you in three days when I have the money. Don't bother trying to contact me until then."

Before he could say another word, Demetrius opened the door and exited the vehicle. *Punk-ass spic out here doing everything his bitch-*

ass boss tells him to, he thought as he watched Adrian leave, *and I shouldn't pay those faggots nothing because they probably were the ones that set me up for all I know*. "Now, let me go back in here and see if these birds are singing yet," he then said to no one in particular.

Demetrius entered the warehouse again and made his way through the maze of crates and furniture until reaching the void; the smell of death filled the air as he drew closer. Upon arrival, the monstrosity he saw was an unpleasant one. Although he might not have looked happy, he was overjoyed inside.

"What the fuck have you all done? I said to torture them, not to kill them! I thought I made that very clear before I left, didn't I? You're all idiots!"

"Boss, they're not dead," the Mark Henry look-alike said in a rather high-pitched voice. "They're just unconscious ... I think."

"I bet they wish they were dead after what y'all did to 'em," Chad said, emerging from behind a crate while wiping his mouth on the hem of his Polo shirt.

"Where did ... Did you just throw up?" Demetrius asked.

"Da lil weak-ass nigga been blowin' chunks since ya left," the tall one said. "You shoulda took his ass wit'cha. This nigga really scared of a lil blood, so he must be scared of pussy. Damn near fainted like a white boy when they see Michael Jackson on stage."

The Clean-up Crew laughed together.

"Fuck y'all! You nasty, sadistic muthafuckas!"

"I can see that ya sellin' some nice furniture, Bossman," the short one said, "but I didn't see any nice cribs for this big-ass baby." He then focused on Chad. "You want bah-bah, son? Or do ya need Uncle to change ya Huggies?"

The laughter continued.

"Alright, stop the foolishness," Demetrius demanded. "Time is money right now. Now, what exactly have you done to these two fools? It reeks in here. And there are body parts and too much blood splattered everywhere for them to not have said something yet."

The tall one described everything that took place while Demetrius was gone. First, the Clean-up Crew all-out slapped the two Jamaicans around to soften them up as both of them spinelessly begged for mercy. After doing that for a few minutes, they mentally fucked them by debating amongst each other about which of them were going to pair up together before choosing their victim, and which one of the tools in the suitcases caused the most pain they going to save for last. Ultimately, they agreed to play Rock, Paper, Scissors to determine teams, and which team got what Jamaican.

Once that was settled, they retrieved a reciprocating saw from a suitcase, a large power drill from another, and a blowtorch from the last one to join the already-used sledgehammer. Before engaging in their mastery of pain and disfigurement, they gave the two men one last, final chance to come clean. The response from both Virgil and Buckey, however, was only more pleading mixed with gibberish -- being reticent was only going to hurt them, literally.

To begin the procedure, they yanked out two handfuls of Virgil's lengthy dreads. The reason for doing that was to gag them both with the knotty locks before duct-taping their mouths in order to muffle the ear splitting screams that were soon to come. The next phase involved the reciprocating saw. They successively removed both Virgil's and Buckey's mutilated appendages. Buckey passed out midway through the cutting of his foot. Their bloody stumps were then blowtorched, and that rancid smell of burning human flesh caused Chad to vomit. The foot-removing process though, was ironic. It was as if they were doctoring the very wounds they inflicted.

Since Buckey was out cold, they decided to remove the gag from Virgil's mouth to ask him if he had a change of heart and wanted to end the mayhem for the both of them. Word for word, Virgil's feeble response was, "Fuck ya an' da pussy dem wit'cha. Me know nutting, me do nutting. Me ah bad man but me do no harm ta Kilo. His Imperial Majesty, Haile Selassie I, know me heart, so Zion me soon come." Then he spat blood in the face of the short one.

No longer interested in obtaining a confession at that point, they viciously smacked the incapacitated Buckey until he was somewhat conscious. They wanted to make sure Buckey was awoke for what came next. They then punctured numerous dime-sized holes all over their bodies. The blood Virgil and Buckey lost during this harrowing procedure made them extremely weak. But that didn't stop the torture, because after the drilling, the short one found a square two-foot long strip of splintered plywood lying around and they improvised by continuously ramming it up their asses until it broke off in Virgil's rectum.

Really enjoying themselves, and just starting to warm up, they then blowtorched the near-death Jamaicans' testicles, causing their nuts to catch a fire. Once they burned the majority of their bodies as well, leaving them virtually unrecognizable, they ended the torturing. They really didn't want to stop though, because they really wanted nothing more at that time than to kill the disloyal, thieving bastards. But instead, they left them within an inch of death, at least until Demetrius heard they weren't giving up any information.

"I'm a diehard Florida Gator fan," Demetrius blurted out. "Do you all think they like the Florida Gators?"

Chad and the Clean-up Crew looked amongst each other with a puzzled expression on all their faces.

Eventually, the Mark Henry look-alike answered, "No, Boss,"

"Well, us Gator fans have a saying: If you're not a Gator fan, then that only means you're Gator bait. So remove them out of here ASAP, and have this area immaculate by noon." He turned to leave. "Chad, let's go!"

***

March 7, 2009 5:15 pm

Coral Gables, FL

"This is Khristal Dansbury of *Channel 8 Fox News*," the middle-aged, gorgeous red-haired woman said on the best and biggest flat-screen television that money could buy, "and I'm reporting live from the Everglades. Behind me is the grisly scene of a body that has been discovered earlier today.

"It is confirmed that at approximately 8:30 this morning, a group of tourists enjoying a pleasant airboat ride through this vast, beautiful swampland, encountered the decapitated and dismembered burnt body. The medical examiner at the scene has released information regarding the victim: a black male in his late thirties, early forties, and he has only been deceased less than ten hours. It is unknown at this time whether the authorities have identified the victim ... Wait, I think the chief is going to release a statement about the victim."

The reporter scrambled to join the swarm of other reporters that gathered around the graying chief. After battling for a good spot, she then thrust her microphone towards the chief's clean-shaven face, along with the other mics.

With a somber expression, the chief sternly said, "The medical examiner has made a key discovery, which may be the victim's identity, or help lead us to identifying our victim. On the victim's person was a card issued by Immigration. The name on the card is one Virgil Brashears of West Palm Beach. We are still unsure whether our victim is actually Mr. Brashears, until we …"

I know for a fact my men searched both Virgil and Buckey for anything that could lead to them being identified, before disposing of their bodies, Demetrius thought as he changed the channel to AMC, *but I know also Virgil kept his green card on him at all times in a pocket somewhere.* "I should've told them to burn their bodies," he said out loud. "Damn!"

"What's wrong?" Beauti inquired, entering Demetrius' room after returning from the bathroom down the hallway.

"Oh ... It's nothing." He paused. "Thank you, Tamara, for stopping by on such short notice. Although I'm very surprised you've actually decided to meet here in my new place, I want to apologize for calling you to discuss things in this unprofessional setting. As you know, from the news, I'm going through a ... tumultuous time."

Beauti came out of the designer sandals on her feet. Her freshly pedicured feet, with toenail tips painted virgin white, sank deep into the plush carpet. In her casual snug white V-neck shirt and khaki capri pants, she sashayed over to the bed. Demetrius was sitting on the edge of the bedstead when she confidently took a seat towards the massive hand-carved oak headboard and got comfortable, leaving a distance of about seven feet between them.

"First of all, business is business, no matter where it's conducted. Secondly, when you called me, I could hear how you sounded stressed out, an' I have never heard you like that, so that kinda ... that worried me. An' lastly, I haven't seen da news, so I have no idea what's going on. However, I would like ta know all you're willin' ta tell me, cuz I'm not a nosey bitch an' …"

Looking back at Beauti, Demetrius seriously said, "Don't say that."

"Don't say what?"

"You're not a bitch. While you are light years away from being the friendliest woman I've dealt with…" He began to display his signature smile "I have come to realize you're not easygoing and you're going to be you, regardless. I have accepted that. So, give me your word you'll refrain from degrading yourself, because you're ... you're a remarkable, phenomenal, and unique woman."

The two locked eyes in silence.

Feeling uncomfortable after a few seconds of staring into Demetrius' inaccessible soul, Beauti cleared her throat while averting her gaze elsewhere. "Well … hmmm … What was it that you wanted ta talk about?"

Withdrawing himself from the physical attraction he felt for Beauti, he stammered once again. O-oh, yes ... let's see, where should I begin?" Since Beauti claimed she didn't know about the cocaine that was found torched in his store -- he had absolutely no plans of telling her about the cocaine either -- he began to fabricate a story about how he made a terrible business deal that had him on the verge of filing for Chapter 11 bankruptcy. He went on by saying how the next three days were going to be extremely overwrought with work and more work, if he wanted to keep his business from going belly up.

He finally explained how he needed her to have his back to the fullest; he was depending on her to help get him out of the ordeal he was facing. And he summed it all up by promising her a bountiful compensation as soon as things were back in order and running smoothly again. "I can guarantee if we—yes, you and I—can make it through the next three days, I will make you the first lady of my organization, which is a prestigious position that has yet to be claimed. So, are you up for three taxing, strenuous, and sleepless days of work?"

This was Beauti's golden opportunity. Out of sheer desperation, Demetrius placed the "First Lady" position on a platinum platter for her. And it was all hers, once she proved herself trustworthy by helping him get out of the grave he had no clue he wasn't going to get out of. So, there was no chance whatsoever she was letting this pivotal opportunity pass by, she was in there like swimwear. *Hmph, I just hope he actually believed me when I told him I didn't know what was going on*, she said unto herself as she looked in Demetrius' eyes again and now saw vulnerability, which was something she had never seen in his eyes before.

The solemn look Beauti had on her face during the ten to fifteen seconds of pretending to think his proposal over, gradually became an ear-to-ear grin. "I got you, Demetrius. This bitch'll ride-an'-die with you!"

He couldn't help but to smile at her inflexibility.

Phone rings

"Oops, that's me," she said as she removed her Blackberry from her pocket. "It ain't nothin' but a text message I received. I wonder who ..."

Demetrius witnessed Beauti's jaw drop after looking at her phone. "What is it, Tamara? Is everything okay?"

"Uh ... uh ..." Before she could say something that made any sense, she hopped off the bed. She then speed-walked to the bathroom inside his bedroom this time and firmly shut the door.

Rather than chasing behind her, and asking twenty-one questions through the door, he just sat there. *Hell, I have my own problems to worry about right now*, he reasoned with himself, *but I hope whatever happened isn't nothing serious.*

CHAPTER TWENTY-FIVE

March 9, 2009 3:17 am

Coral Gables, FL

"Demetrius," the familiar voice reverberated everywhere in the dark room. "Demeeeetriiiiiuussssss," the voice then sang.

"Mel ... is that you?" Demetrius asked fearfully.

"Yes, Demetrius, it is I. It is I, the once beautiful, young, innocent mother you took it upon yourself to ... kill!"

The last remark echoed continually, becoming louder and louder every time it was said. It go so loud in the enclosed cavity, or whatever it was he was in again, that he swore his eardrums were about to blow.

Without caution, and to his pleasure, the echoing ceased. There was complete quietness for a couple of seconds before the voice yelled, "You're a fucking murderer, Kilo, and the end is near for you!"

Demetrius arose entirely clothed, perspiring and quivering like a novice welterweight boxer facing Mike Tyson in his prime. He ardently swiped at the sweat coating his face before he proceeded rectifying his rapid and irregular breathing. Once again, he utilized the technique he picked up from a television show, and he reduced his anxiety attack to a status where he was nearly stable again.

Once composed, he ultimately took in the familiar atmosphere he was exposed to. Although he clearly recognized that he was in the comfort of his own bedroom, his prior anxiety attack gradually culminated after seeing there was some undetermined thing next to him under the covers. In a frightened approach, he tossed back the sopped sheets and discovered that ...

"Damn, I'm really losing my mind," he said to himself as he shoved the many throw pillows onto the floor that were "supposedly" the person in bed with him. "Keep it together, Demetrius. You can make it through this. Don't let people or things drive you crazy when you know it's only walking distance."

After giving himself a pep talk, he looked at the innovative digital clock on the wall opposite the bed and realized how early it was still. Rather than trying to go back to sleep, he simply seized the opportunity to get up and get a head start on the many tasks he had to perform today. *Being optimistic about the outcome of the situation at hand is the only way I'm going to prevail over this predicament*, he thought as he picked up his smartphone and called Chad, *and I have just one day left until the deadline.*

***

March 9, 2009 9:23 am

West Palm Beach, FL

It was less than two weeks before spring, even though it was feeling a lot like summer already. The fresh breeze and low humidity made for a pleasant day, so there had to be a good reason not to be outside, whereas the mood inside of the warehouse at the moment was souring by the second as Demetrius discovered more upsetting information about who may have performed the lick on his coke.

"Are you positive?" Demetrius asked again from behind the desk.

"I'm positive, Big Cuzzo. Like I told ya, I swerved through Pleasant City an' downtown damn near all day yesterday an' da day befo', tryna come 'cross some shit that was outta pocket. An' I'm tellin' ya them lil Triple S niggas out there boomin' our coke ... fo' da low.

"They also been blowin' stacks on everythang, from gettin' grilled up wit platinum an' diamonds, ta puttin' they raggedy-ass Chevys an' Buicks in da shop, ta splurgin' at da Palm Beach Lakes Mall an' da mall in Palm Beach Gardens, ta trickin' wit some bad bitches, ta buyin' pounds of kush an' pills, ta goin'—"

"Okay, okay ... I understand." Demetrius furiously slammed a fist on the desk, causing its contents to shake. Besides hearing the new, disturbing news from Chad, he was mad at the fact that he knew playing in the streets long enough would eventually lead to falling victim to the very ways of the street life. Being considered untouchable was fictitious.

In fact, he'd been robbed once before when he first started pushing major weight for two birds and twenty-five stacks, by two people that knew better than to try him. To save face then, he promptly took care of that baser, after obtaining most of what was taken from him. However, what was taken from him this time was well worth starting a civil war in the streets, so he could only respect the parts of the game he always respected during a time like this.

"Big Cuzzo, they dunno who they fuckin' wit!" Chad exclaimed, trying to match his cousin's fury. "Ain't no way in hell they know they jacked our shit!"

"It's not a coincidence. Now, it's questionable whether Virgil actually had something to do with all of this or not, but I'm certain he told me ... an ignorant me ... a while back that Triple S could've been formulating a way to bring RBF down so they could become the new legion.

"So, they very well know the head of RBF is a living legend in these streets still. And being that I am a legend only means the rookies are going to do whatever it takes to surpass me. Even if it means embarrassing me and making me the laughingstock of my city, by jacking my coke and having a ball in my face, while acting like it's not a big deal. It's the same as when the rookie Allen Iverson crossed over the legendary Michael Jordan without hesitating or thinking about Mike's reputation or ankles, afterwards. So, it's obvious they know who they've jacked. They simply crossed me over, and they can care less about my legendary reputation."

"What're we gonna do then?"

"Well ... Although I have no clue of how much coke was destroyed in the fire, I really doubt they took forty-three million dollars' worth of my coke. If they did take that amount, the coke has been divided amongst more than a dozen of them by now, so all there's left to do is to send out a few expendable goons to try to locate the leader of Triple S, and/or ferret out the true identity of the person inside my organization that has double crossed me. I cannot guarantee I'll find a leader though, because black youths nowadays in Palm Beach County have issues following the orders of one man, so RBF will definitely go down as the last organization with this many blacks taking in hundreds of millions of dollars. But, blood will be shed, I can guarantee that."

"Fuckin' right!" Chad shouted. After a brief pause, he continued, "So, Big Cuzzo, you don't have any dope? I gotta a lotta my peeps in New York an' Georgia lookin' ta score a few blocks."

Demetrius chuckled. "Fortunately, I have two hundred and twenty keys stashed away for a rainy day right here. But, even if I were to sell them all before tomorrow at a high price of thirty per unit, that will only be six-point-six million dollars to the good." He paused. "Now, I can easily gain access to at least three million dollars after a few personal calls, then I could add all that together with the money my accountant is retrieving from all of my various business accounts as we speak. As a matter of fact, he should be phoning me…" He looked at his watch "…in a few minutes, informing me on how much money he'll be able to obtain today. Hopefully, I should have relatively twenty million altogether by the end of the day from my accounts alone."

"Shit! If I woulda never bought that house in O-Town fo' four hundred stacks, dropped my '73 on twenty-eights, an' splurged down here recently befo' da jack move, I woulda had close to one-point-five mill fo' ya." Chad inhaled deeply and exhaled. "Is it possible that'cha man 'cross da water will give ya a break if ya came up wit at least half of that bread?"

"If my accountant is able to garner a third of the cash that's in my business accounts, I don't see why he wouldn't." Demetrius shrugged. "I've been wondering the exact same thing as you are, because that is actually what I planned on doing; buying myself some more time. If he's courteous enough to give me a little leeway, then I'd suggest to him to let me pay him interest."

"An' what's da plan if we can't get da money up by tomorrow?"

"There's no we, Chad," Demetrius said woefully. "If I cannot come up with this money, I will have to gather the ones closest to me and play a game with the man across the water I seriously doubt I can win."

Chad was puzzled by the last statement. "What game ya talkin' 'bout?"

"Hide and seek," Demetrius replied stiffly.

Phone rings

"This should be my accountant. Please, excuse me one second." Demetrius answered the office's telephone. "Hello ... Yes ... They did *what*? Uh ... Hold on, wait a minute. Repeat that once more, because I'm sure I heard you wrong ... You cannot be serious ... How did they find out? Uh ... wait a second, I was never there with my black book ... It's impossible ... I'm fucking positive! ... Goddammit!"

The phone was slammed down, probably breaking it in the process.

"What's da problem now?"

Demetrius ignored the question. Instead, he began erratically shuffling through the drawers of the desk. He swiftly rambled and gathered a few CD-ROMs and files from the numerous drawers, then he said while jumping out of the chair, "We have to go … STAT!"

With a fearful look, Chad also jumped out of his chair, and he followed his cousin. Neither one of them spoke as they walked at an unusually fast pace out of the office and to the back door.

Once at the back door, which led to their parked cars, Chad stood within centimeters of Demetrius. Demetrius carefully and slowly opened the door and peeped outside. He continuously surveyed his field of vision while gradually opening the door further. He then shot out the door, and Chad trailed him.

When they reached their separate vehicles that were parked alongside one another, Chad finally asked again, "What's da problem now?"

Somewhat out of breath, Demetrius said, "I do not have the time to explain right now." He opened his car door. As he climbed into his Benz, he added, "Just know that shit is totally fucked up! I'll call you soon."

Demetrius crunk up and sped off, leaving Chad in the parking lot. *What the fuck is happening*? he thought as he pounded the steering wheel, *I have to be having a nightmare*!

CHAPTER TWENTY-SIX

March 9, 2009 11:53 am

West Palm Beach, FL

A fugitive? No, that was being too subtle.

A destitute fugitive? Uh-uh, that was still being a bit modest.

A wretched, destitute fugitive? Yes, that was more precise. A wretched, destitute fugitive described Demetrius the best at the present time: he was overwhelmed with worries, he was penniless, and he was on the run from the feds. How things were looking, not even the great Matthew O'Hare could get him out of the shit that he was in this time. So he had absolutely nobody to run to for help.

Well, he briefly considered seeking refuge with a member in RBF. But he ultimately knew he'd be a jackass to even try to seek help from anybody that could be linked to RBF, because the feds were surely watching all of his associates, and his associates' associates by now, just waiting for him to show his wanted face.

With just about all of his options exhausted, he had just one more person to call on. The one and only person he was hoping he could run to for help was also the one and only person he trusted outside of RBF. No, it wasn't his son, Bizzy. That one distinctive person he had no choice but to rely on during the lowest point in his life was none other than ... Carter. Tamara Carter, to be exact.

Getting in contact with his Beauti, however, was a mission itself because he didn't have her number at the present time. The reason for this was because as soon as he left the warehouse less than two hours ago, with his mind moving at two hundred miles-per-hour, he immediately began ridding himself of anything that could lead to his whereabouts. So, he trashed his cellphone, credit cards, and even ditched his Benz. He then took the one hundred dollars cash, the only money he had to his name, and hopped on the nearest county transit bus with one goal in mind, and that was to find Beauti, somehow.

Lacking a phone number, a home address, and a mutual friend, he hadn't the slightest idea of where to start his search for Beauti. So all he was able to do for the time being was just ride the PalmTran for hours, while paranoid and relentlessly thinking of a way to get to his Beauti.

Then, it hit him.

He knew a place that might lead him to Beauti.

To begin his quest, he quickly retrieved a bus route map of the whole county from the driver. After exactly two hours and forty-seven minutes of riding a few different buses and walking a dozen blocks, he arrived at his destination in Lake Worth at 2:42 pm. He hurriedly walked into the building with a sign above the entrance that read, The Palace.

Now, he wasn't in the gentlemen's club to blow his last on a lap dance or two before turning himself in. Rather, he was there in high hopes of locating someone that knew how to reach Beauti. And although he didn't think he'd have difficulty finding one of Beauti's friends, since it had only been two months or so from the time when she last worked in The Palace, he thought it would just be miraculous to find someone there at that time of day that would have Beauti's number.

Nevertheless, it seemed that his luck was taking a turn for the better, because he found a friend of Beauti's.

Mystic, a tall and slender, red-boned stripper knew Beauti, and she also happened to have her number. However, she was reluctant to give Beauti's number to Demetrius, because she wasn't for giving out strippers or ex-stripper's info to customers, since that might lead to a stripper being stalked.

But, after Demetrius convinced her he was indeed Beauti's new boss and his acquisition of his employee's number pertained to consequential business, she decided to call Beauti and relay a message from him to her. She took his message and went into the dressing room to make the call, while he sat down at the bar in a corner by himself.

Nearly four and a half minutes passed before Mystic returned and informed Demetrius that Beauti would show up in about ten minutes, since she lived only a few blocks away from the club. Once she relayed the message, she walked off with intentions of making a few rounds to solicit the few customers in the building, yet she stopped and decided whether or not to keep Demetrius company after seeing how uneasy he was at the bar. However, before she accompanied him, she attentively watched him from a distance and saw him constantly checking the door to see who entered and exited the inanimate club, while sporadically looking around like a plump chick lost in the projects. After observing his abnormal behavior for a while, she finally approached him again and offered to take him to a secluded area in the VIP until Beauti arrived.

"I ... ummm ... Uh, that's probably a great idea," Demetrius said rather loudly in order to be heard over the bumping music.

Mystic grabbed Demetrius' sweaty, clammy hand and ushered him to the VIP. Just before they walked beyond the purple strands of sequin beads that led into the VIP, she spun around and asked him, "Do you want something to drink?"

He was almost nose-to-nose with the tall, pretty stripper when he replied, "Yes. Thank you."

"What do you drink? Liquor? Champagne? Beer?"

"Uhh ..." He sighed. "I'll ... Please, just bring me a double shot of the strongest liquor that's served. And it doesn't matter what color it is."

"While I go fetch you and myself a drink, you go right ahead and make yourself comfortable." She winked before releasing his hand. "I'll be right back, Big Man."

Demetrius proceeded ahead. He walked through the beads and swiftly observed the room, and it was of no surprise when he found the room without a soul. But, he still cautiously sought out a spot furthest to the back, and possibly near an emergency exit door. Eventually, he found a suitable couch that wasn't near an exit. However, his spot was way in the back of the spacious VIP room.

He patiently waited for Mystic. While waiting, he commenced to playing out in his head how the rendezvous with Beauti was going to transpire. He was well aware she wasn't going to be too pleased with him popping up at her old job at first, but she should eventually lighten up and become concerned only after he divulged everything. Yes, he was going to tell her about everything that had occurred.

Once he was done spilling the beans, she was more than likely going to scold him as if he were a child caught stealing candy for the first time. And when she was done letting him have it, she should finally agree to let him sleep at her humble abode, until they could figure out what to do. He prayed, which was something he hadn't done in ages, that the foregoing events happened just as he imagined.

Simply saying he had too much on his plate was a major understatement. He tried to reminisce about his life prior to his load being jacked. But all he could recall now was the last couple chaotic days. With one problem leading to another, and that problem leading to a much bigger one, he really hoped he didn't have to face any more problems than the ones that he already had, because he was really tired and fed up with past, present, and future problems. *I can remember when my mother constantly told me when I was young, to ask the Lord not for a lighter burden, but for broader shoulders*, he thought as he sat motionless on the comfy couch, *so I hope the Lord knows this load I'm currently carrying is too heavy for the broadest of shoulders, let alone the narrow shoulders I'm working with.*

In the vacant VIP, with the R&B music keeping the room from being completely quiet, he just stared into ... nothingness. He still couldn't believe every single one of his business accounts were recently seized, putting him back in the Stone Age. He was also still trying to figure out how his treasured black book got from his safe in the wall at his condo in Riviera Beach all the way down to the crime scene at his furniture store in Homestead.

The black book was the key piece in dismantling RBF, so it being discovered at the crime scene was more than just unfortunate. Not only did the black book contain lucrative information on every business Demetrius was involved with, including the store found littered with dead bodies and burning cocaine, it contained personal numbers of every major person that Demetrius dealt with, like the numbers of Kelly Kronkite and Adrian Mendoza. So, how the black book turned up in Homestead was a perplexing mystery, because Demetrius never took it out of the safe, unless he was going to travel outside the country for more than a few days.

The last time he could remember bringing his black book out of the safe was when he traveled to Peru. But, he could also remember not having it with him in Peru, which only meant he left it in the safe at the condo. *So, how in the hell did it get out of my safe and end up more than fifty miles away*? He weighed in his mind.

"Somebody set me up and caused all of this to happen," he mumbled to the man looking at him in the mirror hanging on the wall across from him. "But who would want to see me ruined? Who will gain the most from my demise? It has to be someone right up under my nose. But who?"

"Who you talking to?" Mystic said as she came out of nowhere.

"I-I-I ... umm, I was just thinking out loud."

In three-inch heels, Mystic strutted over in a transparent skimpy, sky blue two-piece stripper fit, with her small perky breasts and semierect nipples on display and her sumptuous forty-inch ass hanging out. She sat down next to Demetrius on the couch, while holding two shot glasses of clear liquor, one in each hand, then she said, "Here's a double shot of Patrón Platinum."

He carefully took the shot she held out to him and throwed it back. After he finished, he simply uttered, "Thank you."

"You're welcome, Big Man." She took the glass from him and placed it on the table next to her. She then took her single shot and continued, "Now, let me help you relax." She threw her long, graceful leg over him and straddled him. "I can see you have a lot on your mind."

Lost in the moment, all Demetrius could do was shake his head pitifully.

She clasped her soft hands around his neck, then began to seductively grind back and forth to the music, while occasionally whipping her shoulder-length hair and staring passionately into his eyes. Although she wasn't drawing any type of reaction from the dormant Demetrius, she persisted to dry hump him until …

"My bad, playa," said a huge white boy with gold teeth. When he saw how Demetrius tossed Mystic to the side in a frightened manner, he added, "Everythin' cool, pot'nah. I work here." He then looked at Mystic. "Yo', someone on da phone fo' ya. They say it's urgent."

"Okay, I'm coming." Once the bouncer left, she said to Demetrius, "That's probably your girl, so I'll be back."

"I hope so," he murmured when Mystic disappeared.

Instead of thinking about what he was going to do if Beauti decided that she wasn't going to help him, he continued to occupy his time by trying to figure out who was behind this well-conceived, elaborate scheme that was ruining him. The more he thought about it, though, the sleepier he became, but the sleepiness didn't deter him from continuing to try to piece together the bothersome puzzle. So, he piously thought long and hard, while he incrementally yawned more and more, which was a clear indication that he didn't get much rest over the last few days due to his excessive thinking.

Still, he didn't plan on resting anytime soon, because it was possible he'd get the chance to rest eternally, if Cesar was to ever catch up with him.

While growing somewhat impatient of waiting for Mystic to return, it suddenly dawned on him that he just might get to go to Beauti's home, only if she agreed to aid and abet him first. That thought eventually led to him wondering about how many people had the privilege to be a guest inside her home. The only reason he wondered this was because of how she always refused to reveal to him where she laid her head at, especially since all he'd ever been to her was a nice guy.

So, it would be a major breakthrough if she invited him to her house. *Let's see, how many people have I invited inside my condo in Riviera*? He wondered as he fought the sleep overcoming him, *because I'm extremely careful about letting people inside my home like she is.*

"Who was it ... I had ... in my condo ... when I recently ... had my ..." He stopped talking to the man in the mirror momentarily, because he was yawning uncontrollably. Then, after a yawn that lasted nearly fifteen seconds, he blurted out, "Oh ... I remember now ... it was ..."

Demetrius, instantly and unknowingly, passed out on the couch and was snoring within seconds.

CHAPTER TWENTY-SEVEN

March 10, 2009 3:43 am

West Palm Beach, FL

"Kilo, wake up!"

I vaguely recognize that voice, Demetrius thought before cracking his eyes open a hair. It took a full five seconds, however, to completely open both eyes. But, just as slow as he opened them, he slowly closed them.

Smack!

Demetrius quickly opened his eyes this time, only because of the loud sound that followed the hand hitting his numb face. What appeared to be a ceiling was all he saw until he tilted his head down. He slowly blinked a few times to adjust his vision, for it was beyond out of focus. It also didn't help that the place was dimly lit by a light coming from an adjacent room. Consequently, his vision wasn't going to get any clearer.

When he started looking around, it was as if he were looking into a kaleidoscope. Then suddenly, his head and the room began to spin in opposite directions. The spinning became faster the longer he kept his eyes open, eventually causing him to shut his eyes again. Finally, he languidly tried to move, but he couldn't. *Am I dreaming*? He wondered as he laid there helplessly, *and if I am dreaming the usual dream, then she is here.*

"Mmm ... Mmmee ... Mmmeellll," he struggled to say just above a whisper.

Smack!

"Bitch-ass nigga, keep my mama name out your mouth!"

Just like the sky was certainly blue, Demetrius certainly felt that last slap, and he certainly heard the person slapping him claim to be Mel's son, which was impossible, unless it was ...

"Byron?" he mumbled as his vision began clearing up by the second. He diligently looked around until he saw the silhouette of a figure standing directly over him to his right. "Son, is that—"

Smack!

Whatever drug that was in his system making him groggy began to progressively wear off after each slap he'd received.

Although he was damn near coherent now, he still couldn't move. And the silhouetted figure was still unrecognizable to him. "Who…" Demetrius cleared his throat. "Who are you? Where am I?"

The silhouetted figure just stood there, motionless and speechless.

Demetrius tried to move again, but he too remained motionless. He slowly turned his head and looked at his left arm and noticed there was rope wrapped firmly around his wrist. In a circular motion, he scanned over his body and saw his other limbs were also wrapped firmly with rope. He finally noted that not only was he tautly tied-up, his naked body also formed a perfect X on the bed he laid on. *Shit, Cesar caught up with me*, he thought as he closed his eyes for good, *I wonder if they got anybody else*?

Smack!

"Motherfucker, just kill me!" Demetrius snapped, with blood spilling from his mouth. "And tell Cesar I said fuck him ... and his money too!"

Boisterous laughter filled the room.

"If I wasn't tied up to this bed, motherfucker, you wouldn't find shit funny!" Demetrius fought to free himself. "I swear I'll beat …"

The oh-so familiar sound of a gun cocking caused Demetrius to shut up.

"You in a fucked-up predicament ta be talkin' all that big boy shit. I should just shoot your bitch-ass 'tween da eyes right now."

"What're you waiting for?"

"Shut da fuck up, Kilo!" the silhouetted figure yelled before pressing the cold barrel onto Demetrius' lips. "Da only reason why I haven't aired ya ass out yet is becuz ... I'm gonna have some fun wit'cha first." The silhouetted figure removed the gun from his lips. "Now, ta answer ya first question, I'm da person that's been anxiously waitin' fo' today."

"Hmph, Cesar sent some dumb nigga from the projects that has probably never killed anyone before to kill me. I say that because you said you're so anxious to kill me. Am I correct? You are a dumb nigga from the projects that has never killed a man, right?"

The silhouetted figure laughed boisterously again. "If you look around, dummy, you'll see exactly who sent me ta kill you. As a matter ah fact, lemme hit da lights so you can get a better look," the silhouetted figure said before turning to hit the light switch by the door.

The bright light directly above Demetrius made him instinctively shut his eyes tightly as soon as the light came on. A few seconds passed before he slowly opened his eyes, and he squinted until he was used to the bright light. When he was finally capable of seeing, he saw the person was gone. He cautiously anticipated something happening, and when nothing happened after a while, he eventually surveyed the room. He looked from one side of the room to the other a couple times, then his jaw felt like it was no longer attached to his skull. *This cannot be the place*, he thought as his jaw rested on his heaving chest, *I know I'm dreaming now.*

"I thought you'd fo'get this place," said the person that was wearing a hoodie with a hat, while stepping into the room with a .380 in hand, "but I see that'cha didn't." The hoodie made it difficult to distinguish facial features, and the hat was tilted down so low it casted a shadow over the face, leaving just a small portion of the mouth to be seen kind of clearly. "It's exactly da same as when you left here da last time," the person added. "Well, da body is gone an' all da blood has been cleaned up, but it's da same."

The voice is really starting to sound familiar, but it's more ... manly, Demetrius reasoned. "Who are you, you timid motherfucker?" he asked aggressively, and one-hundred-percent clear-headed now.

The lights abruptly went off.

Soon after the lights were off, the rattling of a belt buckle being unfastened could be heard. The unzipping of a zipper followed after that.

"What the fuck is going on here?" Demetrius shouted, wishing dearly that his eyesight adjusted rapidly to the darkness so he could actually see what the person was doing. "What're you doing?" he decided to ask, wishing dearly that the person would answer him.

Without replying, the silhouetted figure appeared at the foot of the bed. The person then proceeded to climb onto the bed, eventually positioning himself between Demetrius' wide-open legs.

In a last-ditch effort to free himself, Demetrius mustered up all of the strength he had and began to wriggle and squirm like a worm about to go on a hook. Seeing that he wasn't doing nothing but tiring himself out, he yelled, "Man, get off me! What the fuck are you doing?"

Demetrius still was unable to see. But he did hear the eerie response whispered into his right ear.

"I'm 'bout ta give you a dose of your own medicine, Kilo."

Demetrius didn't get a chance to utter another word, because something was immediately placed forcefully over his swollen, bleeding mouth, stifling his remarks. And thus was the beginning of a brutal act of sodomy.

Approximately forty unforgettable, and unconscionable, minutes of rupturing and battering Demetrius' lower opening of the alimentary canal passed by before an alarm sounded. After the alarm went off, the horrendous sex act ended.

Demetrius was beyond fatigued, and he felt less than a man. Although he determinedly fought to get out of the restraints for the first couple minutes of the hideous deed, he eventually weakened and ceased struggling. It was from that moment forth when he cried, prayed, and wondered why he was enduring the most severe ordeals and afflictions of his entire life during the last couple days. Once that alarm sounded though, and the violation of his body sanctity was over, he finally accepted his fate, which was a big pill to swallow.

Karma is a bitch! he concluded as he silently lie stretched out in excruciating pain.

The smell of pure hate consumed the room as the person slowly exited Demetrius' impaired anus and climbed off the bed, leaving Demetrius to lay in an unsavory mixture of sweat, blood, urine and feces.

Moments later, the light suddenly came on, causing Demetrius to immediately close his puffy eyes. Upon opening his bleary eyes, he observed his molester standing in the middle of the room and facing him. Then he observed that his molester left their pants down around their ankles, giving him a direct view of the long, huge blood- and shit-covered dick that dangled while somewhat still erect.

After further inspection of the unique organ, he saw something was just not right. "What the fuck ....?" was all he got out before his molester began doing something more than rather peculiar. He watched his molester reach down with both hands at the back of both thighs, and the sound of unfastening followed. What happened next caused him to gasp. "Who-who-who are you?" he stammered, as the crude apparatus that took his manhood now rested upon the floor.

Struck with horror, Demetrius then watched the person slowly and dramatically commence to removing their hoodie, while keeping the hat on with their head bowed down. During the process, it seemed as if the person allowed him a quick peek, and that was when he noticed the person had a girl-like countenance. In the same fashion as removing the hoodie, he continued watching the person as they simultaneously began raising their head while lifting off their blacked-out Detroit Tigers fitted hat. The more the person's head raised, the deeper the shock overcame him. If he hadn't already got the shit fucked out of him, literally, he would've surely defecated on himself when he saw standing before him, totally transformed was ...

"It look like you wanna say my name, but I'm tellin' you right now that'cha better not call me by that bitch name!" the person said, fully exposed before pausing briefly. "You should know my real name though, since it was yo' bitch-ass that killed my mama ... an' raped me when I was just four years old!"

"No ... no, you're *dead*!"

"Yes, it's me—alive, an' still thuggin'. But I have ta admit that'cha kinda right 'bout me bein' dead, cuz you did kill da lil girl I was back then when you left me in this house slumped. So, as for my name, my name on da streets now is Devon. See, you killed Devona Herrera a long time ago!"

"No, it couldn't have been you this whole time. You set me up?" Demetrius asked, quivering like a mutt stuck outside during a severe thunderstorm. "I won't believe that."

After confirming with a small nod it was indeed her that orchestrated his downfall, she briefly relived the entire ordeal, starting from the very beginning and only leaving out minor events.

The story started off with her telling how she was supposed to have died that sad, unforgettable day, due to a significant amount of blood loss. She was told by Miss Candace the only reason she didn't perish that day was because of Sheryl, Demetrius' then fourteen-year-old sister.

Around seven that morning, Sheryl was walking home a friend's house, when she stopped by Melina's to see if she could earn a little money by babysitting little Devona later on that morning. Sheryl repetitiously knocked while calling out for Melina. Just before leaving, though, she obscurely glimpsed into the front living room window and saw the motionless body laid out in Melina's room, surrounded by both blood and the early morning sunlight. After that grisly discovery, Sheryl ran next door to get help, and that was unfortunately the last time Devon heard of Sheryl.

Closer to death than life upon arrival to the hospital, she immediately underwent extensive surgery to stop the internal hemorrhaging from having her tiny womb and rectum ruptured. Thereafter, five of the eight months in the hospital were spent in critical condition in ICU. Then, three days after her fifth birthday, she was finally discharged with a womb that was no longer able to create life. Yet, instead of being happy when she left the hospital, she was extremely low in spirit.

From there, she went directly into the custody of the DFACS until Miss Candace gained guardianship of her a few months later. She was then raised to the best of Miss Candace's ability in a rather homely environment.

During her early childhood, though, Miss Candace immediately saw how she deliberately hated being around all men, knowing very well that resentment only derived from what happened to her. As a subsequence, Miss Candace wasn't too surprised when the development of "Devon" materialized around the time she was turning eight years old. And although Miss Candace didn't praise the transition, stopping the transformation itself would've been more selfish than anything, because Devona lacked a personality prior to creating Devon.

RahRah, on the other hand, simply loved the fact that she wanted to be one of the boys. However, RahRah had to gain her confidence first, which took almost two years to accomplish from the day they initially met. He eventually became the only male she completely trusted. While taking on the job to teach her the tricks and trades on how to be the realest of her kind, RahRah began treating her exactly like the rest of the niggas he dealt with, straight up overlooking the fact that she was a pretty and moderately fearful little girl.

As Miss Candace continuously disapproved of and criticized the bad habits she was picking up from her "brother," RahRah persisted to be a terrible influence on her, by teaching her how to smoke weed and snort powder. Making her fight boys that were bigger and older than her. Showing her how to load, hold, and shoot different types of guns. Basically, teaching her how to survive in the wicked, merciless streets. RahRah instinctively knew she appreciated the tough love and her gladiator training as a jit, because that helped spread and enforce her new identity in the hood. And she wouldn't have been widely accepted and well-respected as Devon to this day without RahRah's teachings.

Soon after that, around age eleven, she began to wear sports bras with baggy clothes to conceal the curves she possessed and her feminine features. She also cut her hair low and rocked deep waves for six to seven years, before she started growing dreads. Furthermore, it was around that same period when she found herself sexually attracted to females.

Although she was officially perceived as a *he* in the hood by age twelve, she was often brought back to reality when she had nightmares of that life-changing, traumatizing day. Usually, after every nightmare she had—they occurred less but became more intense and realistic as time progressed, she would awake with an insatiable hunger to seek revenge.

Since the age of thirteen, she'd committed herself to searching for and asking about any man that called himself Kilo. But her search and inquiries gradually lessened after a while, because the few tips she pursued led to the wrong man, or a dead end, so she presumed the Kilo she was looking for was either dead, locked up, or never returning back to the city.

Then, on a night that was supposed to be special, her twenty-fourth birthday, she was caught completely off guard when she confronted Demetrius at her party for the first time since he raped her. And, to this day, she didn't have a reasonable explanation for not killing him that very night, because killing him would've been the best birthday present she'd ever received. However, she admitted she was crazy for playing with him by trying to set him up with the white bitch, Ivory. But once he killed both Ivory and Gudda, she had no choice but to take matters in her own hand, only after she fled the city first.

While fuming in Cocoa Beach about how she may have ruined her only opportunity to get back at him, she came up with the wild idea of transforming back to a ... woman. She knew she and her mother resembled each other, from seeing a couple pictures of Melina that Miss Candace had, so making him fall for her was most definitely the easy part. Yet, the biggest problem she faced was whether the resemblance she shared with her mother would forewarn him, preventing her from attaining her vengeance.

So, basically, her scheme only looked achievable in her mind. Therefore, she commenced to plotting further.

The transition itself was difficult to carry out, because she had no clue at all how to act feminine. Since she didn't know how much longer he was going to remain in the area, although she had people watching him, she had to learn how to do a lot in a little bit of time.

With Rhapsody's integral and resourceful help, she had to first buy an entire new wardrobe that ranged from casual to captivating, which made her very uncomfortable and to think thrice about her "brilliant" idea. Not one to give up, though, she continued by readily chopping off her long dreads before purchasing a few haute couture wigs and other accessories. Secondly, Rhapsody taught her how to apply makeup by herself and how to walk sexily in heels, which was the most difficult to learn. Thirdly, she had to discipline herself on how to speak more femininely, while also toning down the Ebonics and curse words. Finally, and most importantly, she had to really discipline and prepare herself mentally, physically, and emotionally, on how to tolerate being around him, while remaining friendly enough to not cause any suspicions. Her goal was to ultimately gain his trust, because she wasn't only going to kill him at that appointed time, she was going to ruin him first for making her life a living hell.

After twelve days of rigorous around-the-clock training, Beauti made her debut at The Palace. Although she had the club owner's support, it was required that she'd wear a stripper's outfit, but she didn't have to dance for any customers or go up on stage unless she desired. She worked eight hours a day for a full week prior to that highly anticipated "second encounter" in order to get accustomed to the patrons admiring her exclusive never-before-seen body and calling her all types of bitches and ho's.

When that time finally came for the second encounter, she thought it would be much different than the first. Yet, it was just as miserable, because she wanted nothing more in the whole world than to just pull out her .380 and make his soul float. Instead of deviating from her precious plans though, she played her role for the greater goal, to take *everything* from him!

Over time and after practicing daily while alone, she really began to feel like she was Beauti, a competent, business-minded, sexy and independent woman. She found herself struggling with putting her true feelings to the side and becoming the character Beauti at first, until she eventually became so deep into character, she almost forgot Devon had a mission to complete. Plus, at one point in time, it was like she had Stockholm Syndrome, because she started to actually like the character he became.

So again, she came awfully close to aborting the mission of ruining him, and she was just going to settle for killing him by any means. But then she remembered someone once said, "You find a way to go further when there's no way out." And that was exactly what she did.

Finally coping with what she had to do to succeed, she began to take things somewhat less seriously. Easing up a tad clearly worked in her favor because he gradually came to confide in her enough to offer her a job. Once he gave her a top job at one of his contrived stores, giving her the right-of-way to dig for vital information on his illegal ventures, she came close to calling off the mission for a third time. The reason that time was because of him asking her if she knew Melina Herrera. Nevertheless, after feeling she avoided having to answer that question, along with any more questions that pertained to her mother, she felt comfortable enough to proceed.

Thereafter, she went back to work and began obtaining information that was sufficient in bringing his empire down. That meal ticket presented itself when he invited her to his condo to discuss business before he left for Peru.

During that casual visit, she didn't have any intentions of snooping around. However, when she saw the things by the door that he was taking with him to Peru, she seized the opportunity to palm something of importance, which happened to be his treasured black book. Once she was in possession of that book, she was able to thoroughly plan his demise, but she needed help to pull it off.

She immediately called upon her dawgs from around the way known as Sunset Syndicate. After she provided them with all the details on the lick, such as where the coke was hidden in the warehouse and how to disable the alarm, she instructed them to burn the remaining coke that they weren't able to tote, and to place the black book in plain sight once they cleared the scene.

Whereas that heist seemed perfect, the only flaw was that lone Triple S member being killed and left behind at the scene amongst the casualties, causing her to worry that the robbery would eventually lead back to her. So, for a fourth time, she considered pulling out, but she was in way too deep to stop then.

Shortly afterwards, he'd invited her to his Coral Gables estate, which was rather surprising to her because she would've sworn he didn't trust a soul at that point. She was glad he'd invited her though, since she really enjoyed how he practically begged for her help and propositioned her with the First Lady position, after lying about what was really happening to him. She was getting a good laugh inside at his distress while pretending to sympathize with him.

Things took kind of a drastic turn, however, when she received that text message from Miracle saying Virgil's mangled body was found in the Everglades, and she almost panicked again. But after chewing it over in his bathroom, she knew if Virgil did happen to tell him anything before dying, it wasn't enough to implicate either Beauti or Devon.

She then prayed that once he found out the feds seized his accounts, and were also looking for him, he would run to her as a last resort instead of fleeing the state. Receiving that call from her girl Mystic was the answer to her prayer, and she knew the finale was soon to come at that point.

It was a good thing she'd planned ahead by putting a few of her bitches on point at StudioX, Illusions, and The Palace, so that when he showed up at either one of these clubs looking for her, she could further instruct whomever on what to do afterwards. When she got the call from Mystic, her orders were to pour the contents of the little glass vial, which she gave to all the bitches involved on separate occasions, into his drink. She would call back every ten minutes or so, until it was confirmed he drank the liquid, then she would handle everything from there.

When she arrived at The Palace and found him out cold, she had Big Herb carry him out the back of the club, and put him in the back of a rented Tahoe. Big Herb drove until pulling up to a little quaint house she'd bought about six years ago as soon as she had enough money; the same house where the most tragic event of her life took place. Big Herb then assisted her in stringing him up to the bed before he left in the SUV.

There was a brief silence, signaling that the chilling story had come to an end.

"I wanted ta wrap this shit up on August 17," Devon continued, "which is da date my mama died, but that's almost five months from now. So I decided ta end this shit around da time she passed away, which was approximately five in the mornin'." She pulled her pants up over the filthy boxers, reached into her pocket and pulled out her phone. "It was perfect timin' when ya drunk that stuff twelve hours ago, cuz it started wearin' off 'bout a hour an' a half ago.

"Now, I was gonna let Beauti off you so that'cha could see how you let some pussy get'cha trapped up. But since *I* need da closure, I decided ta show you who I am only after I did da same ta you that was done ta me, which was rape you while you couldn't do shit ta stop me!"

Demetrius sympathetically gazed into eyes that he now noticed looked exactly like Melina's and said, "While I was looking for a friend ... I found my enemy." He paused. "Do you want to know why I did what I did that day?" he said as if he had a justifiable reason. "Besides the fact that your mother set me up to get robbed, I was ... fed up. I was fed up and ashamed of being in love with a crackhead, especially one I helped create. I had a hand in making your mother a junkie, so I … I killed what I created, rather than watch the one woman I truly loved disintegrate before my eyes."

"An' what about me, huh? Why did you take my womanhood from me?" Devon began to cry, which was something she found herself doing a lot lately. "You single-handedly fucked up my life. Not only did you take my mama away from me, you took my innocence, my dignity, *and* my ability to be a mother." She wiped the tears from her eyes and regained her composure. "Well, it don't even matter any mo'. I've come ta accept my destiny, an' I'm proud of who I am now. An' once I edit this tape, yo' people gonna be ashamed ta say they even knew you."

Demetrius puzzledly asked, "What tape?"

Devon didn't answer. She simply walked over to the closet, slid open the closet door which was already ajar, and pressed stop on the video camera. She then said, "The tape of some guy fuckin' da shit outta you."

"You bitch!"

"They say blood doesn't wash away blood," Devon said while pulling a .38 special off the top shelf in the closet. "But in this case, that shit don't apply, becuz my mama's blood is thicker than that Kool-Aid runnin' through your veins."

"Wait, since you said that, let me tell you some …"

POW!

One shot was all it took to splatter his brains completely over the headboard, walls, and ceiling. "It's finally over," Devon said unto herself, "and I can hopefully rest peacefully at night now since I know he's in hell."

She began to carefully wipe down everything she may have touched in the house currently leased out under the name of a person that didn't exist. Next, she grabbed the camera and the disgusting bloody strap-on before she double-checked to make sure that she hadn't forgotten anything. She then cut off the light and casually left, leaving Demetrius assed-out, literally.

As she proceeded to walk the two blocks to 20th Street and Beautiful Avenue, to chop it up with whomever was out and about early this morning, she pulled out her phone.

"Hello?"

"What it do, baby?"

"Devon, is that you?" Miracle shrieked.

"Who else you got callin' ya baby? A nigga been outta town fo' a lil while an' you already got somebody else?"

Miracle sucked her teeth. "Better stop playin' with me." She paused. "Is it over?"

"Lemme put it like this. Tell Rhapsody ta brang my lil nigga Kamani home. It's 'bout time you, him an' me live under one roof."

CHAPTER TWENTY-EIGHT

March 14, 2009 9:49 am

Wellington, FL

Life after settling a prolonged beef was usually no better than it was beforehand, because hypothetically speaking, a new wound caused all the old ones to ache again. Indeed, the apprehensiveness may have vanished because of the threat being eliminated, but the misery and uncertainty of life still lingers. Instead of living that carefree life as expected, there was always the possibility retaliation was in the making. So, the expectation of living a laid-back life and happily ever after was going to be a hard pill to swallow.

However, that wasn't the case for Devon. At the moment, she couldn't have been any happier. The last four days were the gayest four days of her life, pun intended. She slept much better, the high she got from doing drugs and drinking seemed more intense. Her days flew by smoother, and her relationship with Miracle was absolutely perfect. And since she returned back to her everyday life of getting money by all means, everything she did now had a newfound joy in it. She simply had a totally new outlook on life because her one and only nemesis was now a memory.

This jubilant morning, she was presently twenty-five minutes into making new, fond memories.

"Aaahhhh, that's it," Miracle gently moaned while sprawled out on the bed. "Eat this good pussy, Dee."

While on both knees at the foot of the bed, Devon majestically lashed and lapped at the good pussy indeed as it barely protruded from the edge of the mattress. Even though Miracle intermittently jerked from numerous overpowering spasms, she persisted to maneuver her unearthly tongue in and out and around Miracle's pink tunnel of love. She then forced her critically acclaimed mouth muscle into overdrive when she felt Miracle was at the threshold of ...

"Bust this good pussy open, Dee," Rhapsody suddenly groaned loudly from the doggystyle position on the floor. "Mmmm, that's right."

Unquestionably, Devon crudely bashed and pummeled the good pussy as it readily poked out in the air. Although Rhapsody occasionally shuddered from multiple devastating orgasms, she continued to work her phenomenal mechanism forward and backwards, into Rhapsody's oozing coral-colored treasure chest. She then drove her top-of-the-line synthetic staff unsparingly once she sensed Rhapsody was on the brink of ...

It was merely a coincidence when both Miracle and Rhapsody sexually erupted at the same time from Devon's proficient multitasking performance. While the number of times they had climaxed may have differed, the explosive feeling that simultaneously overcame them during their most recent orgasm was undeniably identical in intensity, because they both let out emotional grunts as their bodies quivered unsteadily.

Now that Devon had accomplished her difficult mission, which was to make both Miracle and Rhapsody bust an incredible fat nut synchronously, it was her time to be catered to for her award-winning services.

In spite of the fact that both Miracle and Rhapsody had yet to snap out of the euphoric trance they were in, Devon slowly crawled into bed and laid on her back next to a whimpering Miracle, and said, "Aye, it's time ta show me some love now since y'all done got off. An' it's anythang goes. No holds barred!"

"Are you serious?" Miracle asked, full of shock.

"Damn! I changed my mind now since you said it like that, so just do da usual. An' maybe I'll tell you, dependin' on how I feel, ta go all da way," Devon replied.

Rather than being satisfied herself, Devon was the type of butch that naturally loved to give pleasure to her partner. However, the only person she ever allowed access to her exclusive goodies every so often was Miracle. And when she did commission Miracle to please her, there was no penetration of any kind at all. The reason she didn't want her pussy being touched or probed by just anybody in any type of way, had little to do with being insecure. She was just so traumatized by what had happened to her, she was simply scared to feel that agonizing sensation ever again.

Today, nonetheless, she deemed she was no longer scared. So, not only was she going to let two people have access to her rarely tampered-with pussy, she was even considering letting one of them, most likely Miracle, carefully probe her with a vibrator or small dildo. And because of that, today was certainly a landmark in her life either way. *It's about time I live my life to the fullest,* she thought as she inhaled deeply and exhaled, *because I only got one life.*

Miracle began the remarkable event by delicately and passionately pop-kissing Devon's robust lips multiple times. She gradually forced Devon's mouth open by biting and pulling down on her bottom lip, then she proceeded to massage Devon's tongue with hers. She caressed Devon's mouth for a while, before she lightly dragged the tip of her tongue from Devon's lips to her chin, down the length of her neck. Then from the base of her neck over to the left side of her neck, and from her "spot" up to her ear.

She elegantly flicked her tongue in and out of Devon's ear a few times like an energetic lizard before sucking on her pulpy earlobes. After Devon produced an erotic moan and shivered, she then dragged the tip of her tongue from Devon's ear to her collarbone, over to the center of her chest, and down to her left nipple. Upon reaching Devon's atomic nipple, which was centered in a half-dollar-sized shade of dark brown, she lustfully licked all over the breast before finally taking most of the B-cup into her moist mouth.

While Miracle was being all affectionate and tender up top, Rhapsody was down bottom being straight-up nasty and rough.

First, Rhapsody ambitiously sucked off the remaining juices that clung to Devon's strap-on. As soon as the massive dick was spic-and-span, from helmet to balls, she removed it and grasped a mouthful of the outer fatty folds of Devon's tight pussy and sturdily nibbled upon them. She mauled Devon's labia majora for a bit before she ungracefully ran much of her wide, thick tongue from Devon's tightly drawn lips to her dainty inner folds, to her pink pearl, and down to her puckered asshole.

She stiffly stroked her tongue around Devon's contracted asshole a couple times, as if she were licking an ice cream cone on a hot day, before trying to drive her tongue into the snug backdoor. After Devon sexily wailed while twitching, she then ran her wide, thick tongue from Devon's asshole down the crack of her ass, down her right inner thigh to the back of her knee, and from the back of her "other spot" down her right leg to her foot. Upon arriving at Devon's pedicured foot, which was smooth and cotton soft, she aggressively licked all between the toes before finally cramming the five luscious digits into her sultry mouth.

It eventually became obvious between Rhapsody and Miracle that they were immersed in a fierce competition to outdo one another, rather than focusing on having fun and contributing generously to Devon's illustrious breakthrough. Devon, however, didn't notice their rivalry for she was too busy indulging in the well-overdue moment. So, for Devon's sake, neither one of them openly displayed their resurrected displeasure of each other, and they put the beef amongst them on hold and teamed up to kiss, lick, and suck on Devon from head to toe.

"Mmmmm-huh, that shit feels soooooo good," Devon professed as she petted the two heads currently between her thighs. The dual action of the tongues that flickered and slurped her sweet slushy induced her legs to tremble and goosebumps to blanket her body. *I can really get used to this pampering,* she thought as she sensuously bit her bottom lip due to the pleasant sensation that flowed continuously up and down her body. "Aye, y'all come up here an' give me a kiss," she instructed softly, stopping the cunnilingus.

Miracle and Rhapsody both obediently ceased what they were doing and crawled up to Devon's face. With Rhapsody on the left, Devon in the middle and Miracle on the right, the trio then partook in a three-way kiss. As slippery tongues journeyed from mouth to mouth and hands wandered from body to body, the assemblage of unadulterated lust carried on for eleven diligent minutes, until ....

"Sssssssss," Devon hissed before sucking in air through clenched teeth. While wincing in pain, she said, "Ooooowwwww, stop. That shit ..."

"Just go wit it, Dee," Rhapsody whispered into Devon's ear. "I promise, it's gonna feel better once ya get used to it."

Devon panted like an animal outside in South Florida in the month of July. As she bit her lip even harder, she said, "O-o-okay, just go… slow."

Now that Devon was alert, giving Rhapsody approval to continue, Rhapsody proceeded to finger Devon's narrow pussy again. As they all kept on kissing and fondling one another, she slowly inserted two fingers into Devon's exquisite shallowness and worked them in and out. After working two fingers through Devon, she added a third into the now slippery canal and propelled all three nimble fingers back and forth, while gradually picking up speed. Within two minutes of introducing the third finger, she was finger-fucking Devon's pussy as fast as her hand allowed.

The discomfort combined with the unfamiliar feeling of euphoria resulted in Devon's body becoming tense. As Rhapsody firmly finger-fucked her to a point of no return, she became temporarily paralyzed.

Then, suddenly, something strange began happening to Devon, and there was absolutely nothing she could do to stop the occurrence.

Devon's eyes swiftly rolled to the back of her head. Next, her jaws locked like a pair of vise-grips. Then her back arched off the bed as her limbs became stiff as two-by-fours. And finally, her toes curled up like corn chips. All these unknown signs to her only meant she was on the verge of ...

"Aaaaahhhhhhhh … mmmmmmmmmm … oh-oh-oh … oh shit!" Devon screamed at the top of her lungs as the feeling of lava flowing from her pussy subdued her. It was simply a "miracle" when the feeling of "rhapsody" engulfed her body after she experienced her first real orgasm. Wave after wave of a tingling sensation traveled back and forth from her head to her feet afterwards, and she survived a spree of brief spasmodic contractions of her muscles.

After partially recovering from the wonderful feeling that swamped her, Devon said, "Boy, I'm glad that nigga dead cuz I been missin' out on some hellafied shit." She had the biggest grin on her face when she added, "Yes, I'm glad."

"I'm glad, too," Miracle said before leaning over to kiss Devon. "Now your aunt can rest in peace, and you can call your cousin and tell her you took care of her mother's murderer and her molester. That should give your cousin some closure."

Damn, should I finally tell Miracle it was me all that shit happened to? Devon weighed in her mind.

After a quick second of thinking, Devon said, "Yeah ... I'll call my cousin tomorrow."

"I'm gonna turn yo' ass out now, Daddy," Rhapsody declared while sucking Devon's first nut ever off of her fingers. "Or, should I call ya Big Mama now?"

"Hoe, don't get it fucked up now. I'm still Daddy ta you an' er'body else," Devon retorted. "This didn't change a fuckin' thang. I'm just enjoyin' myself now. So you can miss me with that 'Big Mama' bullshit!"

While Rhapsody remained silent after being checked by Devon, Miracle was snickering and smiling at Rhapsody's dumb ass for trying Devon like everything was namby-pamby now.

Knock at door

"Uh-oh," Miracle blurted out before hopping off the bed and putting on some clothes. "Shit! Y'all get under the covers."

"Who that is?" Rhapsody asked fearfully.

Knock at door

Miracle hurriedly walked to the door. She quickly glanced back at Devon and Rhapsody to make sure they were covered, then she opened the door.

"Momma," Lil Kamani said, while wiping his eyes with the back of his hand, "I heard screaming."

"Everythin' okay, baby," Miracle said to her son as he stood in the doorway in his SpongeBob pajamas. She stooped down and hugged Kamani. "I'm sorry we woke you up, but that was crazy Dee screamin' like that because she ... because she …"

"Becuz I just seen this big ole' spider," Devon chimed in. "It ran away somewhere an' …" Her eyes grew wide. "An' it's by your foot, lil man!"

Kamani didn't even bother to see if there was really a big ole' spider by his foot. Instead, he shot down the hallway faster than a crackhead that found an invitation to a free crack giveaway.

"Why you scare my baby, Dee?" Miracle said while giving Devon the evil eye. "You dead wrong. I just hope you know I'm goin' to get you back for that."

"You need ta sign Lil Man up fo' track cuz that boy fast as hell." Devon laughed. "My bad, though, I forgot that my Lil Man hates spiders." She casually shrugged after sitting up. "At least he gone an' we don't have ta do no furtha explainin', right?"

"Ugh, I'm goin' to get you. Mark my words." Miracle frowned. "Now, I'm goin' to go calm him down and wash his face and stuff, then I'm goin' to fix him breakfast."

Devon excitedly said, "Oooh, I want some eggs, grits an' …"

"Hmph, no you don't!" Miracle rolled her eyes. "Well, you ain't gettin' nothin' until you apologize to my baby," she said, before suddenly turning around and disappearing.

"Oh, well, since I have ta get up anyway, I might as well go say sorry ta Lil Man. Besides, I'm hungry as I dunno what, an' I'm not gonna miss out on Miracle's good cookin'." Devon proceeded to get out of the bed. "I have some place ta be in a lil while, so what'chu doin' today?"

"I wanna be wit'chu," Rhapsody said pitifully.

"Naw, you can't slide wit me this mornin'. Maybe ..."

"No, Daddy." Rhapsody sat up in the bed. "I want to be with you. Just you an' me ... forever."

"Girl, you talkin' nonsense."

"Daddy, I'm all you'll ever need." She stared feverishly into Devon's eyes. "Look at all I did for you. Rememba, it was me who gave that guy twenty thousand for ya, an' I ain't want no money back. I did that an' everythang else becuz I love you." She sucked her teeth, then said, "Besides, I'm twice da woman ..."

"Keema, shut da fuck up befo' you say somethin' you gonna regret." Devon walked butt-naked towards the bathroom. "Bitch 'bout ta ruin my beautiful day already wit that fuck shit," she mumbled to no one particular before closing the bathroom door behind her.

Rhapsody sat under the covers and sobbed. "No, it's you that will regret not choosing me over that bitch, Miracle," she said unto herself as tears covered most of her baby doll face, "because there's absolutely nothing worse than a real bitch scorned!"

***

March 14, 2009 11:20 am

West Palm Beach, FL

Even after the delightful episode she'd just had at home this morning, Devon was now ambling through a cemetery, and found herself with conflicting feelings. Because Demetrius was across town being placed in the dirt this lovely morning, she was truly the happiest person on the planet today. But she was also incredibly sad, because she was in Regal Palms Memorial Park, visiting both her mother's and Miss Candace's graves.

The varied feelings she now had was the outcome of a meaningful dilemma she faced just before departing from the house. The dilemma derived from Miracle asking her an earnest question, and that question was whether she was going to visit her mother and Miss Candace as Devon or Devona. After taking some time to think over that damn good question, she considered it pointless to pretend Devona was the person she'd been living as all these years. However, she reasoned with herself that it was perhaps best "Devon" pay respects in a formal black woman's suit with black heels. *I know Miss Candace is certainly going to smile down from Heaven once she sees me looking ladylike,* she thought at that time, *and my mother will, too.*

The first person she decided to visit was Miss Candace. When she arrived at the grave, a cool gust of wind swept by and ruffled up the curly, shoulder-length weave on her head.

"Dang, Miss Candace," she uttered as she stooped down and began clearing the debris and weeds from around the headstone that read, Candace Ann Johnson. "You didn't have ta mess up my new hair just ta say hello." She smiled. "I know it's you becuz you do it er'time I visit. Oh, an' I wanna apologize fo' not comin' by in a while. I been busy wit ... Y'know what I been up to.

"Anyways, how do I look? I know you smilin' right now becuz da last time you saw me dressed up all feminine was when I was around nine or ten." She paused. "I gotta say, though, I can get used to dressin' up like a woman becuz it's not that bad, plus I seen a bunch of cute clothes that fit me. Da only problem I have ta get used ta, howeva, is dudes tryna holla at me when I'm lookin' ... sexy. Ewww!" she concluded before laughing.

She rapped with Miss Candace for the next ten to fifteen minutes. And during the conversation as usual, she avidly thanked Miss Candace for everything, because only God knows where she would've been today if it wasn't for her guardian angel, Miss Candace.

"Well, sweet Miss Candace, it's time ta say goodbye," she mumbled with tears welling up in her eyes. "I really hate this part becuz I miss you sooooo much. You were the mother I never had, an' I hate that'chu gone." She sniffled. "I will truly always love an' miss you, sweet Miss Candace, an' so does RahRah. I'll tell him you said what's up an' that'chu love an' miss him, too." She then kissed her hand and placed it on the headstone. "Bye, Miss Candace. It's time ta go visit my mama now. An' don't you tell her I'm comin' eitha. I wanna surprise her."

As she stood up, another cool gust of wind swept past her. "I know you're always watching over me," she said to herself while walking off. "Thanks, sweet Miss Candace."

Her mother's resting place was on the opposite side of the cemetery, so she moseyed along while thinking about a multitude of things. After about six minutes, her mother's plot came into view. As she drew closer, she could plainly see there were two individuals standing nearby her mother's grave. *They must be visiting somebody close to my mama's grave*, she reasoned as she walked forward.

She was probably twenty feet away when she walked up on the man and woman that had their backs to her, and she noticed the man and woman were looking down at the tombstone that read, Celestine Melina Herrera.

The woman turned around, which also caused the man to turn around, when Devon walked into her peripheral vision. The middle-aged black woman then said, "Hello? Are we in your way, or are you ... Wait a minute …" The woman began to study Devon. "Lord, this can not ... No, it can't be you."

"An' … who are you?" Devon asked kind of rudely.

"Oh, my God, it is you! Devona, I haven't seen you since ... since they took you to the hospital." The woman approached Devon and embraced her. "How are you, baby?"

"Ummm … Excuse me, but who are you?" Devon asked again as she stood stiff in the woman's embrace.

"It's me ... Sheryl. You probably don't remember me because you were a little girl back when ... I was a good friend of your mother's." The woman stepped back from Devon and glanced down at Melina's grave. "Yeah, she was my best friend and I looked up to her as if she was my sister, and I miss her sincerely." She looked at Devon again. "Once they took you to the hospital that day, I never saw or heard from you again. Then, after Melina's funeral, I remember my mother and I just upped and moved to Jacksonville for no reason, and that's where I've been since."

Devon was unable to speak. Here it was, in the flesh, the very person that was responsible for her existence. She could only remember a little about Sheryl from when she was younger. There was so much that she wanted to say to this wonderful woman. But all she could say was ...

"Thank you." The two women embraced each other again, and the only difference this time around was that the embrace was heartfelt from both parties. She then added, "I would be in a grave myself if you didn't stop by da house that day. So, thank you."

After the brief sentimental reunion, Sheryl said, "Oh, I'm being rude. I haven't introduced you to the person that's with me."

In Devon's eyes, the young man that stood behind Sheryl was rather handsome. After a minute of looking over the guy, she began to feel queasy for no apparent cause. *He resembles somebody,* she thought as she stared nauseously at the young man, *he looks kind of like ...*

"Devona," Sheryl said, cutting Devon's thought short. "This is my nephew. He's Demetrius' son, and his name is Byron."

Bizzy stepped forward and said, "How you doin'?"

"I-I-I'm good," Devon stuttered as she examined the man that was a younger version of Demetrius. It was almost as if she was reliving the whole ordeal all over again ... twenty years hence, however.

"I don't know if you heard, but my brother Demetrius was brutally murdered a few days ago in West Palm Beach, and his funeral was held this morning. After the service was over, I decided to bring Byron over to meet…" Sheryl's mouth suddenly flew wide open. "Oh, my sweet Jesus! This is unbelievable! Hallelujah!"

"What's wrong wit'cha, Auntie?" Bizzy asked with a raised brow.

"It didn't occur to me until now." Sheryl smiled, then she faced Bizzy. "Byron, you won't believe this, but this girl right here is your little sister."

"What?" both Devon and Bizzy shouted simultaneously.

"I know, babies, God works in mysterious ways. How is it that Byron and I came from out of town to attend Demetrius' funeral and ran into you, Devona? I only brought Byron out here to visit the grave of the mother he never knew briefly, before we both headed to the reception? That's God, baby. Hah-haaa, Hallelujah! God is good all the time!"

"Hold on, hold on," Bizzy finally said. "My pops told me I was his only child."

"And I told you a while ago you have a sister, remember? I just didn't know if she was dead or alive ... until now."

"Yeah, I rememba, Auntie. An' when I asked my pops 'bout ... her ... he said that'chu didn't know what'chu were talkin' 'bout. Since then, I believed I was his only seed."

As Bizzy and Devon stared at each other without speaking, Sheryl said, "Listen, both of you have the same mother for sure. And it's a ninety-nine percent chance the two of you have the same father as well."

"But—" Bizzy started to say before he was cut off.

"Melina used to tell me all the time my brother Demetrius didn't claim Devona because she didn't resemble him. But, Melina swore up and down Devona was in fact Demetrius' daughter, and I truly believe she is." She faced Devon. "That's why I used to always babysit you, Devona, because Melina assured me you were my niece and I wanted to be around you as much as possible."

She then turned to Bizzy. "Demetrius took you away from your mother when Devona was born, which was when you were about one and a half years old. You never knew your mother or your sister, because you were raised by me and my mother, until your father took you to live with him for good in Tallahassee when you were five."

"Damn," Bizzy said with a hostile expression on his face, "so da man that meant da world ta me had me believin' I was da only child, an' my momma abandoned us ta live to this day, in Mexico wit her new family." He sighed. After a moment of silence, he continued, "My pops may have lied ta me 'bout a lotta thangs, but I know he did so ta protect me becuz he loved me, an' I'll always love him ... no matter what."

"Now, I have both my nephew and niece with me on this glorious day," Sheryl cheered. "I may have lost a family member this week, but our Savior has blessed me today. Hallelujah!"

While Bizzy stared at his long-lost sister in bewilderment, Devon stared back with an uneasy feeling overcoming her. She felt like throwing up, especially after hearing she killed ... her father! *Hell no, I'm not going for that*, she thought as she continued to stare directly at her 'supposedly' full-blooded brother. *There's no way in hell I'm accepting that child molesting, cold-blooded killer as my father, even if what Sheryl said is all true*!

Watching tears roll down Devon's face, Bizzy asked, "What's wrong … sis?"

What was wrong was he had no clue. Little did he know the little girl that had the will to live that sorrowful day, was the same little girl standing before him that had killed their father. And now that little girl was willing to kill her newfound brother, if that brother ever let it be known he wanted to avenge their infamous father's death.

As Devon stood there mute, with black mascara streaks running down her cheeks, she tried to erase the last ten minutes of her life from her mind. While trying not to accept the new, chilling discovery, the deafening sound of her mother's lethal gunshot began to echo in her head. That torturous, repeating gunshot brought on heartbreaking thoughts of the mother she barely knew, along with thoughts of how she would kill Bizzy without flinching if it came down to it. And all because of the hatred she had for the man formerly known as Kilo.

Little did he know.

To Be Continued…
A Gangsta's Karma 2
Coming Soon

Submission Guideline

Submit the first three chapters of your completed manuscript to ldpsubmissions@gmail.com, subject line: Your book's title. The manuscript must be in a .doc file and sent as an attachment. Document should be in Times New Roman, double spaced and in size 12 font. Also, provide your synopsis and full contact information. If sending multiple submissions, they must each be in a separate email.

Have a story but no way to send it electronically? You can still submit to LDP/Ca$h Presents. Send in the first three chapters, written or typed, of your completed manuscript to:

LDP: Submissions Dept
Po Box 944
Stockbridge, Ga 30281

DO NOT send original manuscript. Must be a duplicate.

Provide your synopsis and a cover letter containing your full contact information.

Thanks for considering LDP and Ca$h Presents.

NEW RELEASE

FRIEND OR FOE 3 by MIMI
A GANGSTA'S KARMA by FLAME

Coming Soon from Lock Down Publications/Ca$h Presents

BLOOD OF A BOSS **VI**

SHADOWS OF THE GAME II

TRAP BASTARD II

By **Askari**

LOYAL TO THE GAME **IV**

By **T.J. & Jelissa**

IF TRUE SAVAGE **VIII**

MIDNIGHT CARTEL IV

DOPE BOY MAGIC IV

CITY OF KINGZ III

By **Chris Green**

BLAST FOR ME **III**

A SAVAGE DOPEBOY III

CUTTHROAT MAFIA III

DUFFLE BAG CARTEL VII

HEARTLESS GOON VI

By **Ghost**

A HUSTLER'S DECEIT III

KILL ZONE II

BAE BELONGS TO ME III

A DOPE BOY'S QUEEN III

By **Aryanna**

COKE KINGS V

KING OF THE TRAP III

By **T.J. Edwards**

GORILLAZ IN THE BAY V

3X KRAZY III

De'Kari

KINGPIN KILLAZ IV

STREET KINGS III

PAID IN BLOOD III

Flame

CARTEL KILLAZ IV

DOPE GODS III

Hood Rich

SINS OF A HUSTLA II

ASAD

RICH $AVAGE II

By Troublesome

YAYO V

Bred In The Game 2

S. Allen

CREAM III

By Yolanda Moore

SON OF A DOPE FIEND III

HEAVEN GOT A GHETTO II

By Renta

LOYALTY AIN'T PROMISED III

By Keith Williams

I'M NOTHING WITHOUT HIS LOVE II

SINS OF A THUG II

TO THE THUG I LOVED BEFORE II

By Monet Dragun

QUIET MONEY IV

EXTENDED CLIP III

THUG LIFE IV

By **Trai'Quan**

THE STREETS MADE ME III

By **Larry D. Wright**

IF YOU CROSS ME ONCE II

By **Anthony Fields**

THE STREETS WILL NEVER CLOSE II

By K'ajji

HARD AND RUTHLESS III

A Gangsta's Karma

Von Diesel

KILLA KOUNTY II

By Khufu

MOBBED UP III

By King Rio

MONEY GAME II

By Smoove Dolla

A GANGSTA'S KARMA II

By FLAME

Available Now

RESTRAINING ORDER **I & II**

By **CA$H & Coffee**

LOVE KNOWS NO BOUNDARIES **I II & III**

By **Coffee**

RAISED AS A GOON I, II, III & IV

BRED BY THE SLUMS I, II, III

BLAST FOR ME I & II

ROTTEN TO THE CORE I II III

A BRONX TALE I, II, III

DUFFLE BAG CARTEL I II III IV V VI

HEARTLESS GOON I II III IV V

A SAVAGE DOPEBOY I II

DRUG LORDS I II III

CUTTHROAT MAFIA I II

KING OF THE TRENCHES

By **Ghost**

Flame

LAY IT DOWN **I & II**

LAST OF A DYING BREED I II

BLOOD STAINS OF A SHOTTA I & II III

By **Jamaica**

LOYAL TO THE GAME I II III

LIFE OF SIN I, II III

By **TJ & Jelissa**

BLOODY COMMAS I & II

SKI MASK CARTEL I II & III

KING OF NEW YORK I II,III IV V

RISE TO POWER I II III

COKE KINGS I II III IV

BORN HEARTLESS I II III IV

KING OF THE TRAP I II

By **T.J. Edwards**

IF LOVING HIM IS WRONG…I & II

LOVE ME EVEN WHEN IT HURTS I II III

By **Jelissa**

WHEN THE STREETS CLAP BACK I & II III

THE HEART OF A SAVAGE I II III

By **Jibril Williams**

A DISTINGUISHED THUG STOLE MY HEART I II & III

LOVE SHOULDN'T HURT I II III IV

RENEGADE BOYS I II III IV

PAID IN KARMA I II III

SAVAGE STORMS I II

AN UNFORESEEN LOVE

By **Meesha**

A GANGSTER'S CODE I &, II III

A GANGSTER'S SYN I II III

THE SAVAGE LIFE I II III

CHAINED TO THE STREETS I II III

BLOOD ON THE MONEY I II III

By J-Blunt

PUSH IT TO THE LIMIT

By **Bre' Hayes**

BLOOD OF A BOSS **I, II, III, IV, V**

SHADOWS OF THE GAME

TRAP BASTARD

By **Askari**

THE STREETS BLEED MURDER **I, II & III**

THE HEART OF A GANGSTA I II& III

By **Jerry Jackson**

CUM FOR ME I II III IV V VI VII

An **LDP Erotica Collaboration**

BRIDE OF A HUSTLA **I II & II**

THE FETTI GIRLS **I, II& III**

CORRUPTED BY A GANGSTA I, II III, IV

BLINDED BY HIS LOVE

THE PRICE YOU PAY FOR LOVE I, II ,III

DOPE GIRL MAGIC I II III

By **Destiny Skai**

WHEN A GOOD GIRL GOES BAD

By **Adrienne**

THE COST OF LOYALTY I II III

By Kweli

A GANGSTER'S REVENGE **I II III & IV**

THE BOSS MAN'S DAUGHTERS I II III IV V

A SAVAGE LOVE **I & II**

BAE BELONGS TO ME I II

A HUSTLER'S DECEIT I, II, III

WHAT BAD BITCHES DO I, II, III

SOUL OF A MONSTER I II III

KILL ZONE

A DOPE BOY'S QUEEN I II

By **Aryanna**

A KINGPIN'S AMBITON

A KINGPIN'S AMBITION **II**

I MURDER FOR THE DOUGH

By **Ambitious**

TRUE SAVAGE I II III IV V VI VII

DOPE BOY MAGIC I, II, III

MIDNIGHT CARTEL I II III

CITY OF KINGZ I II

By **Chris Green**

A DOPEBOY'S PRAYER

By **Eddie "Wolf" Lee**

THE KING CARTEL **I, II & III**

By **Frank Gresham**

THESE NIGGAS AIN'T LOYAL **I, II & III**

By **Nikki Tee**

GANGSTA SHYT **I II &III**

By **CATO**

THE ULTIMATE BETRAYAL

By **Phoenix**

BOSS'N UP **I , II & III**

By **Royal Nicole**

I LOVE YOU TO DEATH

By **Destiny J**

I RIDE FOR MY HITTA

I STILL RIDE FOR MY HITTA

By **Misty Holt**

LOVE & CHASIN' PAPER

By **Qay Crockett**

TO DIE IN VAIN

SINS OF A HUSTLA

A Gangsta's Karma

By **ASAD**

BROOKLYN HUSTLAZ

By **Boogsy Morina**

BROOKLYN ON LOCK I & II

By **Sonovia**

GANGSTA CITY

By **Teddy Duke**

A DRUG KING AND HIS DIAMOND I & II III

A DOPEMAN'S RICHES

HER MAN, MINE'S TOO I, II

CASH MONEY HO'S

THE WIFEY I USED TO BE I II

By Nicole Goosby

TRAPHOUSE KING **I II & III**

KINGPIN KILLAZ I II III

STREET KINGS I II

PAID IN BLOOD **I II**

CARTEL KILLAZ I II III

DOPE GODS I II

By **Hood Rich**

LIPSTICK KILLAH **I, II, III**

CRIME OF PASSION I II & III

FRIEND OR FOE I II III

By **Mimi**

STEADY MOBBN' **I, II, III**

THE STREETS STAINED MY SOUL I II

By **Marcellus Allen**

WHO SHOT YA **I, II, III**

SON OF A DOPE FIEND I II

HEAVEN GOT A GHETTO

Renta

GORILLAZ IN THE BAY **I II III IV**

Flame

TEARS OF A GANGSTA I II

3X KRAZY I II

DE'KARI

TRIGGADALE I II III

Elijah R. Freeman

GOD BLESS THE TRAPPERS I, II, III

THESE SCANDALOUS STREETS I, II, III

FEAR MY GANGSTA I, II, III IV, V

THESE STREETS DON'T LOVE NOBODY I, II

BURY ME A G I, II, III, IV, V

A GANGSTA'S EMPIRE I, II, III, IV

THE DOPEMAN'S BODYGAURD I II

THE REALEST KILLAZ I II III

THE LAST OF THE OGS I II III

Tranay Adams

THE STREETS ARE CALLING

Duquie Wilson

MARRIED TO A BOSS I II III

By Destiny Skai & Chris Green

KINGZ OF THE GAME I II III IV V

Playa Ray

SLAUGHTER GANG I II III

RUTHLESS HEART I II III

By Willie Slaughter

FUK SHYT

By Blakk Diamond

DON'T F#CK WITH MY HEART I II

By Linnea

ADDICTED TO THE DRAMA I II III

IN THE ARM OF HIS BOSS II

By Jamila

YAYO I II III IV

A SHOOTER'S AMBITION I II

BRED IN THE GAME

By S. Allen

TRAP GOD I II III

RICH $AVAGE

By Troublesome

FOREVER GANGSTA

GLOCKS ON SATIN SHEETS I II

By Adrian Dulan

TOE TAGZ I II III

LEVELS TO THIS SHYT I II

By Ah'Million

KINGPIN DREAMS I II III

By Paper Boi Rari

CONFESSIONS OF A GANGSTA I II III

By Nicholas Lock

I'M NOTHING WITHOUT HIS LOVE

SINS OF A THUG

TO THE THUG I LOVED BEFORE

By Monet Dragun

CAUGHT UP IN THE LIFE I II III

By Robert Baptiste

NEW TO THE GAME I II III

MONEY, MURDER & MEMORIES I II III

By **Malik D. Rice**

LIFE OF A SAVAGE I II III

A GANGSTA'S QUR'AN I II III

MURDA SEASON I II III

GANGLAND CARTEL I II III

CHI'RAQ GANGSTAS I II III

KILLERS ON ELM STREET I II III

Flame

JACK BOYZ N DA BRONX I II III

A DOPEBOY'S DREAM

By **Romell Tukes**

LOYALTY AIN'T PROMISED I II

By Keith Williams

QUIET MONEY I II III

THUG LIFE I II III

EXTENDED CLIP I II

By **Trai'Quan**

THE STREETS MADE ME I II

By **Larry D. Wright**

THE ULTIMATE SACRIFICE I, II, III, IV, V, VI

KHADIFI

IF YOU CROSS ME ONCE

ANGEL I II

IN THE BLINK OF AN EYE

By **Anthony Fields**

THE LIFE OF A HOOD STAR

By Ca$h & Rashia Wilson

THE STREETS WILL NEVER CLOSE

By K'ajji

CREAM I II

By Yolanda Moore

NIGHTMARES OF A HUSTLA I II III

By King Dream

CONCRETE KILLA I II

By Kingpen

HARD AND RUTHLESS I II

MOB TOWN 251

By Von Diesel

GHOST MOB

Stilloan Robinson

MOB TIES I II

By SayNoMore

BODYMORE MURDERLAND I II III

By Delmont Player

FOR THE LOVE OF A BOSS

By C. D. Blue

MOBBED UP I II

By King Rio

KILLA KOUNTY

By Khufu

MONEY GAME

By Smoove Dolla

A GANGSTA'S KARMA

By FLAME

BOOKS BY LDP'S CEO, CA$H

TRUST IN NO MAN

TRUST IN NO MAN 2

TRUST IN NO MAN 3

BONDED BY BLOOD

SHORTY GOT A THUG

THUGS CRY

THUGS CRY 2

THUGS CRY 3

TRUST NO BITCH

TRUST NO BITCH 2

TRUST NO BITCH 3

TIL MY CASKET DROPS

RESTRAINING ORDER

RESTRAINING ORDER 2

IN LOVE WITH A CONVICT

LIFE OF A HOOD STAR

CPSIA information can be obtained
at www.ICGtesting.com
Printed in the USA
LVHW051139120122
708210LV00013B/453